MOON SHELL BEACH

**Center Point
Large Print**

**This Large Print Book carries the
Seal of Approval of N.A.V.H.**

MOON SHELL BEACH

Nancy Thayer

CENTER POINT PUBLISHING
THORNDIKE, MAINE

This Center Point Large Print edition
is published in the year 2008 by arrangement with
The Random House Publishing Group,
a division of Random House.

Copyright © 2008 by Nancy Thayer.

All rights reserved.

The text of this Large Print edition is unabridged. In other
aspects, this book may vary from the original edition.
Printed in the United States of America.
Set in 16-point Times New Roman type.

ISBN: 978-1-60285-223-5

Library of Congress Cataloging-in-Publication Data

Thayer, Nancy, 1943–
    Moon Shell Beach / Nancy Thayer—Center Point large print ed.
        p. cm.
    ISBN 978-1-60285-223-5 (lib. bdg. : alk. paper)
    1. Female friendship—Fiction. 2. Divorced women—Fiction. 3. Homecoming—Fiction.
    4. Nantucket Island (Mass.)—Fiction. 5. Large type books. I. Title.

PS3570.H3475M66 2008b
813'.54--dc22

2008007556

For My Beloved

Charles Walters

Joshua Thayer

David Raymond Gillum

Sam Wilde Forbes

and

Ellias Samuel Steep Forbes

Acknowledgments

My thanks to John West, brilliant chocolatier of Sweet Inspirations, and beautiful Cheryl Fudge of Cheryl Fudge Designs. Thanks to the glamorous Anastassia Izioumova and the gorgeous Viktoriya Krivonosova. I'm so glad you're on Nantucket. Thank you, Josh Thayer, for your swift, precise information about business matters. Thanks to Libby McGuire for her insight. Thanks to the very cool Dan Mallory. Enormous gratitude to my virtuoso agent and friend, Meg Ruley.

And to my editor Linda Marrow, genuine on-my-knees idolatry for her genius, inspiration, and editing.

One morning when I was six years old, my father said to me, "Son, today Charles Lindbergh is going to try to fly solo across the Atlantic Ocean. Let's hope he makes it." My father left for work. I wanted to do as he said, but I realized my father hadn't told me how to hope. So all day long, I thought, over and over again, "I hope he makes it. I hope he makes it. I hope he makes it."

—U.S. Ambassador William Butts Macomber, *speaking at the Nantucket Atheneum, 1990* prologue

1987

Clare and Lexi discovered the beach when they were ten. Hidden away off a country road, it was a small crescent of sand at the creek end of the harbor, so concealed by a tangle of beach grass, cattails, and wild rosebushes that no one would ever find it unless they were young and supple and small, creeping low to the ground, pretending to be Wampanoag Indian scouts.

Spider crabs scuttled along the sand, which was speckled with scallop shells and mussels and coiled moon shells, each shell spotted or banded, the far ends peaked like a woman's breasts. Gulls cruised low over the beach and elegant white herons occasionally stalked in the gleaming waters. They could see the long town pier and, in the distance, the arrival and departure of stately ferries and sailboat races and regattas, but no boats, not even rustic wooden rowboats, came close to their beach. It was far too shallow.

They never saw signs of other people—no footprints in the sand, no discarded bits of paper. On the hottest days they swam far out in the cool, translucent water, looking for mermaids, sometimes pretending they were mermaids themselves, as their long hair waved around their faces like fronds and their skin took on a greenish underwater hue. They collected shells to make jewelry, carved designs in driftwood as secret codes, sent messages off in bottles, hid treasures in the woods around the marsh.

It was their own fairy-tale thicket, their fantasy world. Best friends since they were five, they told no one else about the place, not other girls, not Lexi's brother, Adam, nor their parents. It was not just a place to them, it was a kind of reality, and a possession of a bond deeper than words could say.

They met at the beach almost every day, biking out from their homes, hiding their bikes behind trees. They wore bathing suits and flip-flops and T-shirts, their skin grew brown as nuts, and their noses were always sunburned red. During the school year, they met at Moon Shell Beach in the late afternoon or weekend mornings, to tell each other the important things.

When it rained, and during the worst of the winter months, they had to play inside. The inside games were never quite as satisfactory—they were too close to the real world. When they were at Clare's house, they played *her* choice—elaborate games of house, transforming Clare's bedroom into a home complete with sometimes as many as twelve children made from Clare's stuffed animals and dolls. In later years, they spent entire weekends experimenting with elaborate meals that Clare would store for her own real family—her literary, artistic, and absentminded parents and only child Clare—to eat over the course of the next week. Clare loved the coziness of baking on a rainy day, filling the kitchen with smells of cinnamon and butter. She even took pleasure in the way the windows steamed over when she did the dishes.

Lexi always grew bored with such domesticity. *She* wanted to see outside. *She* wanted to travel to far-away lands, she wanted *adventure,* so when Clare came to her house, they turned the backs of sofas into camels and elephants and dressed up like belly dancers or gypsies.

They respected their differences and even envied each other a bit. Lexi wished her mother were an artist like Clare's mother, who spent most of her time in her studio at the back of the yard and forgot to shop for groceries or clean the house but sometimes sat with the girls, leafing through her art books, explaining in intricate and entrancing detail the works of Monet or Sargent or Childe Hassam. Every now and then Ellen Hart took the girls to a lecture on the island about Nantucket artists—Anne Ramsdell Congdon, Maginel Wright Barney, Frank Swift Chase—and Lexi's passions stirred. When she compared her own family, she was ashamed of how cranky she felt about her own parents, so exhausted from running their shop that they never went out in the evenings but collapsed at home, watching anything and everything on television.

In turn, Clare envied Lexi her slightly larger and much more present family. Lexi had an older brother,

Adam, who filled the house with noise and movement and slamming doors and bouncing basketballs and hoarse squawking laughter. Sometimes on winter Saturday nights the four Laneys gathered around the kitchen table to play Monopoly or Scrabble or Clue, and if Clare was invited to stay over, she grabbed the opportunity, loving the teasing and tumble of family life. Clare would bake brownies or cookies or even a pie to bring over with her for a Saturday night at the Laneys.

The summer of their thirteenth year, they were filled with an unexpected restlessness, like air before a storm, charged, tense, and irritable. They started their periods, and Lexi shot up to almost six feet, and both girls suddenly found themselves with the unmistakable mixed blessing of breasts. Oh, they tried to stave off the transformations of adolescence. They gave each other lighthearted pet names—shorter, dark-eyed Clare was "Doe," and Clare called tall, lean Lexi "Stork." They wore loose clothing to cover their changing bodies, but they soon discovered they were helpless before the force that swept them up like driftwood in the sea.

Clare developed a passionate crush on Lexi's older brother, Adam. He was fifteen, tall, broad-shouldered, with hair and eyebrows bleached white by the sun and Lexi's aquamarine eyes. He had a deep voice and an easy laugh that made Clare feel shivery.

Lexi was infatuated with Adam's best friend, Tris, who had broad shoulders, flaming red hair, and a deep rumbling voice.

Sometimes Adam went over to Tris's house, or played soccer or baseball with friends. Some days Tris came over to hang out with Adam. Then the girls would leave Lexi's bedroom to creep around the house, spying on the guys, peeking around door-ways, ducking behind furniture, pinching each other's arms so hard they left marks.

One Saturday afternoon, Adam and Tris and three other guys sat at the kitchen table playing poker. Clare and Lexi pretended to watch TV in the family room, but they went into the kitchen as many times as their dignity would allow, on the pretense of get-ting some chips, or some Coke, and then apples. When the game broke up, the five guys rose and clomped out of the kitchen on their huge hairy male legs, laughing in their deep male voices. Lexi and Clare stormed the room like a pair of spies, then raced outside and jumped on their bikes and pedaled to Moon Shell Beach.

They tucked their bikes down in the brush and made their way through bushes of rosa rugosa, tupelo trees, and tall, razor-edged grasses. Beneath their feet, the ground made squelching noises. Small twigs from the beach plum bushes scratched their skin, but they pushed on through the undergrowth until they suddenly arrived at the hidden cove. Before them spread the blue waters of the harbor. Behind them, the marsh curved like a green curtain, shielding them from the real world.

They sank on their knees in the sand and took out their stolen treasures.

Wrapped in a paper napkin lay the leftover part of a sandwich, the bread curved in a half circle where Tris's mouth had bitten.

Clare had an apple, partially eaten by Adam.

"His mouth was here," Lexi whispered. She held the sandwich to her lips and closed her eyes, thinking of Tris's breath.

Clare ran her fingers over the moist white flesh of the apple and thought of Adam's straight white teeth.

After a while, Lexi giggled, trying to lighten the intensity of the moment. "We're kind of insane, aren't we?"

But Clare remained serious. Across the water, by the town pier, islanders were painting the bottoms of their rowboats turquoise or scarlet. The sun dazzled like fireworks on the water and the air smelled of salt and spring. All around them in trees and shrubs, small buds unfolded like thousands of tiny hands opening slowly, releasing secrets. And something urgent was unfolding in Clare, something was waking.

"Lexi, let's make a pact. Let's promise never to bring a guy out here unless he's the man we're going to marry."

"Marriage!" Lexi shouted. "*Ugh*. Marriage is about a million years away, Clare."

"I know. But still . . ." Clare spread out her arms, including the beach, the water, the moment, so private, so rich. "This is really *our* place, Lexi. And things are changing. *We're* changing, don't you feel it?"

Lexi squirmed and shrugged her shoulders.

Clare ran her fingertip over the red skin of the apple. "We're *playing* now, kind of. You know? But someday it will all be serious. And I don't want to, oh, I don't know, *spoil* this place."

Lexi shifted on the sand. "I know what you mean. And you're right."

Clare continued, "This is *our* beach, and we won't bring just *any* guy out here—"

"—cuz you *know*," Lexi teased, "babes like us are going to be dating so many guys!"

Clare's face remained solemn. "So I swear I won't bring a man out here unless he's the man I'm going to marry."

Lexi settled down. "I swear, too."

Both girls dipped their hands into the clear waters of Nantucket Harbor, then with wet palms, solemnly shook.

Lexi giggled again. "Clare. You said *man*."

They looked at each other, awed, and frightened, and eager.

part one

ONE

1994

"Hi, Mrs. Laney, where's Lexi?" Clare ambled into Laney's Dry Goods Emporium, bringing a gust of crisp October air with her. Her curly brown hair was held back with a tartan headband and she was glowing from the morning's game. Her sophomore year in high school, she was throwing herself wholeheartedly into team sports.

Myrna Laney was ringing up a sale. "Did we win?"

Clare pumped her fist. "Whalers four, Wareham a big fat egg!"

"Good for you girls!" Mrs. Moody, who led the community chorus, looked up from signing the charge card. "Only one more game before the tournament, right?"

"Right." Clare held up crossed fingers.

Myrna slipped Patricia Moody's purchase into a bag. "Lexi's just cleaning up the dressing rooms," she told Clare. "Go on back."

At the far end of the store were four dressing rooms. Lexi was there, scooping up discarded clothing and fastening them back onto the hangers. "Hey, Doe." Seeing Clare's face, she said, "Well, I can tell you guys won."

21

"Victory is sweet!" Clare did a little dance, then picked up a sweater and folded it, helping Lexi. "I really wish you'd try out for the field hockey team."

"Right. Because I'm such a jock."

"I think you could be if you tried."

Gangly Lexi gave her a stare.

"Well," Clare amended, "I think you could be better than you think you are."

"Doesn't matter," Lexi said. "I've got to work here after school and on Saturdays. I don't even have time to *watch* field hockey. The only time my parents let me off is for the homecoming football game."

"I know." Clare ran her hands down a pair of wool slacks, smoothing them. "It's not fair."

"Oh, Clare, it's fine," Lexi argued amiably. "I'm such a spaz, I don't enjoy sports. Besides, I'm saving money for the class trip to New York."

"New York? I thought you were going with the French class to Paris in the spring."

Lexi slumped against the wall. "Didn't I tell you? That's out. No way can I make enough money for that."

"But I thought the school was paying for part of the trip. What have we been holding the car washes and lotteries for?"

"Mom and Dad got a letter from the school. We still have to come up with a thousand dollars. No way can we raise that."

"That *sucks*." Clare chewed her lip, thinking. "Well, if you don't go, I won't go."

"You have a chance to go to Paris and you won't take it! That's crazy."

"I won't have any fun if you're not there," Clare said loyally. With a pile of clothing over her arms, she followed Lexi out of the dressing room area back into the store. "Anyway, I don't care about Paris. What I really want is for you to come cheer for us at the Division II tournament in November."

"If the Whalers win next weekend."

"We will. So you have to come to the tournament, okay?" She tugged on Lexi's shirt, doing her best annoying child imitation. "Please, pretty please?"

Lexi laughed. "Go harass my mother. She makes the scheduling decisions."

The bell over the door chimed as Mrs. Moody left. Now that no customers were around, Clare approached Lexi's mother. "Mrs. Laney, can Lexi have Saturday off in two weeks to come to our tournament?"

"I'm already letting Lexi off on Thursday afternoon so she can go to the Cape while you get your braces tightened," Myrna reminded Clare.

"But if we play the Vineyard?" Martha's Vineyard, "the other island," was Nantucket's fiercest rival for all sports.

Myrna gave in. "All right. If you play the Vineyard."

"Yes!" Clare leaned over the counter and hugged Lexi's mother. "You're the best."

"We're having chili tonight," Myrna told her. "And Fred and I were thinking it was time for you two girls to learn to play bridge."

"Because we can't play board games because *Adam* never stays home on Saturdays now that he's a big fat senior," Lexi called from the other side of the store.

"I'd love to learn bridge!" Clare said. "And I love your chili. I'll bring dessert."

"Something chocolate?" Lexi called.

"You got it. A cake . . . or maybe brownies . . ." Clare waved and headed out into the brilliant autumn day.

ᴛᴡᴏ

1996

Clare ran her tongue over the smooth surface of her teeth as she stood in line to board the Hy-Line fast ferry. She was a senior in high school, and *finally,* her heinous braces were off ! She felt teary and celebratory and kind of shaky. And weirdly lonely.

When she'd first had the braces put on, two years ago, the orthodontist had been on Nantucket, but he moved to the Cape, so she had to make trips off-island for her appointments. Sometimes it was fun. Sometimes Lexi came with her and they went shopping at the Cape Cod Mall. But today was a Saturday, early in October, and Lexi had to help her parents in their store.

Clare looked around the cabin. The wind had risen during the day and the seas were choppy, so she didn't want to sit on the upper deck. Her favorite seat up front was already taken. She dumped her backpack on one of the small round tables and dropped into a chair. It was just beginning to rain, long drops streaking down the ferry windows. The line of passengers coming up the ramp and into the boat moved faster as the rain increased from spatters to a heavy downpour.

At the end of the line shuffled a tiny old woman, so uncoordinated it seemed she took two steps back for every step she took forward. Old Mrs. Gill, one of the island's more eccentric characters. A cranky, suspicious old hermit, she lived by herself in a spooky old falling-apart house just outside town, the same house she'd grown up in and never left. Clare remembered when she was in seventh grade, when she went with a church group singing Christmas carols. At Mrs. Gill's house, instead of offering them hot chocolate or cookies, the old nutcase had switched on the porch light and yelled at them to leave before she called the cops. Clare had seen her around town occasionally since then and felt sorry for her, the way age was bending the old woman's back and curving her hands into claws. Elementary school kids made up songs about her—she really was the island's hag. She had even begun to grow a mustache and a bit of a beard. And she was getting meaner and meaner. If you said hello to her on the street, she'd just snarl.

But now Clare wondered if she should go help her up the ramp. She rose from her seat. Then she saw Jesse Gray say something to the boat attendant and run out into the rain.

Jesse Gray, *wow*. He was the handsomest, coolest, sexiest guy in the senior class. She knew he'd slept with half the girls in high school, and a lot of older women, too. He was just awesome. Clare almost fainted whenever he nodded at her in the hallway.

Now there he was, putting his arm around old Mrs. Gill and ushering her patiently up the ramp. The rain darkened Jesse's blue jeans and plastered his Red Sox T-shirt against his chest. Lucky old Mrs. Gill!

When they finally made it into the dry harbor of the cabin, Mrs. Gill wrenched her arm away from Jesse. "Get your hands off me, young man!" she snapped. "I don't need your help!"

Heads turned. You could tell right away who was an islander and who wasn't. The tourists looked puzzled, but the islanders rolled their eyes. Some of them gave Jesse a thumbs-up.

Mrs. Gill sidled over to a bench and plopped down. Immediately she began to dig around in the enormous plastic bag she carried with her everywhere.

Jesse watched to be sure she was settled, then looked around the cabin.

His eyes met Clare's.

He smiled.

Clare smiled back.

"Hey, Clare." Jesse ambled over. "What's up?" He dropped into the chair opposite her.

Omigod omigod, Clare thought. He knew her name! Part of her was so overwhelmed by his presence she wanted to squeal. Jesse Gray coming over to talk to her?

Snap out of it, Clare told herself. "I just got my braces off."

"Let me see," Jesse said, leaning forward.

Nervously, she showed him her teeth.

"Awesome. You've got a great smile."

"Thanks." Her heart was triple-timing in her chest. "Why were you off-island?"

"My truck. Had to take it to the Jeep place for an overhaul."

Clare grinned. Jesse's truck, a 1975 Chevy pickup, was famous in town. "It must cost a lot to keep it going."

"You have no idea. My whole life's devoted to that old gal. I've had to work after school and on weekends down at Don Allen Auto. I have the social life of a piece of wood."

"That's not what I've heard," Clare said, surprising herself with the flirtation in her tone. Without even thinking about it, she'd relaxed back into her chair with her arms crossed behind her neck, unconsciously sticking out her breasts. Flushing, she changed positions, digging around in her backpack for her water bottle, even though she wasn't thirsty.

"Don't believe everything you hear," Jesse told her. Raindrops dripped down from his hair onto his face and chest.

Clare pulled a sweatshirt from her backpack. "You're soaked. Put this on."

"Well, thanks, Mom," Jesse said with a grin.

Then he raised his arms and drew off his wet T-shirt, exposing his muscular chest. Blond hair lightly

28

matted his skin and longer hair furred his armpits. He slid Clare's sweatshirt over his head. Jesse was slender and not much taller than Clare; still the sweatshirt was ridiculously tight.

He noticed Clare staring. "What do you think?"

Her throat had gone dry. "About what?"

He held up his arms as if he were a model. "A fashion statement?"

"More like a fashion cry for help."

They both laughed.

"Want some hot chocolate?" Jesse asked.

Clare nodded. "Sure." As Jesse walked to the snack bar, the ferry left the harbor for the open waters of the Sound. Jesse was going to sit with her for the whole trip! *Clare,* she ordered herself, *you are not allowed to act like a geek.*

Jesse returned with two paper cups of hot chocolate. They lifted the lids. Steam rolled up into the air.

"So," Jesse said, "are you contributing anything to the school literary review?"

"Nope. Literature's not my talent, even though my dad teaches English."

"Are you artistic?"

So Jesse knew about her family. Jesse was *aware* of her.

She shook her head. "Can't draw, either." She leaned forward. "You know what I can do? I can cook, and I love to cook."

"You'll have to show me sometime," Jesse said.

And something about the way he looked at her, his blue eyes so warm on her face, his whole presence focused on her, made her say, "Sure. I'd like to do that." And she wasn't even afraid when she said the words. She was ready.

The Saturday after she met Jesse on the ferry, she invited him to her house for dinner and a video. She told her parents about it, and they gave her their approval in their vague way. Clare didn't tell Lexi because, well, she wasn't even sure this was a *date*. Whatever it was, it was exciting, and frightening, and it was *hers*.

Probably nothing would happen. Probably tomorrow she'd tell Lexi, and they'd laugh at what a geek she was.

Still, she went schizo dressing. She tried on a pretty sweater, then cast it aside—too dressy. She finally chose a long-sleeved red tee that set off her dark hair and eyes.

The evening before, she'd made a stew, so the flavors could mingle overnight. She was glad she'd prepared, because when Jesse arrived at her house, his presence took her breath away. He wore jeans and a white button-down shirt, a dress-up shirt that made him look like such a *man*. Her mind was completely befuddled.

"Hi, Jesse, come in, dinner's ready, I thought we'd eat in the living room, want to watch MTV?" She knew she was babbling; she couldn't help herself.

"Sure." Jesse ambled behind her, completely calm.

In the kitchen, she ladled out the stew and handed Jesse a plate. "I didn't make a salad, guys usually hate salads, and besides, the stew has lots of veggies . . ." *What was she, a fifty-year-old nutritionist?* She wanted to clamp her own hands over her blithering mouth.

"Smells great." Jesse's fingers brushed hers as he took his bowl.

She nearly fainted. "Drink?" Her voice came out in a squeak.

"Milk's fine. Or water."

Clare led him into the den, and suddenly she was embarrassed by how alone they were in the room. "My dad's off-island for a teacher's conference," she explained. She'd already set up the TV tables, and she put out the utensils and napkins with shaking hands. "And Mom's in her bedroom—" Oops, *bedroom.* "She always goes up early, she takes a cup of chamomile tea and a book. She has a bad back from painting."

"My parents are off-island, too." Jesse settled onto the sofa and pulled the tray toward him.

The sofa! Clare thought, her face burning, why had she put the trays side by side on the sofa? Why didn't she just wear a big sign saying, *I hope my thigh touches yours!* She sat down, squeezing herself as far away from him as she could.

"This is delicious, Clare," Jesse told her.

"Thanks." She watched him lick his lips and her breath caught in her throat.

"I like this song," Jesse said, nodding toward the television.

"Oh, me too." She had to eat; she couldn't sit there and gape at him.

Somehow they got through the meal. When they were through eating, they moved the trays aside. Jesse helped her carry the dishes into the kitchen.

"Um, ice cream?" She'd considered making a pie or a cake, but decided that would be too dorky.

"Sure."

As Clare moved around the room, her every movement was defined by how close it brought her to Jesse. Finally she managed to hand him a bowl of ice cream without dropping it, and then they went back into the living room, where the television flickered and the lights were low.

She sat on the sofa. Jesse sat, too, but closer to her than before. He ate his dessert, then put the bowl on his TV tray. He shifted to look at her full on.

"Want to watch another channel?" she asked nervously.

"Not really," Jesse said. "You?"

Clare shook her head. He was close to her. It was all so intense she felt she was about to cry.

"Hey," Jesse said. "Don't look so serious. Let me see your million-dollar smile."

Clare blinked as she managed a tremulous smile.

Jesse ran the tips of his fingers lightly over her teeth. "Very nice." He ran his fingertips over her lips.

"Also very nice." Leaning forward, he kissed her gently.

She was afraid she'd do something wrong. She didn't know how to kiss. She knew Jesse was experienced and she didn't want to seem pathetic and naive.

It was amazing, how natural the kiss was, how warm and right. She drew back, looking into Jesse's blue eyes.

"Jesse. I don't want to be just another . . . *girl* for you."

His smile was like an angel's. "Hey, Clare. I know that. You're special. Trust me."

She trusted him.

Monday, Clare sauntered into the cafeteria for lunch. She wasn't the least bit hungry. She was so full of happiness she had no appetite for anything else. She drifted toward the table where she usually sat with Lexi and a bunch of other girls who weren't cheerleaders but weren't The Hopeless and the Damned, either. She smiled, thinking of how she would casually mention that she was going out with Jesse Gray.

Someone grabbed her elbow, hard. Clare turned. "Hi, Lexi."

Lexi seemed ready to explode. "Are you dating Jesse Gray?"

Clare winced. "Lex, we just had one date. I didn't know it was going to get so serious so fast."

"So *serious?*" Lexi looked stricken. "I can't

believe you didn't tell me."

"Lex." Clare took Lexi's arm and led her toward the cafeteria line. "Chill. Everyone's looking at us. Look, I'll call you, I'll tell you all about it."

Lexi nodded. "Come over after school."

Clare winced. "Um . . . I'm doing something with Jesse after school."

Two days later, they met at Moon Shell Beach. It was one of those golden autumn days that made Nantucket seem like paradise, as if summer would always be suspended like this, ripe with beach plums, warm air on your skin, the blue waters sparkling back at the sun.

Lexi was agitated. "Clare, are you nuts?" She paced over the sand. She didn't know why she was so upset, so frightened.

"Lexi, you don't know him," Clare protested. Lexi's reaction was not at all what she'd expected. "Jesse's really nice."

"Jesse Gray is really *sexy,* that's what you mean." In spite of the warmth of the day, Lexi hugged her sweater to her chest as she talked. "Clare, Jesse is a hound dog, you know that."

Clare pleaded, "Lexi, don't be this way. Come on. This is important to me. I really really like Jesse."

"But that's what's so awful, Clare. *You like* him, but *he* just wants to get in your pants."

"You don't know that." Clare jutted out her chin defensively. "Besides, what if he does? It's time I lost my virginity."

"But you don't want to be just another notch on this guy's belt," Lexi insisted.

Clare smiled radiantly. "Look at it from my point of view. Maybe I want him to be my first lover."

"Lover," Lexi spit the word out scornfully. "Clare, you're going to get hurt."

"If I do, it will be worth it."

Lexi gaped. "I don't even know you."

"Oh, stop it, Lex!"

Lexi looked stricken. "Promise this much," she said solemnly. "Promise me you won't bring him to Moon Shell Beach."

"Oh, Lexi . . ." And all at once her friend seemed childish. Clare felt ages more experienced and wise.

Lexi chewed her thumbnail, thinking. "Maybe you can bring him *someday*. When you know you're going to marry him."

Clare laughed. "Who cares about silly old Moon Shell Beach!" She was shocked at the hurt in Lexi's eyes. "Oh, Lexi, I'm sorry. I didn't mean— Look, I promise I won't bring him to Moon Shell Beach."

Clare's senior year of high school was all about Clare and Jesse. She went to class, she did her homework, she applied to colleges and got accepted, but none of that was real to her. Only Jesse was real.

Jesse worked after school and on weekends, so they had very little time together, but what time they had was sweet.

It wasn't just sex. It was more than that. It was warmth, and security, it was home. Clare could be leaning over the sink, rinsing the dishes, and he'd say something, and she'd bend her head to hear him over the water, and he'd go to her, put his arms around her waist. She'd lean back against him, her head against his chest. He'd tuck his chin down onto her forehead. They'd stand there like that, as warmly satisfied as bread rising in the oven.

There was no hesitancy between them, no awkwardness, no games. Everything was clear and pure and clean. After three weeks, Jesse told Clare he loved her. She told him she loved him, too. At Christmas he gave her a necklace with a diamond heart. They talked about their futures. Clare was going to UMass, but she wasn't sure about what she wanted to major in. Jesse admitted with adorable shyness that he wanted to start a band. He'd like to spend a few years concentrating on his guitar and vocals, maybe even cut some CDs, see what happened. When he talked about this, Clare encouraged him, but her heart went chilly with fear. She'd heard about musicians, how they slept with women at every gig. The future was complicated and unclear, full of danger and changes. Clare was so engrossed with Jesse, she didn't even notice how little she saw Lexi anymore. Besides, it was difficult now. It would have been better if Lexi had been in love with someone, but Lexi wasn't dating anyone. Clare tried to be sympathetic, but her days and her life and her heart and soul were devoted to Jesse.

ТНREE

It took about five hours to get from Nantucket to the University of Massachusetts at Amherst, depending on the weather. If it was too windy, the ferries didn't run and the planes didn't fly, and if the state was hit with one of its extreme blizzards, driving was impossible. Perhaps that was why Clare had felt such panic, every single day her first year of college. She'd enjoyed her courses, she loved meeting the other girls in her dorm, and she was only slightly intimidated by living and studying on a campus that had a larger population than Nantucket. All that she could take in her stride. It helped to have Lexi on the same campus; it was like having a security blanket clutched in her hand.

The distance from Nantucket troubled Clare because of Jesse. Because she could see Jesse so seldom. Because some weekends she traveled home to see him and some weekends he traveled to Amherst to see her . . . but most weekends, and all week, she was here and Jesse was on the island, careless and sensual and ranging free.

Somehow, in spite of the distance, rumors made their way to Clare that fall. Jesse was seen at the Muse

Friday night, flirting with Eleanor Hoston. Jesse danced at the Chicken Box with Sandy Jones, who was practically climbing all over him. Jesse was seen at Fast Forward, sipping a cup of coffee and flirting with Alice Coffin. But those were only rumors. When Clare came home for Christmas, Jesse confessed that he'd slept with Donna Tyler a couple of times. That was fact, and all of that Christmas was eclipsed for Clare by a whirlwind of misery. She and Jesse fought, and Lexi consoled Clare, and then Clare and Jesse made up, but when she went back to college, she knew in her heart that Jesse would weaken again.

In an odd way, Clare became closer to Lexi during this year than she had been since they were children. When Clare wept, hating herself, feeling ugly and worthless, Lexi championed Clare. She sat up for hours with Clare, late into the night, reassuring her that she was the same spectacular, fascinating creature she'd always been, that Jesse's infidelities had everything to do with Jesse's wiring and nothing to do with how Clare looked or acted or thought. Lexi encouraged Clare to go out with other guys, even if she didn't find them attractive. "It's part of your college education, Clare," Lexi had teased. Lexi was dating one of the varsity quarterbacks; she was feeling *fine.*

Clare envied Lexi's emotional freedom. Lexi liked her classes and was discovering a passion for art, while Clare's grades suffered as she worried and obsessed about Jesse. It seemed that Lexi was diving into her off-island life like a seal in surf while Clare could only paddle at the edge of the waves, tempted by the water but afraid to leave the glistening safety of the sandy shore. She knew so many people who had left Nantucket only to come back, because they couldn't make it somehow in the real world, and she didn't want to be like them. She knew she wanted to live all her life on Nantucket, but she wanted to at least be capable of surviving elsewhere.

She was nearly weak with relief when summer came. She took a job at a gourmet shop, and worked as many hours as they would give her, but most of her days and all of her nights were about being with Jesse. Jesse was repentant about his sleeping around, and swore it wouldn't happen ever again, and that summer, when they were together every single night, Clare began, cautiously, to trust him. They talked about a future together, agreeing that they had to save up a pile of money before they could make any serious plans. Jesse wanted to build his own house, and Clare was thrilled with that idea. But land on the island was expensive. Clare told Jesse she'd put all her summer money in a special bank account earmarked for their future house. Her parents paid her tuition and other expenses, but for new clothes, movie tickets, an occasional latte, she'd taken a part-time job at the university.

At first, it was a golden summer. She lived at home, and since her parents were so self-absorbed, they hardly noticed when Jesse slept over. The days were hot, humid, and bright with light, and Clare loved wearing the pretty little sundresses she wore to work. She loved the sun on her skin, the breeze in her hair. Most nights she and Jesse went to one of the parties on the beaches undiscovered by the tourists. They would drink beer or wine, catch up on the day's gossip, perhaps walk hand in hand along the water's edge, and sometimes, on the hottest nights, swim in their clothes, coming out of the water with the cloth slicked against their bodies. "I've got goose bumps," Clare would tell Jesse, and Jesse would wrap his arms around her and hold her against him all up and down, warming her, grinning down at her as she became aware, through the material, of his erection.

Lexi was never at the townie parties because she was working at a posh restaurant, and in a way, Clare was glad. In spite of Lexi's kindness and support their freshman year, it was awkward when the three of them were around one another. Lexi had a way of standing back from Jesse, as if he were riddled with some contagious disease, and Jesse, who threw his arm around all his friends, male or female, got clumsy around Lexi. The most he would give Lexi was a curt nod. The truth was, Clare was secretly relieved to see so little of Lexi.

FOUR

Lexi had always loved summers, especially the beginning, when the sky was full of light and the season stretched ahead like the sea, glittering with promise.

After one year of college, Lexi was flying high. She'd just finished her first year at UMass/Amherst, her grades were stellar, and she'd found her vocation—she wanted to major in art. Painting, sculpting, graphic arts, photography, design—she wanted to study *everything*. Still, she was nineteen, and it was summer—she wanted to have fun. She planned to work in her parents' store, catch the beach when she had time off, and party every night.

But just a few days into June, Lexi realized with a terrible plummet of her heart that Laney's Dry Goods Emporium was failing, losing business to the chic boutiques that had crowded into the small town. Days would pass with only a handful of people drifting into her parents' store, and then all they wanted was a pair of cotton socks or a sun hat. Adam was off in Boston, in veterinary college at Tufts, which was taking all his money and a lot of their parents' savings. One night, Lexi overheard her parents talking in strained whispers, trying to figure out how they could pay their mortgage and still help Adam with his tuition.

The next day, as she worked in the store, dusting shelves and straightening merchandise that no one ever looked at, she studied her parents' faces. Fred and Myrna both looked tired, and Fred's shoulders slumped—although he straightened if a customer entered. Myrna's hair was growing white.

That night, Lexi opened her bedroom door and strained to hear her parents' conversation.

"We'll have to close the store at the end of the summer." Her father's voice was grim.

Her mother began to cry. "The business your grandfather started . . ."

Her father's voice got defensive, and choked with emotion, "Well, tell me, Myrna, what else can we do? Already, we've got to tell Adam he has to deal with his tuition himself."

After a few moments, her mother heaved a great sigh. "At least when Adam gets out of vet school he'll make enough money to support himself. I can't imagine how Lexi can support herself with an art degree."

Perhaps that was the moment Lexi grew up. Certainly it was the moment she understood that she was responsible for her life. Her parents had all they could handle. But what could she do? She was frightened. She longed to talk it over with Clare, but Clare was all about Jesse these days—she scarcely had time to talk to Lexi on the phone. Anyway, Lexi wasn't sure she should talk about her family's finances even with Clare. To the island community, money was as popular and crucial a subject as the weather. Zillionaire summer people who lived in sprawling trophy houses for one month a year drove housing costs out of reach of the normal family. Town newspapers headlined articles every week about the jump in real estate prices. But Clare didn't have to worry. Clare's father taught at the high school and Clare's mother was an artist, and the financial pressure of their lives was immeasurably softened for them because Clare's father had inherited their house from his mother. They had no mortgage. That gave them a freedom most people could only imagine.

And if she did talk with Clare, what help could Clare provide? Sympathy, of course, but lots of islanders were aware of the fading fortunes of the Laneys, and their sympathy was almost like pity, and being pitied was a very hard thing to bear.

She decided that there was one way she could help her parents.

So one evening, at home, as they were eating their Crock-Pot dinner, Lexi casually announced, "I don't think I'll go back to college this year."

"Oh, honey!" Lexi's mother leaned over the kitchen table toward her. "Sweetie, you've got to stay in college."

But the look of relief that passed over Fred Laney's face told Lexi all she needed to know. Her determination doubled. "It's no big deal. I can always go back. Lots of kids I know take a year off. I'll stay here and work and pile up some money."

Her father's voice was somber. "You won't pile up money working at the store."

"That's all right, Dad." At that moment she simply wanted to erase the worry from his face. "I want to take a job waitressing. I can make a ton that way."

"Well." After a moment, her father nodded. "That's a good idea, Lexi."

"A very good idea," her mother echoed.

Lexi was proud of herself, and deeply sad. She felt as if her future had been floating above her like a brilliantly colored hot-air balloon, tethered to the ground, waiting to lift her away . . . and she had just cut the line and could only watch helplessly as her hopes drifted up and out of sight while she remained stranded on the earth.

Later that evening, Lexi shut the door to her bedroom and hid away, phoning Clare.

But Clare wasn't home.

Clare was with Jesse.

Lexi couldn't blame Clare for being infatuated with Jesse. It wasn't just his blond hair, blue eyes, and easy smile, it was his entire *Jesse-ness* that made him irresistible. Still, when Clare and Jesse had hooked up in their senior year of high school, Lexi had quietly assumed they wouldn't last. Jesse never stayed with anyone for more than a few weeks. So she had listened patiently while Clare sang Jesse's praises and confided that they were making love— she'd said "making love," not "having sex," and confessed that she was madly in love with him. Lexi thought Clare was deluded, and would be hurt when Jesse dumped her for someone else, but she humored Clare and vowed to herself she would be there for Clare when things fell apart.

But that didn't happen. As their senior year wore on, Jesse stuck with Clare, and stopped sleeping around. They became a real couple, *the* couple in the school. Lexi found herself relegated to the background. Clare never had time to be with Lexi; she was always with Jesse. Clare stopped confiding in Lexi; she didn't want to betray Jesse's confidences, although she did tell Lexi that Jesse secretly wanted to be a folk singer, but everyone knew that, he was getting a band together. Lexi felt rejected by Clare, even betrayed, which made her feel inferior to Clare, and, in truth, wasn't she inferior? Popular Jesse had plucked Clare out of the crowd. No one had chosen Lexi. Oh, she had dates, and plenty of guys tried to get in her pants, but no one was in love with her.

While Clare and Lexi were at UMass together, Jesse stayed on the island, working as a carpenter. Clare had more time for Lexi, and their friendship had grown strong again. Then, what Lexi had half feared, half hoped would happen came about. Clare got news that Jesse was sleeping around. She came to Lexi with her tears and anger and grief, and Lexi felt a mixture of sorrow and relief. She told Clare what she truly believed—that Jesse wasn't right for her, that he wasn't good enough for her, that she would find real love, true love, with someone else.

And now Clare and Lexi were home from college. Jesse had snapped his fingers, and Clare had gone to him as quickly as if he were a hypnotist and she his subject. Clare got a job working for a gourmet shop, and what free time Clare had, she spent with Jesse.

This summer Lexi was determined not to be so lame. After all, this past year she'd gained enough confidence to have her first love affair, with a hunky UMass quarterback, and *she*'d been the one to break up with him. So she was experienced, less dependent on Clare. She had other friends on the island, after all. She stopped phoning Clare and sought them out, and when she wasn't working, or collapsing after work, she met friends at the beach or at a bar for a drink.

She also quit working at her parents' store and got a job cleaning houses during the day. At night, she waitressed at a posh restaurant, La Maison. She stopped buying celebrity magazines and nail polish, and slowly her small bank account began to grow. She was determined to be optimistic.

But in her new jobs she recognized, more than ever before, that the distance between her life and the lives of the really rich was immense—an almost unbridgeable chasm.

The houses she cleaned were stunning, with paintings and sculptures that took her breath away. Each room was a work of art all by itself, the colors so perfectly coordinated, even the island landscape was framed by windows to appear as another masterpiece money could buy. She didn't mind cleaning the houses—they were so flawlessly decorated, it was like playing house.

She thought she'd enjoy working at the posh French restaurant, too, but the other waitstaff and the chef at La Maison were a chummy, tight little club who spoke French with one another and snubbed Lexi. And the customers were from another galaxy. Some were older couples, the women with coiffed hair and a Queen Elizabeth kind of style, but lots of diners were in their twenties or early thirties, and these women, just a bit older than Lexi, took her breath away with their expensive clothing and casual elegance. She envied their looks, their laughter—she envied the way they *smelled*. But most of all, she envied them their experiences.

As she attended to their every need, offering them menus, pouring more water or wine, setting plates before them, brushing crumbs away, she couldn't help but hear them talk about their trips to Paris, or the opening of the Impressionist show at the Met, or their little jaunt over to Tuscany. They weren't all empty-headed bimbos, either, although Lexi wished they were. Some of the most dazzling women were archaeologists, or lawyers, or art historians. *Art historian!* Lexi thought. It seemed the most splendid thing she'd ever heard of.

The men who squired these glittering women were

handsome, too, some of them, and all of them accustomed to being in command. Lexi was aware of the way the men's eyes slid over her, taking in her long legs and sleek figure, and occasionally a guy winked at her or smiled as he met her eyes, and Lexi's hopes would waken. But the men always returned their gaze to the women they were with, and Lexi knew—it was an old, old story on this island—that the most she could ever be to one of these men was, at best, a summer's dalliance; at worst, an easy lay.

She resigned herself. At least she made great tips. Yet every evening after serving people with good educations and wealthy backgrounds, she went home to a house that was becoming shabby with neglect, and she would hear her parents in the kitchen, going over the books, trying to cope with the failure of the store that had supported them all their lives.

She didn't want to become bitter like some of her high school friends, who made up nasty names for the women whose homes they cleaned, whose parties they catered, whose children they tended. Once or twice she managed to wrench Clare away from Jesse, and that helped. Clare wasn't bitter. Clare was so in love with Jesse, she didn't want any life but her own.

But Clare also loved the island more than Lexi did, or loved it in a different way; that was becoming more and more clear to Lexi. Clare wanted to live on Nantucket after college, but Lexi wanted to travel, she wanted to see the Louvre and the Coliseum, she wanted to hear symphonies and attend theater. At least she wanted the chance to see other places and live a little before settling down to spend her life serving the wealthy.

One Saturday night early in June, when they weren't full, Lexi was surprised to see Lauren, the hostess, whip away from the front door and meet in a buzz with the other waiters and the owner/chef.

"What's going on?" Lexi asked Peter, a waiter who would at least speak to her in English.

"It's Ed Hardin," Peter said. "Lauren doesn't want to seat him."

"Ed Hardin?" Lexi peered around the corner at the group of men standing by the door. "Wow."

That summer the Nantucket community hated Ed Hardin. A real estate mogul, he was cunning, ruthless, and powerful. During the winter, Hardin had bought up luxuriant, unspoiled acreage between the moors and the ocean and developed it into a minisuburb of enormous, expensive trophy mansions that drove the wildlife out of their shelter and towered arrogantly above the landscape, blocking the views of longtime residents, providing nothing good for the island and lots of money for Ed Hardin.

"We can refuse service to anyone!" Lauren was hissing.

"Get a grip," Phil, the chef/owner, snapped. "If you want to be moralistic, go to divinity school. We're here to make money, and Ed Hardin has more money than Midas, so shut up and smile."

Angrily, Lauren glared around at the waitstaff. "Lexi," she said, "*you're* getting him."

Ed Hardin was handsome for a man nearing forty. He was almost bald, but his eyebrows were black and bushy over a raptor's piercing dark eyes. When he looked at Lexi, his gaze was like a judgment. Then he smiled at her.

"Well, *hello,*" he said.

Over the summer, he dined at La Maison at least once a week, sometimes with men, sometimes with lovely young women. He always flirted with Lexi, who beamed back appreciatively—he left fabulous tips. He requested Lexi's table every time he came, and when he was with a man, he leaned back in his chair and asked Lexi about herself. It would have been rude not to respond, and she secretly enjoyed having the attention of this powerful man. She knew she looked good—finally she accepted how her long legs and slim torso, which had earned her the name of "Stork" in school, had become assets. She wore a white button-down shirt and a short black skirt to work. Her blond hair was almost white from the sun. She wore it simply tied back with a black ribbon, a long tail hanging down her back, swinging as she walked.

One evening, he asked, "Do you work every night?"

Cool, she thought, he wants to come here only

when I can be his waitress. "Not Mondays and Tuesdays."

"Great. Let me take you out to dinner on Monday."

"Oh." Lexi was so surprised, she almost dropped the bread basket. Flustered, she stuttered, "Oh . . . I, uh, I can't. Sorry." And she hurried away.

That night, she casually told her parents that Ed Hardin had asked her out.

Her father snorted. "I hope you said no!"

Her mother patted her hand gently. "Lexi, he's much too old for you, honey. A man like him, well, he would only take advantage of a small-town girl like you."

Lexi knew her mother only meant to be helpful, but her words cut deep. And by morning, she found something in her rebelling. Did her parents think she was *stupid?* That she'd be so grateful to be asked out by a wealthy man that she'd do anything he asked? And yet her mother was right. Her life and Ed Hardin's were worlds apart.

A week later, Ed dined at La Maison again. Again, Lexi was his waitress. When she placed the leather folder holding the tab on his table, he put his hand on it, near her hand. "Lexi, I'd really like to take you out to dinner. Any evening you're free."

Lexi pulled back her hand. "I don't know what to say."

"You have Monday off?" He really did have a nice smile.

She was aware of the eyes of the other staff and diners on her. She capitulated. "All right. Monday." As they made arrangements, she knew she was flushing. She felt like a heroine accepting a challenge from a fascinating enemy.

He took her to the Chanticleer, the best restaurant on the island, and the most expensive. He ordered fabulous wine and amazing food. He was sophisticated, imposing, witty, and well-traveled. But he also seemed genuinely interested in her. When he discovered that she loved art, he drew her out, asking her which painter she liked best, which style, what painting she'd buy if she could buy anything in the world. He asked whether she'd been to the Clark Museum in Williamstown. He asked if he could take her there sometime.

When he drove her home, he said he wanted to come in. She grinned, finally having a little power of her own, and told him, "I live here with my parents." She slipped out of his Mercedes before he could kiss her.

In her room that night, she paced the floor, trying to work off the energy of her conflicting emotions. She was not sexually attracted to Ed Hardin. He was almost twenty years older than she, and even a little shorter, and portly. But she was attracted to *who she became* when she was with him. He hadn't laughed at her opinions about art, even though she hardly knew enough to have an opinion. He'd made her seem interesting, even knowledgeable.

She really needed to talk to Clare.

"Are you nuts?" Clare yelled.

It was a hot July afternoon. They were sitting in an alley behind the gourmet shop. Lexi had convinced Clare to spend her precious few lunchtime minutes here so they could talk.

"Clare, let me explain. Ed treats me—"

"There is nothing to explain!" Clare was so upset, she tossed her sandwich aside and stood up, pacing in her frustration. "Lexi, first, Ed Hardin is a terrible, terrible man. How can you even let yourself get sucked in by talk about all this *art*—this man has single-handedly ruined acres and acres of the island!"

Lexi nodded, miserable. "I know—"

"And second, which, actually, ought to be first, because I love you and don't want to see you used and tossed aside like a piece of soiled tissue: all this man wants to do is seduce you."

"Maybe not," Lexi objected quietly.

"Really? You think he likes you for your mind? You think you're *interesting?* Lexi, Ed Hardin is a carnivore! To him, you're just one more pretty young gazelle in a herd of thousands!"

Lexi folded her arms over her chest stubbornly. "I don't think that's true."

"Then you're kidding yourself." Tears flew from Clare's eyes as she paced in a circle. "Lexi, Lexi, come *on!* Don't do this to yourself." She glared at Lexi as if she were repellent. "Honey, if you date that man, you might as well hang a sign on your back saying 'If you have money, you can do me.'"

"Clare, don't be so mean!" Lexi begged.

"Lexi, don't be so stupid," Clare shot back.

Lexi opened her mouth to retort—*and Jesse's sign says "if you're female, you can do me!"* She wanted to be just as vulgar and demeaning as Clare had been. But she bit her tongue. She wasn't with Ed Hardin the way Clare was with Jesse.

Ed phoned her to ask her out again. She politely refused, saying she was busy.

He said, "Well, what night are you free?"

She hesitated. "Look. I can't—I'm not—"

"It's just dinner, Lexi. And conversation. I enjoy your company."

He seemed so mild, so reasonable. He didn't seem like a monster at all. He wasn't a monster, really.

"Well . . ."

On their next date, over dinner at Toppers, Ed told her about his life. He'd grown up in a suburb of Kansas City, he'd had a happy life with a loving family, he'd gone to college in the Midwest, married young, and had three children who were now teenagers. He was divorced. He seldom saw his ex-wife, but their relationship was amicable.

"I like what I do," he told her. "I'm proud of what I do."

"But how can you be?" she countered. "You . . . you ruin the earth. You're like a scourge on the island."

He smiled gently, not in the least offended. "It all depends on your perspective, Lexi. I provide luxurious residences for people who work hard at important jobs—a transplant surgeon bought one of my houses, and a civil rights lawyer bought one. They need a place to escape to, a place to catch their breath, away from the harsh realities of the world. Where they can unwind. Even dream again. Where better than in one of my homes among the dazzling, sheltering scenery? They go back to work recharged."

He was like a word wizard, an enchanter. She could see his point of view.

He continued mildly, "And there are other places as spectacular as Nantucket Island. If you could see the big picture—I've built my estates outside Vail and Palm Springs and Miami. People can trust me to provide them with homes that nurture them."

She nodded, thinking that what he said was true. There were other places as spectacular as Nantucket. She just had never seen any. She wished she could.

"What do you think?" Clare leaned forward, eager to hear Lexi's verdict. She wore an apron over her sundress, and the apron was covered with chocolate stains.

Lexi sat at the kitchen table in Clare's kitchen. "Delicious. But maybe a little . . ."

"Too much cinnamon, right?"

It was a hot Sunday morning at the end of August. Miraculously, Clare had phoned Lexi to invite her over for breakfast. Both Lexi and Clare had the day off and Jesse had gone to an all-guys' party the night before and was sleeping in today.

"I'm sure he's hung over," Clare told Lexi earlier that morning. "Anyway, I haven't seen you forever, plus I'd love your opinion on a chocolate breakfast brioche I'm inventing."

Lexi had jumped at the chance to spend time with her best friend. She'd thrown on shorts and a T-shirt and biked over to Clare's. Clare's father was off-island, doing research for his book, and Clare's mother was already out in her studio, painting.

Now Lexi tilted her head as she let the tastes meld in her mouth. "Yeah, yeah, perhaps too much cinnamon."

"I know. Right." Clare grabbed a journal and scribbled notes. When she looked up at Lexi, her face was radiant. "Oh, Lexi, I'm having so much fun working at the gourmet shop! Especially creating new recipes. I'm toying with the idea of leaving UMass and going to a culinary college." She buzzed around the kitchen, setting pans in to soak, wiping down the counters.

This seemed like a good time to tell Clare, Lexi decided, while they were both in a good mood and the sun shone through the window. "Well, you know, I'm not going back."

"Back where?" Clare bent over to put a pan in the dishwasher. "La Maison?"

"College. UMass."

Clare stood up and gawked at Lexi. "Oh, come on! You've got to go back, are you *kidding* me? You don't want to clean houses forever, do you?"

Lexi took a deep breath. "Clare, my parents can't afford it."

"Oh." Clare sat down in a chair with a thump. "Oh. Wow. That's awful, Lexi."

Lexi was grateful for her concern, but at the same time, she felt herself bristling, straightening in her chair. "Well, it's not *tragic,* for heaven's sake. I mean, well, look at Jesse. He's not going to college."

Clare snorted. "Jesse in college? Ouch, can't even imagine it. Of course some people just aren't meant for college, but you, Lexi, the way you love art and stuff . . ." She looked at Lexi with affection and sympathy. "What are you going to do?"

Lexi toyed with her fork. "I'm not sure."

Clare squinted her eyes at Lexi. "Are you dating Hardin?"

Lexi looked away. "He wants to take me to Williamstown in September. To see the Clark Art Museum."

"Please, Lexi. He wants to get in your pants, that's all."

Lexi lifted her chin defiantly. "It wouldn't be the worst thing in the world if he did. Anyway, Clare, I don't think that's true. I think he likes me."

"Lexi, come on, don't tell me he likes you for your mind! You're a baby compared to him!"

"No, I don't think that. I do think he likes the way I look—and I don't mean," she hastened to add, "just that he wants to screw me. I think he likes it that I'm tall and lean and young. He likes being seen with me."

"Yeah, because it's another way of giving it to the islanders. It's like saying, not only can I buy up your land and trash it, but I can buy up your women and trash them."

"Clare, you're being really harsh about him."

"Lexi, if you want to know why, just drive out on the Polpis Road and look at his development. And it's not as if he's going to live here and funnel some of his gazillions back into the town, no, he's just flying over like . . . like a stealth bomber or something, blasting the hell out of the land and then disappearing."

"He's providing tranquil places for stressed-out people," Lexi argued weakly.

"Look," Clare snapped, "just sleep with the man, okay? Sleep with him, so he can add another notch to his belt, and then maybe he'll leave you alone!"

After Labor Day, the island was suddenly quieter. Most of the summer people had gone back to their homes to ready their children for school or to gear up for work. Lexi's cleaning jobs ended after she helped close up the houses for the off-season, and her hours at La Maison were cut drastically. She knew she had to find a full-time job, but this was just exactly the wrong season to look for one.

Perhaps because she had time on her hands, perhaps because a lot of her friends, including Clare, had left the island for college, and perhaps because she actually truly wanted to, she accepted Ed's invitation to go to Williamstown to see the Impressionist paintings at the Clark Art Museum.

In a fit of madness, Lexi spent half of her hard-earned money on three dresses and a pair of fabulous shoes at one of the most expensive boutiques on the island. Now, as she walked through the cool, hushed rooms of the museum with Ed at her side, she knew she looked absolutely *classy*. She saw the way other people looked at her, their eyes lingering, and she felt so elegant, so special, it almost seemed that even the eyes of the people in the portraits were looking at her, too.

That night Ed took her to a restaurant with the dark, mysterious, leathery ambience of a world-class library. The menus were even larger than the ones at La Maison, and no prices were listed. Roses floated in a low bowl in the middle of their table and candles flickered in silver holders and on sconces on walls around the room. Lexi shivered with the realization that here, now, in her marvelous, simple black dress, she must seem to others like the well-educated, well-traveled women she had waited on all summer at La Maison.

Ed gazed approvingly at Lexi. "I hope you've noticed, you're the object of much admiration."

Lexi tried to be cool. She felt both triumphant and frightened. Ed had reserved two rooms for them—with an adjoining door. She took a sip of the champagne Ed had ordered and forced herself to calm down. She wanted to be *more* than she was.

"This has been a wonderful day, Ed," she told him.

Did he actually blush? He seemed almost embarrassed by her sincerity. "Yes, it has. Which painting did you like best?"

She laughed. "I couldn't possibly choose!" Then, more seriously, she said, "But the pictures that most interested me were by Mary Cassatt. I've been reading about her, and about the Paris Salon in the 1880s. Mary Cassatt was one of only a few women who exhibited with the men whom we now regard as masters. Renoir. Monet. Degas. And poor Degas! Did you know he never married? And he hated the term *Impressionist* and he believed that no painter could possibly have a private life. He was blind when he was older, and lonely—" She paused, suddenly embarrassed by her own fervency.

"Go on," Ed prompted. "Please. I'm fascinated. I've never taken the time to study the personal lives of artists."

"Oh, well," Lexi sipped more champagne. What was she thinking, telling this real estate mogul anything at all?

"Really," Ed insisted. He smiled his charming smile. "I find the lives of all successful people of interest."

After dinner, they strolled around the formal grounds of the hotel. The air was hot and humid and lush with the scent of roses. For a few moments they watched the waters of a fountain spill over the marble. This would be a good time for Ed to kiss her, Lexi thought. To hold her hand . . .

But he only took her arm, lightly. "It's late," Ed said. "We have to get up early tomorrow to drive back to the ferry."

She walked along helplessly as they returned to the hotel and took the elevator to their floor. At the door of her room, he said formally, "Good night, Lexi. Thank you for a delightful evening."

"Oh." She felt awkward, uncertain. "I thought—"

Calmly, he told her, "Anything else that happens tonight is your choice. The door between us stays locked, or you can open it. It's up to you."

"Well, okay . . ."

"See you in the morning."

Ed walked away, down the corridor to his own room. As he did, Lexi experienced an unexpected twinge of disappointment. A sense of loss, almost.

In her bedroom, she crossed to stand in front of the full-length mirror. She had twisted her blond hair into

61

a simple, classic chignon. Her makeup was only a touch of lipstick, but her cheeks were rosy from the champagne. She was sleek and slim and, yes, she was elegant, standing there in the black dress and high heels.

And she was glowing. From champagne, or nervousness, whatever—she was glowing.

And now she thought: why *shouldn't* she sleep with him? Probably she would never see him again in her entire life. Or perhaps next summer she would see him, and she would be waitressing at La Maison, and he would be courting and seducing another, younger waitress, and Lexi would be cast aside just like Clare predicted.

But next summer was far away. And until this trip, she had been feeling so lonely. Her brother was in school in Boston, her parents were in the process of closing their store, and most of her friends were back at college. She was young, after all; why shouldn't she be foolish while she was young? Why shouldn't she have a night of frivolous sexual passion with a wealthy, fascinating man?

She rechecked her image in the mirror. Should she change into her sexy little nightie? No. No, if she didn't unlock that door right this very minute, she'd have second thoughts and freeze up with terror. She looked as good as she was going to, and so she took a deep breath, and she unlocked the adjoining door.

Ed was standing by his bed. He was just removing

his dinner jacket. His white shirt gleamed like snow. "Well, hello."

She crossed over the threshold into his room. "I thought . . ." Suddenly she was trembling. She'd had sex with boys before—with *boys,* inexperienced, clumsy boys. She clenched her fists and struggled to remain dignified. "I thought I'd like to go to bed with you."

"Did you, now." Ed's face softened. "I was rather hoping you'd decide that."

She walked toward him slowly. She could feel her thighs brushing the silk of her dress. "Do you —Would you like me to undress?"

He pulled her to him in a gentle hug. "Lexi." He kissed her face and ran his hands down her arms. "Yes, Lexi, I'd like you to undress. But first, I'd like you to sit down. Here." He gestured to one of the chairs in the sitting area of his room.

Puzzled, she obeyed. Ed sat next to her. He studied her for a moment. "You really are lovely."

Her throat was so dry she was afraid to respond.

"Lexi," Ed said, "what would you think about marrying me?" And from his pocket he brought out a small black velvet box holding a large emerald-cut diamond ring.

Clare was nearly shaking with anger. It was very early Sunday morning, a muggy hot morning in early September. "I can't believe you made me come out to Moon Shell Beach to tell me this!"

Lexi hugged herself defensively. "We agreed we'd tell each other the important things here!"

Clare stamped her foot. "You'll never forgive me for not telling you the *moment* after I first slept with Jesse, will you?"

Lexi kicked off her thongs and drew a design in the sand with her toe as she gathered her thoughts. After a moment, she said, "Clare, this isn't about you and Jesse. This is about you and me. Our friendship. I thought it was special."

"It *is*." Clare held out her hands. "I love you, Lex, you know that. You'll always be my best friend. And we always knew we'd fall in love—it's part of growing up."

"So, that's why I asked you here to meet me. So I could tell you I'm going to marry Ed Hardin."

Clare protested, "But Lexi, he's a *horrible* man! What kind of woman have you become that you'd marry him? You know you *can't* love him. So you're marrying him for his money, and that makes you no better than a whore!"

Stung, Lexi shot back, "You should know. You're sleeping with the town slut. Jesse can't keep his trousers zipped, plus oh, right, he's really going to be able to support you with his awesome band that never quite gets formed."

"This isn't about Jesse," Clare said between clenched teeth. "It's about you marrying Ed Hardin. He's just an immoral, greedy, saga-sized *turd!*"

Lexi retorted, "And you're just a provincial little

peasant whose ambitions end at Jesse Gray's ass!"

Clare bit her cheek to stop the tears. She took a deep breath and struggled for dignity. "Well, I'm so glad you invited me out here to our *special* place to have this conversation," she said sardonically. Slapping bushes out of her way, she stormed along the path to her car.

Lexi held herself tightly for a long moment, then sank onto the sand and wept. Her parents were having financial troubles, her best friend hated her, she was alone—she was lost. You can only take what life offers you, Lexi thought. Clare wanted Jesse. Ed Hardin wanted her. She would marry him.

part two

FIVE

2006

Clare leaned against the bathroom door, watching Jesse shave. "Honestly, Jesse, I don't want to do this."

"Come on, babe. It's disrespectful if you don't show up." Jesse made a face as he scraped the delicate skin between his mouth and nose.

Tony Kostner's fishing boat had gone down in a storm on Georges Bank a week ago and Clare was trying to decide whether she was obligated to attend Tony's memorial service. "Well, I never did *respect* Anthony," Clare reminded him. "He was a drunk and an arrogant, bad-tempered lout."

Jesse dipped his face toward the basin, splashing it with cold water. Grabbing a towel, he rubbed his face dry. "We went to school with him, Clare." He scowled at her. "Anyway, this isn't just about Tony. It's about Georgeann."

The name opened between them like a black bog, indistinct and dangerous. One step into it and they'd be mired, thrashing around through their past in a frantic attempt to get back to the surface, clear and free.

Jesse brushed past Clare, out of the bathroom. She closed her eyes and tried counting to ten. All of her

69

life, every decision, every deed, seemed tied to her love for Jesse and his philandering.

For the past twelve years, Clare had based her whole life on the conviction that she and Jesse were meant for each other. It seemed right—until good-looking, easygoing, sweet-smiling Jesse once again confessed he'd sort of, kind of, had a *little*—oh, you couldn't even call it a fling, he'd just made one more tiny, purely *meaningless* mistake—in the arms of yet another woman, in yet another woman's bed. Laid-back Jesse, indeed.

Clare had broken off with Jesse every time. And sooner or later, the irresistible force that had drawn them together in high school brought them back together again.

At the end of last summer, when Clare's mother, whom Jesse had adored, was dying, Jesse had proposed marriage to Clare. He'd sworn off other women once and for all. He wanted to get married, he wanted to have children with Clare, he was ready to settle down. Oh, and I can believe you this time *because?* Clare had retorted. *No, thanks.* She knew he was just trying to make her mother happy—that was one of the lovable things about Jesse, he was in his heart a truly sweet guy. Two months later, in front of her father, Jesse had proposed again. This time, she'd accepted.

She was sure Jesse hadn't strayed since then. But the sight of one of Jesse's former flings always stung, and Georgeann Kostner had been his last mistake.

Jesse had been hired by the Kostners to renovate the space above their garage into a small rental apartment. Tony was always out fishing. Georgeann had brought mugs of hot coffee to Jesse, and stayed to talk, and one day she asked Jesse for help opening a stuck window in the bedroom, and then, as was often the case with Jesse, one thing led to another.

After a few weeks, Clare heard the gossip from a friend who had heard it from a friend who had seen Jesse's truck parked in front of the Kostners' house for exceptionally long lunch hours. Clare had confronted Jesse. Jesse had confessed and pleaded for forgiveness. It wasn't that he'd found Georgeann so irresistible, he swore, it wasn't that he cared for her in even the smallest way; it was just that the woman had come on to him so strongly, and she had been so needy, and he had been so weak.

After Jesse's affair with Georgeann, Clare had told Jesse she was through with him, this time *forever.* She'd packed up his possessions and dumped them in the bed of his truck. She'd gotten Caller ID and refused to pick up the phone when his number came up. She refused to open the door when he knocked.

And she had her own affair, with Jesse's best friend, the painfully shy Amos. When he found out, Jesse had given Amos a black eye. Clare had been surprised at how guilty she'd felt when she heard about that. She thought she'd be *pleased* by Jesse's jealousy. Instead she felt sad for both Jesse and Amos.

Then her mother had gotten ill, and Jesse had come

around to visit her, and she and Jesse had grown close again, and now here they were, engaged. Here they were, and she was convinced Jesse was through with wandering. She believed he would keep his promise to her, she trusted him when he said he loved her and wanted to live the rest of his life with her, but she still couldn't find a good reason in her heart or mind to attend this memorial service.

She followed Jesse into the bedroom and shut the door so her father wouldn't hear them arguing. "I doubt Georgeann would even want me to come."

Jesse gawked. "Are you nuts? You think she's going to come on to me at her husband's memorial service?"

"No. No, I didn't mean that. I just meant that Georgeann and I were never close. And she's got to know that I never cared for Tony."

Jesse grabbed his white shirt and yanked it on, buttoning up the front and the cuffs. Jesse looked really good in a white shirt. "His parents will be there, too, and his brother and sister. You like Rena."

Clare conceded the point. "I do like Rena. But it's not like we're close. She won't notice if I'm there or not."

"Sure she will. Come on, Clare, this isn't just about Tony, it's about the community. We've lost one of ours. Whether we respected him or not, he is still one of ours. It's like . . . like . . . like how we all take care of Lillian O'Malley. We don't say, oh, the dumb broad took too many drugs and broke her brain and can't walk across the street without getting lost. If anyone sees her wandering around, we take the time to cajole her into our car and we drive her home, we take the time to do that, even though on this island time is money. Tony was a dumb grunt in high school, I admit that, and he never did get much smarter, but he was a fisherman, he was an island son, and you're an island daughter, and it's just not *right* for you not to attend this service."

Clare looked at Jesse, who had slipped on the trousers to his best and only dark suit and was now working on a tie. His newly washed hair gleamed like the sun. He was beautiful. And he was right, too, about Tony and the island community, and this was one of the reasons she loved Jesse, because he was such a profound part of the island, and the island, land and people, were part of him.

"You're right, Jesse. I should go. I will go. Give me a moment, I'll find my black dress."

The Congregational church was crowded to standing-room only. As Clare sat next to Jesse in the last row, a deep welling of pain told her the real reason she'd wanted to avoid this service. It reminded her of being seated in the first row, next to her father, at the memorial service for her mother.

During the days just after her mother's death, Clare had felt almost coddled by a blanket of exhaustion and relief. Her mother's death had been short but hard, and Clare was grateful simply to have her mother lifted away from her pain. Clare's father, dumbfounded by the sudden illness and death of the woman he adored, became confused and lethargic. Clare had had to do everything, make all the arrangements, patiently accept the sympathies and consolations of the town.

Now she was able to settle into a reflective mood. It was almost Christmas. The year was drawing toward its final days. Night inked out the sky before five o'clock, and plunging temperatures and rising winds drove people into the refuge of their homes. Her shop did little business. Just before Christmas, there would be a sudden explosion of customers needing stocking stuffers and a few grand luxury boxes of truffles, but until then, Clare found herself often alone for hours in Sweet Hart's. There was always something she could do, but recently she found herself just leaning on her counter, remembering.

Ellen Hart had not been particularly maternal. She loved her husband and daughter, but the early years of nurturing a baby and raising a child had been difficult for her. Around the time Clare turned nine, Ellen had her studio built, and with each passing week she escaped more and more completely into her art. Somehow the three of them bumbled along together, and while Clare never starved, she seldom sat down to the dinner table with both her parents, and after a while, if the house needed cleaning, it was Clare who cleaned it. Clare didn't resent her mother.

No one could resent Ellen, who was lovely in a wistful way, with her long brown and white hair floating around her shoulders as she drifted out to the studio in her jeans, painter's smock, and bedroom slippers. When she focused, she was charming. Jesse could usually get Ellen's attention. He could make Ellen light up the way most women did around him, and when Ellen let her head fall back as she laughed, she was enchanting.

In the quiet moments since her mother's death, Clare was visited by memories of earlier years, when she was a little girl, when her mother's attentions were more fully engaged on her family. On rainy days, her mother dressed Clare up in one of her romantic filmy negligees or satin robes, put ballet music on the stereo, and danced, swooping, around the house with Clare, and then the rain would disappear, and the walls of the house would melt, and Clare would be with a Fairy Queen, and she would be the Fairy Princess, and they would be waltzing among the clouds.

One year, when Clare was seven or perhaps eight, a girl in their class gave a Halloween party. Clare wanted to be a mermaid, and her artistic mother had concocted a costume from turquoise satin with a tail that trailed behind her like a shining blue arrow. A small slit on the side made it possible for her to walk in tiny steps, like a mermaid would have to take. In her curly brown hair glittered a tiara her mother had made by gluing shells and sparkles on a headband.

Clare wished she could wear the tiara every moment of her life.

The day before the party, Clare had invited Lexi over to play, and unable to contain the thrill of having such a fabulous costume, she'd tried it on for Lexi. Lexi reacted with wonder, circling Clare slowly, gently touching her long blue tail, and then Lexi had sat right down on the floor and cried. Her parents were both busy in their store. They had no time to create an outfit for Lexi, and had ordered her a generic princess gown that was ugly, too large, and exactly like the one Spring Macmillan said she had.

Clare's mother had been in the hallway at that moment. She'd swept into the room to announce that she would make Lexi her very own singular mermaid costume. Clare was delighted to see her friend's excitement, but worried, too. She didn't want Lexi to have a costume like hers. It would diminish the originality of her own.

But Ellen constructed Lexi's costume from a one-piece emerald bathing suit, draped with scarves of sea green, foam white, and blue that fell to Lexi's ankles, where they were gathered around into a frothy tail. Ellen sat the two girls down at the kitchen table with slender silk ribbons of green and blue and glued tiny silver and gold shells to the end of each ribbon. She phoned Lexi's mother to ask if Lexi could spend the night, and Saturday, just before the party, she braided the ribbons into Lexi's shoulder-length white-blond hair. She drove the girls to the party, and Clare would never forget the thrill of entering the room with Lexi at her side, both of them mermaids, extraordinary, glamorous, creatures from another world. At the very bottom of her heart, Clare was especially pleased that she was the one with the glittering, shell-studded tiara. Her costume was just a little bit better.

The congregation rose now to sing a hymn. As Clare rose with the others, she wondered whether Lexi even knew that Ellen had died. Clare had received no letter of condolence, and that seemed a little odd. Wouldn't Lexi's parents have told Lexi about Clare's mother's death?

Perhaps Lexi hadn't written a note of condolence because Clare had never answered any of Lexi's earlier letters. It had been ten years since she and Lexi had had their bitter, name-calling argument. For a few years after that, Lexi had written brief notes to Clare. And Clare hadn't answered. Lexi's letters had seemed like a kind of bragging. *Here I am in Paris, here I am in Rome.* During those years Clare had gotten a college degree in business, attended a culinary college for two years, worked three jobs every summer to save money, and started Sweet Hart's. She'd had no time to spend on regrets and memories, and what free time she did have she'd spent with Jesse. Loving Jesse—and hating him, whenever she found out he was sleeping with someone else. Now she had agreed to marry Jesse. She'd managed to forgive Jesse for all his philandering. Couldn't she forgive Lexi for an argument that had been every bit as much Clare's fault?

The truth was, she missed Lexi, and yet it was possible that the Lexi she missed didn't even exist anymore. Lexi lived in New York with a wealthy, important man. Lexi's brother, Adam, had left the island, too, to work with a veterinary practice outside Boston. Their parents were both retired now, so Clare never ran into them. She scanned the rows in front of her, but didn't spot the Laneys, although she might not recognize them from the back.

If they had come, and if they were at the reception after the service, she might ask them how Lexi was doing. In the past ten years, she'd never spoken to them about Lexi. Perhaps they might tell Lexi that Clare had asked after her. It might be seen as an overture for reconciliation, and Clare was stunned at how much the thought appealed to her.

But no matter how hard she looked, she didn't see the Laneys.

SIX

2006

Lexi was in the climate-controlled walk-in closet in her husband's Park Avenue home. Funny, how she still thought of this place as Ed's home, not hers. Partly that was because she'd never been given permission to redecorate any of the rooms. Ed preferred a dark palette of colors, and heavy, massive furniture that loomed against the walls, seeming somehow judicial. Their judgment on Lexi was: *you don't belong here.* In the early years, Lexi thought that, with time, she would feel at home in this place. She had *tried* to feel at home here. But now, ten years later, she was still an intruder or, at best, a guest in the gallery of her husband's life.

This one enclosed room in the large, formal house was hers. Her closet, hushed and orderly, was her refuge. Opening the glossy teak closet doors, she ran her fingertips over her silk shirts, skirts, and dresses, organized by color into a rainbow of luxury. With a touch of her finger, custom-built drawers glided open like silk, exposing layer after layer of perfectly folded sweaters, T-shirts, leotards. In other drawers, on velvet pads, lay her glittering treasure hoard of jewelry—the jewelry not valuable enough to be in the vault.

So much beauty. So much perfection.

And all of it cold and mute and still.

She sank down on the floor, pulled her knees up to her chest, and buried her face in her arms. She'd started her period again today, perhaps that was why she was in such a dark mood. Ed would never have approved of her seeing a therapist, so recently she'd taken to reading self-help books. Now she called upon their advice. One exercise had been to look for the positive, to count her blessings. She could do that, couldn't she?

Okay, then. To start with, she lived in luxury, that was certain. And she had to admit that she traveled as much as she wanted. With Ed, she vacationed in Tuscany, sunned on private Caribbean islands, and skied in Switzerland or Vail. She heard operas and symphonies in London, Amsterdam, and New York, and attended private parties for the conductors and divas afterward. She gazed upon breathtaking paintings in Paris and St. Petersburg. She even spent a few summer weeks on the Vineyard, which was kind of funny, since Nantucketers considered it a rival island. The only vacation spot she never went to was Nantucket. Because her marriage to Ed had caused such a rift with her parents, Ed never wanted to spend time on Nantucket, and Lexi didn't push it. In a way, she didn't want to go there when she was with him, because if she was with him she wouldn't be herself, the self people on Nantucket knew and loved.

Or, rather, used to love.

Oh, how she missed the island. She missed her parents, she missed the beaches, she missed Clare.

Stop it, Lexi told herself. Stop obsessing about what you don't have. Focus on what you have.

She looked around the closet. The clothes. It was such fun, choosing and wearing the clothes she was *supposed* to wear, the more expensive, the better, because it all reflected on her husband. Ed valued her lanky, sleek body, and people around him gushed with compliments when Lexi attended a charity ball in a simple gown and big jewels. She knew the admiration was really only a kind of suck-up to her wealthy husband, but that didn't dim the pleasure. At the best of times, she felt like her husband's colleague. Ed would brief her on the people they would be dining with and prime her on whom to flatter, whom to ignore. Earlier in their marriage, he'd liked to have sex after an important business-related event and, in a weird way, that had made her feel useful. But after all these years of marriage, the sex was irregular and brief. She was afraid Ed was bored with her.

And she was unhappy and deeply lonely. Ed traveled constantly and she missed his company, but more than that, she missed having women friends. Most of the women Lexi met were the wives of Ed's colleagues, and those women were older, or first wives who disliked Lexi on principle. Or they were women with children.

Children. Oh, how she wanted a child.

For a few years, Lexi had been on the Pill. Ed didn't like condoms, and she knew she was too inexperienced in this new life to be a good mother. When she stopped taking the Pill, after they'd been married for four years, she assumed she'd get pregnant within months. And she did. Two months later, she miscarried.

Ed was kind to her, on his way out the door to another meeting. He didn't want more children—he already had three. So Lexi never told him about the two other miscarriages. She could never tell him how, as the months passed, with the rise of hope and the plunge of disappointment, she came to hate her body, not for the way it looked but because of what it could not seem to do.

It was impossible to share these deep and intimate emotions with him. She quickly learned, and constantly was reminded, that Ed liked her when she was perfect and distant, but in her imperfect neediness, she was on her own. Lexi had tried to find friends. She gave dinner parties, and networked with other women by doing charity work. She invited women for lunch. Sometimes they invited her back. After a while, with committee meetings and luncheons, she had at least the illusion of friendships. But never did she have that flash of connection she had had with Clare, that sense of being immediately at home, in the same pack. She could never talk about what really mattered to her.

Focus on the positive, she ordered herself.

Okay, she *did* have one friend. She did have Gloria. Thank goodness for Gloria. Two years ago, bored with herself and tired of feeling insecure because she was less knowledgeable than Ed's older, more experienced crowd, Lexi told him she wanted to go back to college. Nonsense, Ed said. In the first place, that would tie her down so she couldn't travel with him, and in the second place, how embarrassing would it be for him to have a wife in college? He had *children* in college!

But he agreed she could have a tutor.

So brilliant, funny, warmhearted Gloria Ruben entered her life—and changed her life. Gloria was ten years older than Lexi, plump, maternal, and energetic. She taught literature and theater criticism at CCNY and supplemented her income with tutoring. Gloria had been divorced twice, she had two teenage children and a constellation of relatives and friends and old and new lovers who were always needing her, but as Lexi and Gloria got to know each other, Gloria made time to accompany Lexi to a new off-Broadway play or a concert at Carnegie Hall.

And when Lexi had a miscarriage, Gloria mourned with her, and nursed her, tucking her in bed with pillows and bringing her chocolates and a pile of new novels. Gloria was the one who insisted Lexi see an ob-gyn about these miscarriages, and when the medical verdict came—Lexi was fine, there was no reason she couldn't have a baby—it was Gloria who celebrated with Lexi, drinking Taittinger champagne.

Lexi could certainly use Gloria's warmth and generosity today. Once again a sudden flood of blood and an agonizing clench of pain announced the end to the hopes she'd nourished over the past two months. She'd been scheduled to attend a luncheon for the hospital committee, but she'd phoned and left her regrets.

Her regrets. What a concept, *to leave her regrets.*

With each passing day, she regretted the way she'd left the island. In her defense, she had been so young. And she'd gotten carried away with herself, the brand-new fabulous Lexi who'd been proposed to by one of the masters of the universe. In the sanctuary of her closet, helped by ten years' experience, she burned with shame to remember that last vitriolic battle with her parents. She'd called them narrow-minded, mediocre ignoramuses with a worldview too limited to even comprehend her dreams. She'd raged at them so terribly, she'd been a whirling spitfire, fueled by her fears. But even with all the horrible things she said to them, she had managed to contain her most grievous complaint, knowing how it would have wounded them. She had not said to her parents: *I would not be doing this if you weren't failing financially! If you could send me to college, if you weren't so depressed and anxious and burdened, if* I weren't such a burden to you,

I wouldn't marry this man. That would have been the cruelest thing to say, and Lexi was glad she had not said it, even though she believed that when she left, her parents must have felt some relief mixed with their consternation and anger. She'd said horrible things to Clare, too, although Clare—Lexi couldn't help but smile—had given as good as she'd got.

Those final arguments had been so savage that when she left the island to marry Ed, she'd done it all alone. She'd slammed out of her house, carrying only a small suitcase. No one drove her to the airport, no one waved good-bye or wished her good luck. She'd been delighted to get away from them all. They would have held her back, she told herself. She was going to a more exciting world. She thought she'd escaped from her island life like a butterfly sloughing off its chrysalis.

For a long time, she had enjoyed her new life, and if she ever found herself feeling sad or lonely or homesick, she put that down to sheer exhaustion. She'd had so much to learn, she was always on the run, boarding airplanes, hearing operas, smiling at important people who didn't speak her language, it was as if time danced along, carrying her with it, and she was engrossed, learning the moves as she went. In those early days she didn't miss her parents or Clare, because, in an odd way, she brought them with her, as if they were tucked away in a compact in her purse, and every time she opened it, they could see her, sleek, glossy, and having the time of her life.

Those first few years she'd been quite impressed with her new self in her amazing clothes, drinking champagne in exotic places. Looking back, she saw how the communications she'd attempted with her parents and with Clare had been one-part genuine attempt for connection and three-parts sheer show-off bragging. She sent postcards to her parents and Clare, and Christmas cards with photos of her and Ed posed on camels or llamas. She sent her parents expensive coffee-table books about the Louvre or spices from the Nile Valley for Christmas. Her parents returned Christmas cards with stiff messages. "We're glad you're happy." They never thanked her for the presents. That first Christmas, she sent Clare an amazing silk scarf from Bangkok. Clare never responded. She stopped sending presents. If they could live without her, she could live without them.

But the gloss of Lexi's grand new life was dimming. Her relationship with her husband, never hot, was growing even cooler. Sometimes she thought she received the most attention from him when they were being settled into their first-class seats on an airplane. Ed fussed over her then, being sure she had magazines, champagne, a light blanket. They were very seldom alone in the apartment together, and when they were, he was working, or sleeping. He still found her sexually attractive, but her attempts at pillow talk afterward were thwarted. She was amazed at his ability to fall asleep during her most earnest attempts to gain his interest. She was saddened that he didn't want children with her, and then, when she stopped taking the Pill and tried to get pregnant, she was even more heartbroken, because she could not share her loss with him. She couldn't even turn to him for comfort.

She had no one to turn to. Somehow, the worse she felt, the more she felt walled in by her own youthful mistake—for now she understood that marrying Ed had been a terrible mistake. She hadn't sent her parents postcards for years. Even the briefest note—"Having a wonderful time!"—would have been a lie. And telling them the truth would have been humiliating.

One morning, lying on the lonely expanse of their king-sized bed, she closed her eyes and found herself yearning not for the cosmopolitan streets of Paris or the exotic landscape of Bali, but for the comforts of her childhood room, the soft pillow with the lavender case, the companionship of her stuffed animals, the apple tree swaying just outside her window, the smell of simmering pot roast, her brother's loud laughter. She recalled being foolish with Clare, both of them laughing like hyenas, literally falling out of their chairs with laughter. *"You girls,"* Lexi's mother would say fondly.

She daydreamed of phoning Clare, but they had been so mean to each other that last summer, equally mean, Lexi thought, like children in a rage. And after all these years, living so far apart, could they ever get that kind of friendship back again?

Could she get back in touch with her parents and still keep up the pretense of having a happy marriage? She thought perhaps Adam might be a good mediator. He hadn't been on the island the summer she met Ed, he hadn't been involved in the arguments, and he'd never weighed in with an opinion. One rainy January when Ed was off on yet another business trip, Lexi had Googled her brother. Adam was working at a veterinary practice in Boston. She e-mailed him just a "Hey, how's it going?" kind of message. He responded, and from then on, they kept up a casual online correspondence. But Adam was busy, usually having time for only a brief answer to her longer e-mails, and it was clear that while he hoped she'd reunite with their parents, he wasn't going to volunteer to arrange it.

So she was on her own. No one got to erase the mistakes she'd made in life. The self-help books advocated taking positive action. So she would not allow herself to lurk like a spoiled four-year-old, hiding in her closet, feeling sorry for herself. She'd get out, she'd do something, she'd have fun. She'd phone Gloria.

Ed didn't like Lexi socializing with Gloria—he said she *shouldn't be so chummy with the help*. She had argued with him about that, and while she rarely stood up for her own opinions against Ed, she was proud that she'd risked his anger and his contempt by insisting that Gloria was her friend. Today, Lexi could really use a friend.

Just making the decision made her feel better. It was a Thursday, and Gloria didn't teach at the college on Thursdays. She would take Gloria to lunch at that new Asian restaurant on East 70th Street, and afterward they could take a stroll through the Met—that always cheered Lexi. Wiping her tears away, Lexi left her closet. She walked through the small dressing room that connected it to the master bedroom, and opened the door.

And stopped short.

She saw a gleam of skin, and a blur of movement. A man and a woman were in bed together, naked, so closely entwined they seemed like one creature.

She put a hand out to the wall for support. "Ed?"

"Jesus Christ!" Ed unceremoniously dumped the naked woman on her side as he yanked the covers up over both of them. He sat up in bed, his face red with anger. "What are you doing here? I thought you were at that hospital luncheon today."

"I . . . I canceled." Her head seemed to be full of sparks. She couldn't stop staring.

"Look," Ed's tone was exasperated, "get out of here, Lexi. Go on, damn it. Let us get dressed."

"Okay," Lexi said reasonably. "I will. But first . . ." She inched forward. "Gloria? Is that you?"

Gloria peeked out from behind a sheet. "Lexi, I'm sorry." Her black hair was mussed, her face mottled with embarrassment.

Lexi stared. For a moment she was helpless; she was like something whirled and abraded by a natural

89

violence, like a shell sucked out of dark depths and tossed up into full, glaring sunlight. The oddest thing was that she didn't cry.

She walked out of the bedroom, leaving the door open, and down the hall, and down the magnificent staircase, and into the living room. It was as if she'd been injected with a marvelous drug that made her see more clearly and think more brilliantly. She looked around the living room with all its deep burgundy and gilt furnishings and thought how much she disliked this somber room.

Footsteps clattered down the stairs. The front door opened. Voices murmured. The door closed. More footsteps, and then Ed was in the room with Lexi. He'd pulled on a pair of chinos and a pink-and-white-striped shirt, and he was rolling up the sleeves as he talked.

"Lexi, look, I didn't mean for you to see that. I thought you were out of the house."

She stared at him. He was almost fifty now and almost completely bald. In spite of his personal trainer and the hours he put in at the gym, he was gaining weight and growing a belly. But that didn't matter. It wouldn't have mattered if she loved him. She did not love him, but she didn't hate him, either. She only seemed to see him very clearly.

She took a deep breath. "Ed, I want a divorce."

"Don't be ridiculous. Gloria means nothing to me."

"She meant something to me."

"Oh, grow up."

"Actually, I have. Grown up. And you've been very kind to me. But now I want a divorce."

He waved his hands in a "stop" motion. "Lexi, calm down a moment."

"Don't I look calm?" She was lucid and composed. "You've been cheating on me all along, haven't you?"

"Don't be so dramatic. It never means anything. I married *you*." That was true, and Lexi knew it was important. For a moment she hesitated, considering his needs and her responsibilities. Then he did the thing that really set her free. He sneaked a glance at his watch.

"Ed," she said firmly, "I really do want a divorce."

part three

SEVEN

2007

When the phone rang, Clare was idly doing the breakfast dishes, gazing from the kitchen window to the end of the yard, where two bird feeders stood, their platforms heaped with sunflower seeds and cracked corn. The cardinal couple was there, the vivid male eating while the duller female perched on the rim, keeping watch. It was April, a shimmery quicksilver month, with days of wind and rain interrupted by long, surprisingly warm twilights and a come-hither sun winking promises as it set.

"Hello?" She clamped the handset between her shoulder and ear, leaving her hands free to finish scrubbing the skillet. Even if, during the rest of the day, her father forgot to eat, she knew she'd started him off well with a stack of bacon, a huge pile of cheesy eggs, and thickly buttered rye toast.

Penny's voice exploded over the air waves. *"Scoop,* honey! *Big scoop!"*

Clare grinned. "What? Has the Little Genius started walking?"

"Stop it." In the background, Penny's baby boy was making the funny guzzling noises he made when he nursed. "This is so not about babies. And it's going to make your eyes pop, I promise. But you have to come over to hear about it."

"Tell me now. Pleeeeese? You know you want to." The large handsome blue jay she'd privately named Johnny Depp swooped down, claiming the bird feeder, and the cardinal couple flew off in a flash of red.

"No way. I want to see your face when you hear this."

Clare hesitated.

"Are you still there?" Penny demanded.

"Yeah, just thinking. How about this. I'll come over for coffee this afternoon. Four-ish. I'll bring some clam chowder and corn bread and salad for dinner tonight."

"You're an angel." Little Mike let out a wail. "Oops. Burp time. See you later."

Clare moved around the kitchen, mixing the corn bread, enough for Penny and her father. Since her mother's death last fall, her father had become even more vague and forgetful. Retired from teaching high school English, he was sixty-two years old and lost in sorrow. On good days he stayed in his study, researching and writing his book on island mythology, but on bad days he roamed the house, restless in his loneliness and misery, forgetting to shave, dress properly, or eat sensibly. Clare had become the one to nurture him.

She put a batch in the oven, set the timer, then raced upstairs to take a quick shower and dress. Sweet

Hart's was closed for two more weeks, so she had time to play around with a new recipe. Jesse would be working today, custom building cabinets for a gazillion-dollar new house, and he might come by for dinner and a video tonight, but even if he did, she could slop around in these jeans and the comfy blue cashmere pullover she'd bought on sale two Januarys ago at Murray's Toggery. It had been washed so many times it felt like satin, and it set off her dark eyes and short, tousled brown hair.

She slid her feet into her felt clogs, clomped down the stairs, and entered the kitchen just as the buzzer sounded. A heavenly buttery aroma filled the air. She took the corn bread out of the oven and was stacking various cartons into a straw tote when the phone rang again.

"Hey, babe."

Clare rolled her eyes at the sound of that "babe." She continually asked Jesse not to call her *babe*. It was such an anonymous, generalized designation. *Any* woman could be *babe*. And for Jesse, countless women had been. Perhaps that was the price Clare had to pay for being in love with such a handsome man. "Hey, Jesse, what's up?"

"Just wanted to say good morning." A chorus of hammer falls and whining saws created background music to his voice.

"Good morning, sweetie." Clare curled up in an ancient wooden captain's chair at the end of the kitchen table, pulled her knees up to her chest, and leaned into the sound of his voice. She could envision Jesse at work in his flannel shirt, jeans, and work boots, his thick blond hair tied back in a ponytail with some old rubber band. Perhaps by now—the crew started work early—he'd have warmed up and tossed off the flannel shirt. So he'd be wearing only an old white short-sleeved T-shirt. She thought of the muscles in his arms, the lean stretch of his torso.

"How's your father?"

His thoughtfulness warmed her. "Better, I think. He's showered and dressed in clean clothes. I fixed him a big fat breakfast."

"Yum. I wish someone would fix me a big fat breakfast."

When we're married, I'll make you breakfast every day, Clare thought. But she didn't want to seem eager. She wanted *him* to be the one to push to set the wedding date. So she kept it light. "How about a big fat dinner tonight?"

Jesse made a kind of purring noise in his throat. "Sounds good."

"And I might have some gossip."

"Oh, yeah?"

"Penny phoned. I'm going over later for coffee. She said she's got a major scoop."

Jesse snorted. "On this island in April? Not likely."

"Wait and see."

"What's for dinner?" Jesse asked. "Talk sexy to me, baby."

Clare smiled. "What about a nice juicy steak with fried potatoes and onions and a big salad to keep us healthy?"

"Sounds great. And just the kind of thing to provide me with a little extra energy for . . . other activities."

Clare closed her eyes, soaking in the sexiness of his voice. Through the phone she heard someone yell.

"Hey, babe, I gotta go. I'll see you tonight. Sixish."

"See you then."

"I love you," Jesse spoke quietly. He'd been ragged on too many times by his friends for being mushy.

"Love you." Clare smiled. She tried not to be the one to say "I love you" first. It always lifted her heart, made her feel more secure, when Jesse said "I love you" without any kind of prompting.

€IGH₺

On an ordinary April day, the blue and white Hy-Line catamaran sped toward Nantucket Island. Lexi leaned on the rail, letting the wind whip her hair against her cheeks, not minding the cold damp lashing. She was returning home.

Her heart raced as the boat skipped over the waves. Two weeks ago she'd made a quick trip to the island to find a building to rent and also to see how she liked being back on Nantucket again. It had felt absolutely *right,* and the building was a dream come true. She'd negotiated the rental agreement by mail and e-mail and now here she was, with the keys to her new home on Commercial Wharf in her pocket. She hadn't called her parents or Clare yet. She wanted them back in her life again, but first, she simply wanted to be on Nantucket.

In the distance, a gray smudge on the horizon indicated the presence of land. Lexi laughed out loud. How had she managed to live without her island? Only now was she grasping how much she had missed Main Street at Christmas, Daffodil Weekend, and the crowds packing the bleachers at the football games. She remembered loving the island for its sun-drenched beaches and bright surging waters, yes, but more than that, she loved it because it was a small town. She loved that babies were born in the Nantucket Cottage Hospital tucked away near the Old Mill, and that those who died rested in the cemetery on a street aptly named Prospect Hill, with its gentle reminder that those still between birth and death might want to take a moment to consider their afterlife prospects and adjust their actions accordingly. She loved it that the island had no malls or McDonald's. She loved it that the only movie house open in the nine months of the off-season was the Starlight, and she was sorry the new owners had changed the name from the Gaslight, which had always provided the youngest males something to joke about. She loved it that one of the busiest streets in town curved past a pond where a community of spoiled mallards and a few marauding herring gulls lived, and when more people crowded onto the island with their cars, the town put up a sign: *Duck Crossing. Please Drive Carefully*. As far as she knew, not one duck had been killed on that busy curve. She loved that women had always been influential on this island —all that history she'd yawned over in school now meant something to her.

The ferry slowed, gliding into the boat basin on the sheltered side of the island. She saw the white spire of the Congregational church rising above the village sheltering along the shore, and the stubby white Brant Point lighthouse, and the curve of Children's Beach. She saw, in the distance, the golden blur of Moon Shell Beach.

The ferry bumped gently against the pilings. Chains sang as they were slung and fastened while ramps were dropped into place, and the passengers filed off the boat, onto shore.

Lexi stepped onto the island. Her new Range Rover would arrive on the big, slow car ferry at eleven-thirty. She'd pick it up then.

She tugged her cashmere cap down over her blond hair and wrapped her scarf around her face, nestling her chin and mouth down inside for warmth. Instead of going right to her building, she took a detour along Water Street, up past the library and post office, and down Main Street. Even after all her years away, she could make this walk blindfolded. On an April Monday, many businesses were closed, but the lights were on in the post office. An old man limped down the sidewalk, accompanied by an extremely fat bulldog that was almost dancing in its attempt to keep its paws off the cold bricks. Could that be Marvin Meriweather? Could he have aged so much? The dog did look like Moses. The pair disappeared inside the Hub before Lexi could make up her mind.

Across the street, a woman with a baby in a Bjorn and a three-year-old child clutching her hand struggled up the path to the children's library. South Water Street was a row of dark, silent buildings. The Dreamland Theater was boarded up for the winter. The various T-shirt shops and art galleries were closed but Fog Island, a restaurant new to Lexi, had a light on far in the back and a sign stating they would be open at eleven-thirty, for lunch.

She hurried on through the Grand Union parking lot, past Old South Wharf where a few private fishing boats berthed along the pier rocked and bounced in the sloshing seas, and finally she walked out on Commercial Wharf and stood in front of the building for which she had just signed a three-year lease.

A two-story wooden structure, it was shingled and gray and as square and forthright as a Puritan with its white trim and granite stoop. It was a duplex, with fifteen hundred feet of open space on ground level, and another fifteen hundred feet on the second floor, where she would make her new home.

It was ironic—and perhaps some kind of omen? —that Clare Hart's chocolate shop occupied the space next to Lexi's.

She would call Clare soon. She *would*.

But for now she just turned the key in the lock and pushed open the door, entering her new space. *Her* new space. The floors were hardwood, sanded and stained golden, and polyurethaned against damage. The walls were a white plasterboard, pitted with holes because the last occupant had been an antiques dealer who'd had mirrors, oil paintings, and several display cabinets nailed to the walls. Lexi walked the length of the room, envisioning changes. Dressing rooms at the back, with full-length mirrors, little benches, and doors or curtains for privacy. Racks for the clothing would hang along the two side walls, and she'd display the jewelry in two glass cases along the middle aisle, where she'd keep the cash register and shopping bags.

She had very little money left—she'd had to sell the good stuff in order to start her new life. When she divorced Ed, she discovered that before their marriage, she'd witlessly signed a prenuptial agreement Ed's lawyers had drawn up, an ironclad document that left her with no alimony, no assets whatsoever, except for the clothes and some of the jewelry.

But that was all right, that was fine. She felt rejuvenated, ready to roll. The depression she had muddled in like a gluey swamp had dissolved the moment she told Ed she wanted a divorce. With the divorce she changed her last name back to Laney. Every day since then, she had felt stronger, braver, and more complete. She knew what she loved, and she knew what she was good at, and she knew what she wanted to do. She was free of Ed and that bizarre mistake of a life. She was clear, large, and in charge. She wanted to run a fabulous little boutique that would make every woman who walked in the door feel special.

So, she needed to find a carpenter right away. Not a contractor—this wasn't a big job. But someone good at designing and envisioning space as well as sawing and pounding nails.

She needed to get her new apartment at least minimally furnished so she could eat and sleep. Unwinding her scarf as she went, Lexi climbed up the stairs at the back of the building. She paused on the landing to unlock the door, then stepped inside her new home. This was an amazing, spectacular place. Oh, it was tiny and bland compared to the homes she'd lived in for the past decade, but this place was *hers*, hers alone, and that made it a palace.

It was one long room with golden floors, white walls, and the best view in the universe, windows looking out over the dancing blue waters of the harbor, the town pier, and the low rise of buildings along the opposite shore. No one lived here in the winter—the cost of heat would be prohibitive—but she knew she'd survive the cold spring and luxuriate in the summer.

The bathroom and kitchenette were at the back of the building. She opened the cupboards, which were bare. She had to go to the grocery store—no problem, with the Grand Union just a short walk away. The moving van was scheduled to come tomorrow.

Now was the moment she'd been both longing for and dreading. Lexi opened her cell phone. She'd already programmed in the number. She hit the button. Her heart raced as she heard the phone ring.

"Hello?"

It took a moment for her to recognize her brother's voice. "Adam! What are you doing there?"

NINE

Penny and her husband lived in a small cottage on a rutted dirt road out in Tom Nevers Head near the eastern tip of the island. Clare arrived to find Penny curled up on the sofa, nursing her gigantic baby. In high school, copper-haired, muscular, sensible Penny had been field hockey captain, star of the swim team, working summers as a lifeguard, so it was no surprise that her square-headed baby looked like a miniature quarterback.

Clare unloaded the chowder and salad, then made them both mugs of hot chocolate—chocolate was, Penny informed her, okay for nursing mothers. Clare allowed herself a moment of yearning pleasure as she gazed down at the baby, with his sweet bald head, then she kicked off her clogs, settled in a chair, and tucked her feet under her.

"Okay"—she blew on her hot chocolate to cool it—"spill."

Penny paused dramatically, enjoying her moment of power, before announcing, "Lexi's come back."

"Get out!" Clare almost slopped her cocoa out of its mug.

"It's true. Mom heard it from Rhoda Rollins, the receptionist at Paul's real estate agency. And there's more. *Big* more. Lexi's opening a boutique, and guess where it's going to be."

Clare's eyes widened. "No."

"Yes."

Clare looked stunned. "I knew that space was for rent. But I never saw anyone looking at it."

"She was here the weekend you went shopping in Boston."

"Holy shit."

"I know." With practiced ease, Penny brought Mikey to a sitting position on her knees and patted his back gently. "You haven't been in touch with Lexi?"

Clare ran her finger over the plaid pattern in the chair cover. "Oh, after she left, I got a few letters. I never wrote her back. Which, I hasten to add, was not my fault. Her letters were always postmarked from some exotic spot in Europe." Sipping her hot chocolate, she reflected a moment, then admitted, "To be honest, I didn't want to get back in touch. She made me feel like what she'd called me, a provincial peasant with no ambitions."

"I'd say starting your own chocolate business is pretty ambitious," Penny argued loyally.

"Yeah, but Lexi was long gone by the time I opened the shop. First, I had to slave away for years, saving money. While I was up to my elbows in loans and hard work, Lexi was swanning around like a princess, showing up in newspapers and magazines, remember? 'Ed Hardin's wife in Oscar de la Renta at the opening of the Met.' "

"I wonder what happened."

"What do you mean?"

"Why is she moving back here?"

"Well, you know they got divorced."

Penny shifted her heavy sleeping baby to her other arm. "I didn't know that, actually. I haven't exactly been tracking her career."

Clare blushed. "I haven't, either! I just read about it when I was in line at the Stop and Shop. It was in one of the tabloids. Must have been a slow news day, no real celebrity divorces."

Penny thought for a moment. A registered nurse, she'd worked at the hospital before marrying Mike Stockwell, a contractor so square-shouldered and bulky he looked like Penny's brother. She'd left the hospital to be a stay-at-home mom. Penny liked to do things slowly and thoroughly. "She must have missed the island. Since she's coming back here. She must have missed *you*. You were her best friend. And gosh, *you* must have missed *her*."

"Truthfully? I really don't know, Penny. I guess I miss who she used to be when we were kids."

Penny grinned. "I'll bet she'll have some tales to tell. All the traveling she's done. The people she's met."

"You're assuming she'll want to spend time with us. The island peasants."

"Come on, give her a chance."

"If she wants to be friends again, why didn't she

tell me she was moving back here?"

Calmly Penny suggested, "Maybe she was afraid of the reception she'd get."

"Look," Clare snapped, "I'm not the one who started it all. I'm not the one who called me names and left."

"No, you were the one who called her names and stayed."

Clare snorted. "Motherhood has made you disgustingly rational."

Penny gazed down on her sleeping baby. "*Rational,* no. Some days I'm so sleep-deprived I nearly walk into the walls. But mellow, yes. Really really happy and just, oh, *creamy* with love, and I want everyone else in the world to be happy, too. Besides, you're a big girl now, Clare. You've got your own great business, and you're engaged to Jesse. Lexi can't hurt you ever again as much as she did before."

"Right. Because she's not going to get the chance."

TEN

The house Lexi had grown up in was tucked away down a winding dirt lane off Polpis Road, behind a thick stand of evergreen trees. Lexi parked her Range Rover on the white shell driveway and sat for a moment, collecting her thoughts. The old ranch house looked great, tidy and welcoming, and dozens of crocuses dotted the flower beds on either side of the blue door.

Deep breath. Lexi got out, crunched up the shell walkway, and knocked on the door. How odd it felt, to have to *knock* at her own front door. A younger Lexi wavered ghostily around her like a hologram, barreling up the steps, throwing open the door, stomping snow off her boots as she yelled, "Hi, guys!"

An explosion of barks, yips, yaps, and an odd baritone honk detonated within the house, storming toward the door. Lexi's family had always had a dog, but this sounded like a kennel. The door opened, and there stood her mother, clad in jeans and a brightly striped sweater, her legs circled by four highly excited canines.

Lexi felt tears rush to her eyes. Myrna was almost sixty, Lexi knew that, but even though it had been years since she'd seen her mother, she hadn't expected Myrna to have aged quite so noticeably. Her blond hair was thinner, her face lined, her shoulders rounded.

Myrna's face flushed and her voice was clogged when she said, "Alexandra. Well, well."

Of course her parents suspected that Lexi was still the arrogant little snot she'd been ten years ago. She had to win their trust back. She sucked in a deep breath.

"Oh, Mom, it's so good to see you." Leaning forward over the wriggling mass of canines, Lexi grabbed her mother and hugged her tightly. The dogs sniffed Lexi's ankles, their tails wagging like metronomes.

Myrna scrabbled around in her sweater pocket for one of the endless tissues she kept handy, and blew her nose. "Let's go into the living room."

"Lexi!" Her huge handsome brother rose to crush Lexi in a bear hug, then held her at arm's length to study her. "Good to see you."

"You, too." Adam had gotten bulkier, and his thick blond hair was brown now, streaked with a bit of gray, but he was still her older brother, good-humored, affectionate, strong, the guy who had taught her how to ride a bike and told their parents he was the one smoking the cigarettes in the basement.

Lexi's father was the last to greet her. He was bald and jowly, and he looked wary.

"Hi, Dad." She closed the space between them

and hugged him. He stood stonily, not returning the embrace.

Lexi spoke earnestly. "I'm really glad to be back on the island. It's so beautiful here. It's really home."

Her parents exchanged a look, but didn't reply. The uncomfortable silence stretched in the room until Adam asked, "Drink?"

Both her parents had highball glasses filled with ice and scotch. "White wine?" Lexi asked.

"Coming right up." Adam went off into the kitchen.

The living room was exactly the same. Moss green wall-to-wall carpet, growing thin near her father's recliner. A brick fireplace with an antique brass bucket holding logs and kindling. Photos of Adam and Lexi as children lined up on the mantel. The latest picture had been taken when Lexi graduated from high school. Gad, what a bean pole she had been!

Her mother sank down onto the ancient brown corduroy sofa. Immediately the Jack Russells scrambled to get in her lap, nipping and shoving each other for dominance.

Lexi sat at the other end of the sofa. "Who are these handsome fellows?"

"Fellows?" Myrna stroked their little pointed heads. "These are my *girls,* can't you tell? Buddha and Pest." She adjusted them so they lay belly up in her arms. Fondly she gazed down on them, making little kissey faces.

"Mother wants a grandchild," Adam informed her drily as he handed her a glass of white wine.

"Well, it's a good thing she's got *two* children, isn't it!" Lexi shot back. *Wow,* she thought, *it came back fast, this family thing.*

Adam settled in the armchair with the wonky back leg. Immediately the other two dogs who'd been shadowing his every move lay at his feet. On his feet.

"Um, Adam, your dog is bald," Lexi whispered over the top of the dogs' heads.

Adam nodded. "Yeah, Bella's got skin problems."

"Bella?" Lexi snorted. "And is that other creature a *dog?* He looks like a hyena. Not that I'm criticizing."

"Poor Lucky"—Adam bent to pat the dog—"we can't all be beauties."

Was that a barb? Lexi wondered. A reference to her vanity? She couldn't interpret every remark anyone made, she'd go mad. She asked her brother, "So you've moved back to the island?"

"Two months ago. I was working up in Boston, at Angell Memorial, and heard they needed a vet at the MSPCA on the island, and here I am."

"That's so great! Where are you living?"

"I bought a small cottage on Crooked Lane."

"He knows he could live here," Myrna interjected with a sniff.

"Mom," Adam said patiently, "I'm thirty-three years old."

"So," Lexi asked, "how's your love life?"

Adam groaned.

Myrna's face lit up. "He's dating Melanie Clark!"

"I'm hungry," Fred said. "I'm going to order pizzas. Two large deluxe, okay? No one's become a vegetarian recently?"

"Okay," Lexi told her father, then turned her attention back to Adam. "Melanie Clark. I remember her. The sweetest girl, and so pretty. What's she doing now?"

"Teaching elementary school," Adam told them. "Fourth grade."

"Is this serious?"

"Maybe!" Myrna said hopefully.

Adam was firm. "No."

Fred ordered the pizzas, then carried the phone with him as he settled back in his chair. "Twenty minutes. I'll pick it up."

"How's Clare?" Lexi asked.

Myrna smiled fondly. "She's doing very well. Her shop, Sweet Hart's, is thriving, and I heard she got a ring from Jesse this Christmas."

"Has Jesse grown up any?" Lexi asked.

Adam gave her a look. "Do you mean has he stopped sleeping around?"

Lexi's father made a face. He hated sex talk.

"So," Myrna changed the subject, turning toward Lexi. "Tell us about you."

Lexi hesitated. "Well, you know I'm divorced. I'm not sorry I got divorced. But I'm not sorry I married Ed, either. I had a few amazing years."

"You certainly got to travel a lot," Myrna said coolly.

"The traveling was the best part of the marriage, actually. And I suppose I grew up a bit. But I always missed Nantucket. I didn't expect to, and yet, when I had to decide where to live, I knew at once I wanted to come home."

Adam nodded. "I know just what you mean. You can't wait to leave, and then you can't stand to live anywhere else."

"It's true. Nantucket is, well, magical."

"But how do you intend to make a living?" Her mother's face wrinkled with concern.

"Believe me, I've given this a lot of thought. I know what I love and what I'm good at. I'm opening a clothing shop."

Her father frowned. "I'm not sure that's such a workable idea, Lexi. You know what happened to our shop. And rents have gotten exorbitantly expensive around here."

Lexi nodded. "Yes, I know. That's why my shop will be upscale. And my merchandise will be special."

Adam lifted his wineglass to her in a toast. "Good for you, Lex."

"Thanks, Adam."

Myrna squinted her eyes. "How special?"

"My own designs. I've got a seamstress I know in New York who will be making the clothes. Well, she and her staff. She did a lot of alterations and custom work for me when we lived in New York, and I got to know her and respect her work."

"It's a lot of work, running a business," her father warned her. "Not much glamour, lots of window washing and paperwork."

Lexi leaned forward. "I know, Dad, I remember how it was at the store. I'm not afraid of hard work."

"If you don't mind my asking," Fred continued, "how are you paying for your inventory?"

Lexi wasn't surprised by the question. She knew money would always be a touchy subject with her parents. "I'm not rich," she admitted. "I stupidly signed a prenuptial agreement when I married Ed that leaves me with, basically, nothing. No alimony, nothing like that. But I did come away with a lot of amazing jewelry and designer clothing. I sold most of it, and that's what I'm using to start this store."

Her father was quiet a moment, considering. "Well," he said slowly, "this all sounds very exciting."

Lexi's eyes filled with tears. "Oh, Dad, I know I was a horrible little snot when I was nineteen. I know I said a lot of really stupid, hurtful things, and I'm so so sorry about that. Perhaps I was just too young to know how much I loved my family, or how much I love this island."

Fred was beginning to get that pinched look he got when things got too emotional. He cleared his throat. Myrna's attention was fixated on the dogs.

Again, Adam came to the rescue. "About your shop, Lex. You'll have to join the Chamber of Commerce."

"Good idea, Adam!" Lexi brightened, glad to be out of the Slough of Remorse and up on firmer emotional ground. "I need all the advice I can get. But I have a shop space and a living space. I came to the island two weeks ago and looked at rental properties, and I've signed the contract, and tonight I'll sleep in my new apartment and tomorrow I'll start organizing my shop for its grand opening in July!"

"Where is it?" Fred asked.

"On Commercial Wharf. The brick building."

"You mean the duplex where Clare's shop is?" Myrna asked. When Lexi nodded, she said, "Well, have you spoken to Clare?"

"Not yet," Lexi said. "I've got some apologies to make there, too."

Her father rose. "Time to get the pizza."

"I'll ride in with you," Adam said.

"Come into the kitchen with me," Myrna told Lexi. "We can make a salad."

At the end of the evening, Lexi drove back to her new home on the wharf. Her parents didn't invite her to stay in her old room, and that was fine. She wanted to be on her own. She was the new, improved, grown-up Lexi, and as she drove along Lower Orange Street, past Marine Home Center and

Hatch's and Orange Street Video, she looked at it with affection, remembering how, when she was nineteen, this same street, these same buildings, all weathered gray shingles and low to the ground, had seemed shabby to her, and unfashionable—*rural*. She had craved city lights, skyscrapers, opera houses, fabulous shops.

And now here she was, back on the island. True, the island itself had changed in the past eleven years, becoming more sophisticated—and more expensive. But she had changed, too.

She parked her car on the cobblestones, crossed the narrow lane, slid her key into the lock, and went into the silent building. She climbed the stairs, opened the door, and entered the long empty room. Moonlight spilled in from the wide windows. For a while she leaned against the window, entranced by the shimmering path of white moonlight on black water. She had missed this so.

She wished she could stay awake all night, just staring out at the harbor.

But an enormous yawn overtook her, making her eyes water and her jaw nearly crack, so she unloaded her duffel bag and shoved her clothing around to make a kind of nest on the floor. She folded up some sweaters for a pillow, and spread her coat over her for a blanket, and as she curled up on her funny little pallet, she was deeply content.

ELEVEN

"So what's the scoop?" Jesse demanded.

"Hang on." Clare untied her apron, settled in her chair, and looked around, savoring this moment. Jesse stared at her like a sleek tawny-pelted mountain lion, captured and tamed at her table.

Clare waited an extra beat, enjoying the power of possessing good gossip. Outside, the spring wind whirled, but it was cozy in the kitchen, and her father was in a good mood, really enjoying his steak.

"Come on," Jesse said. "The suspense is killing me."

Clare announced, "Lexi's back in town."

Jesse looked puzzled. "In April?"

"She's not here to visit. She's moving back."

Jesse snorted. "What? She and Daddy Warbucks building a McMansion so she can lord it over the rest of us?"

"Not at all." Clare was surprised to find a hot spurt of protectiveness warm her blood. *Where did that come from after all these years?* "They're divorced. She's moving back here by herself. She's going to open a business here. In fact, she's rented the shop space next to mine."

Jesse put his fork down. He looked at Clare. "Babe, don't get your hopes up."

Clare arched an eyebrow. "What hopes would that be?"

"That you and Lexi are going to be best buddies again. That she won't be the snob she was when she met that crook and left the island."

"Oh, come off it, Jesse." Clare sipped her wine and gave her fiancé a knowing look. "You didn't like Lexi even before she met Ed Hardin. You never liked Lexi."

Jesse grumbled, "Lexi's arrogant."

Clare argued, "Jesse, Lexi was *shy,* not arrogant. Remember, Jesse, those friends of yours who went drooling after her trying to get in her pants when she turned sixteen were the same guys who made fun of her when she hit five foot ten at age twelve and wore braces and had no boobs." The memory made her mad all over again. "When she turned sixteen, suddenly all those guys wanted to"—she glanced at her father and toned down her language —"get her in bed. They didn't know her. They didn't care for her."

"They didn't get the chance to *know* her," Jesse shot back. "Since she never spoke to anyone. And I don't buy that shy stuff. If she was so shy, why wasn't she *shy* around Ed Hardin?"

"I don't know," Clare admitted. Those last few weeks with Lexi had been so messed up. "Anyway, the rest of us sure made plenty of mistakes when we were young."

Jesse responded by stuffing salad in his face like a

rabbit machine, and Jesse hated salad. Clare knew he was trying to think of a way to change the direction the conversation was taking, away from the topic of all the mistakes *he'd* made, all the times he'd been unfaithful to Clare. She didn't want to go there, either. And she remembered how jealous Jesse had been of her closeness to Lexi. The bad thing about Jesse disliking Lexi had been that she was always torn between the two people she loved most. The good thing was that Lexi was the one island female who'd never slept with Jesse.

She cut a bite of steak and chewed. "Good steak, huh, Dad?"

"Your mother always liked Lexi," her father said. "Even when Lexi went off with that Hardin bastard, she stuck up for her." His face softened with memory.

"That's right, Dad." Clare was pleased that her father had joined the conversation.

"Your mother was as nice as they come." Deftly, Jesse changed the subject. "Clare, there's a storm story on the Weather Channel I've been wanting to see. Would you mind if your father and I had our dessert in the den?"

Clare flashed a grateful smile at Jesse. "That's fine. I'll bring it in."

Jesse pushed back his chair and stood up, lean and lanky in his jeans and flannel shirt. "Come on, George. Time for the men to put their feet up." He waited by Clare's father's chair as the older man mentally regrouped. It was an almost physical act for George to retreat from his thoughts about his deceased wife and pay attention to the here and now, but he finally dropped his napkin next to his plate, rose, and allowed Jesse to usher him out of the room.

Clare finished her dinner in silence. It was sweet of Jesse to be so protective of her. What she hadn't told him, because she was a grown woman now and no one needed to know, was that the thought of seeing Lexi again thrilled her—and made her just a little nervous.

TWELVE

Clare was in the kitchen above her shop, banging around pots and stainless-steel mixing bowls and whisks and ladles and spoons. In the spring, she always cleaned out the shop's kitchen, repainted the walls, and scrubbed the very back inches of every cupboard, shelf, and drawer, but she never did it this early in the spring. Since she woke up this morning, she'd wrestled with herself like a cartoon split personality, half of her desperate to get out the door, the other half trying to force her to stay. Now she was here, so she might as well use all this crazy energy to accomplish something. She tossed a mix of CDs into her player—Faith Hill, U2, Alanis Morissette—so the music could rev up her blood and lighten her mood, and she worked fast and efficiently, but deep inside she remained seriously cranky.

She felt so damned childish! She felt like Lexi would think Clare was in her shop because she'd heard that Lexi had rented the space next door and that Clare was so pathetically *eager* to see Lexi again that she'd come down to the shop and was making all this noise so Lexi would know she was here!

And that was true.

How embarrassing!

Ever since she'd heard of Lexi's return to the island, Clare's emotions had frothed like cream in a double boiler. Bubbles circled to the surface—excitement—Lexi! Her Lexi! Here again! Then *Pop!* Lexi, snotty Lexi, bad Lexi, gorgeous Lexi, shooting Clare a look that would make a giraffe feel short. Clare screamed along to Alanis Morissette's "You Ought to Know" as she pushed and pulled one of the work stations away from the kitchen wall.

A moment of silence fell when the song ended and in that silence, someone said, "Hello."

"Aah!" Startled, Clare stumbled backward, knocking her elbow on the wall.

Right there in the doorway between the kitchen and the packaging room stood Lexi, all grown up and looking like three hundred million dollars. Her shoulder-length white-blond hair was sliced in a sharp blunt cut that gave her a trendy, urban air, not that she needed it, wearing those hip-hugging black stovepipe pants with the ornate beaded belt and a cashmere cardigan sweater. It looked like her boots had seven-inch heels, but that was only because Lexi was so tall and thin. Just a slice of her sleek belly peeked between sweater and pants, a fad that Clare considered one of the fashion world's most significant errors of judgment, but on Lexi even this looked good.

Clare thought how *she* must look to Lexi in her old baggy athletic pants and one of Jesse's faded blue work shirts, unironed, her normal cleaning garb. Her brown hair was rumpled and she hadn't bothered to put on lipstick.

Oh, very nice, she told herself. *You came here expecting to see Lexi, so you made yourself look as sloppy as possible. How perfectly self-defeating.*

Alanis started yelling about something being perfect. Clare stabbed the Off button and the room went quiet.

"How did you get in here?"

Lexi produced a shy smile. "Through the connecting door." She waved her hand vaguely toward the wall.

Clare bent to drop the sponge in the bucket, to grab a moment to hide her confusion. "You might have phoned first."

"Um, but your sign says *Closed.* I didn't know you were going to be here until I heard the music." She hesitated, then said in a rush. "I rented the place next door. I'm going to live upstairs, and have a shop downstairs. I . . . I didn't know this was your shop."

Clare squinted her eyes at Lexi. "It's called Sweet *Hart's* and you didn't guess?"

Lexi blushed. "Well, I suppose I assumed . . . but that's not why I rented this particular space. It's just so perfect for what I need." She shifted her weight, flapping her hands around awkwardly like she'd done when she was younger. She looked like a stork on roller skates. Like she always had. "You look great, Clare."

Clare bridled. "Right. I'm a fashion classic."

Lexi waved her hand again. "I mean, not your clothes, I mean, we all look like that when we clean, I mean, you just look great. Happy. Healthy."

"Well." Clare rubbed an imaginary spot on the counter. "You look good yourself. Sensational, actually."

"I look like a moron," Lexi corrected. "High-heeled boots on cobblestone streets? What was I thinking?"

Clare grinned in spite of herself at the thought of Lexi stumbling her way over the brick sidewalks and cobblestones in those boots, flapping her hands for balance.

Her smile encouraged Lexi. "Hey, would you like to . . . maybe some coffee?"

Clare paused. "Well . . . I could use some coffee right now." She stripped off her rubber gloves.

"Oh!" Lexi jerked her head, did a kind of full body quiver, and waved both hands. "I don't have any coffee! I don't have any cups, either. I mean, I just got here yesterday and the movers are coming today and I haven't been to the grocery store . . ."

Clare tried to work up some resentment because wasn't it clever how Lexi had manipulated things so that Clare had to be the one to serve Lexi, but after all, the Lexi she'd known, the old Lexi, was always going off half-assed like this.

Plus, as she moved around the kitchen, Clare was secretly pleased at this opportunity to show off her shop. *She* might look like the bottom of a bedroom slipper, but her shop and its upstairs quarters looked great. The kitchen, except for the island she'd pulled out from the wall, was tidy and spotless. She glided from cupboard to counter, grinding the beans, organizing the coffeemaker, filling the creamer with fresh cream, setting everything on a vintage Coca-Cola tray.

She carried everything through the door into the larger packaging room. Near the windows overlooking the street she'd made a kind of employees' lounge, with a small sofa, two overstuffed chairs, and a coffee table piled with the latest magazines— *People* and *US* as well as *Gourmet*, *Bon Appétit*, and *Chocolatier.*

Lexi scanned the work table, piled high with glossy dark green boxes waiting to be folded. "I like your design. Very clever."

Clare didn't mind admitting, "I think so, too."

As a chocolatier with the last name of Hart, she couldn't *not* name the shop Sweet Hart's. It had been tempting to make her logo and decorations a chocolate heart, but Clare had chosen to go in another, less obvious and, she hoped, more distinctive direction. So all her boxes were dark woodsy green, with a hart's head on them, and hanging from an antler by a gold cord was one glossy dark chocolate truffle. The mocha-cream-colored hart was very endearing, his antlers slightly lighter brown, his dark eyes huge, his nose velvety soft. The tip of his tongue touched the corner of his mouth, his expression delighted, as if he'd just tasted something delicious. On Christmas, Clare had the boxes made with a round gold ornament hanging from his antler. On Valentine's Day, of course, a heart. For special orders, and she was getting more and more of these each year, she'd had the box maker emboss the antler with a small wrapped birthday present, or a gold ring, or a seashell.

Lexi traced the hart's antlers with the tip of her finger. "This place is really cool, Clare."

"Thanks." Clare set the tray on the coffee table and curled up in a chair. She'd put a few hand-made chocolates on a plate. "Try one."

Lexi sank into the other chair, crossing her endless legs and swinging them to the side so she could reach the truffle. She took a bite. "Wow."

Clare smiled.

"This is amazing."

"Thanks."

"You make these yourself?"

"I do. Well, in the summer I have help making them, but I've created every recipe. You're eating the Nantucket Knock-Out Truffle."

Lexi laughed. "Cool."

"I've had the shop for five years. I love it."

"Mmm, I can see why." She licked a bit of chocolate off her lip and when she grinned at Clare, she looked just like she had when they were both sixteen.

"So," Clare asked bluntly, "why'd you come back?"

THIRTEEN

The wind whined around the building, and for a moment a shaft of light splintered down from the cloudy white sky, streaking the room with a ripple of sunlight and shadows.

"Last year was hard . . ." she stopped. She took a deep cleansing breath. She started over. "Clare . . . Clare, I'm so sorry about the way I was when I left. I saw my family last night, and I apologized to them, and geez, I guess I ought to take out a full-page ad in the newspaper apologizing in general to everyone in town."

Clare quirked an eyebrow at Lexi. "A full page might be excessive."

Clare was giving her a break! Lexi laughed with relief. "Do you really want to hear some stuff?" She waved her hands, indicating the room with its tables laden with boxes waiting to be folded and bows waiting to be tied. "I mean, I don't want to keep you if you're busy."

"Now's fine. I've got plenty of time for cleaning."

"Looks pretty clean to me."

"Yes, but I like it to be spotless. Sterile. The State Board of Health inspects, but never mind—I want to hear about you." Clare drew her legs up and tucked them sideways beneath her, settling in.

Now that the moment was here, Lexi felt suddenly reluctant. "Could I ask you not to tell anyone?" She cleared her throat, surprised at how little-girl her voice sounded. "I mean, I don't mind looking pathetic to you, you're used to it, but I just don't think I could live on this island with everyone else thinking I'm pathetic, and I really want to be here."

Clare made a face. "Pathetic? You're afraid you're going to look pathetic? Give me a break." Then she softened. "All right, fine, I won't tell anyone."

"Not even Jesse."

"Oh, come on. I've got to tell Jesse something! I can't say, well I saw Lexi and we talked and I have no idea what the past ten years were like." Clare folded her arms stubbornly over her chest.

Lexi looked down at her various rings and turned them this way and that. "Well, could you give him a sort of expurgated version?"

"You mean this is going to be an X-rated tale?" Clare waggled her eyebrows.

Lexi hedged, "You know what I mean, Clare."

"All right," Clare agreed. "Just spill."

A truck rumbled past, clanking and banging like the timpani section of an orchestra.

"My gosh!" Lexi strained to stare down at the truck. "I can't believe old Mr. Wallins is still doing trash removal."

"That's not old Mr. Wallins," Clare informed her.

But I saw—"

"That's Dougie Wallins."

"I don't believe it."

"He's thirty-three now. He married Alyssa Santos. They have three kids. One is ten years old." Clare waited until the last bang and rattle faded into the distance. "You've been gone a long time, Lexi. A lot has happened."

Lexi shook her head, trying to take it all in.

"You were saying?" Clare prompted.

Lexi capitulated. "Okay. Remember that summer. How it was for me. My parents were overworked at the shop, and totally freaked out about money. They were going to have to take a second mortgage out on the house to pay my tuition at UMass. Adam was off in veterinary school. And you were totally with Jesse."

"Not totally," Clare started to object, but shrugged and grinned ruefully.

Lexi continued, "So I didn't have you. I didn't have *anyone*. At La Maison I was the outsider who couldn't do anything right." She unzipped her boots and kicked them off, then pulled her knees up against her chest. She hugged her knees and nestled her chin in her arms and sat there for a moment, reflecting. "I was so lonely."

"Have another chocolate," Clare suggested quietly. "Try this one."

Lexi accepted it, took a small bite, and closed her eyes while she savored the taste. "Nice." She ate the rest of it and this time she licked her fingers. "So that's how it was for me that summer. It was

131

like I was invisible. Then Ed came into the restaurant and *saw* me. Chose me. A wealthy, important, *powerful* man like that."

Clare made a noise of disgust, then immediately waved a hand. "Sorry. Sorry. So he whisked you away on a cloud to Shangri-La."

Lexi smiled. "In a way, yes. I mean, Clare, it was amazing. Listen, I have traveled *everywhere*. Stick a pin in a map, and I've been there. I've met some important people, Clare, curators of museums and conductors of European orchestras. And everything was first class, too." She hugged herself. "And the clothes. Oh, I wish you could have seen my clothes! It wasn't just that I *could* buy the newest breathtaking outfit, I was *supposed* to. It was my *job* as his wife to show up looking fabulous."

"I saw pictures of you a few times. In the Style section of the *Times* or *Boston Magazine*. You looked like an American princess. I remember thinking you must be having so much fun, finally getting to play dress-up with the big kids. It made me happy for you."

"That's nice to know. That you thought I was having fun, that you were glad I was having fun." Lexi ran her hands through her long blond hair. "You never answered my letters."

Clare shrugged. "While you were sunning in Bali or skiing in the Alps, I was in college, working nights and weekends, trying to learn bookkeeping, or I was on the island, working two jobs, sixty hours a week, trying to save money to start my shop. I was still pissed off at you for marrying that douche bag. And I didn't think you, out there sipping champagne in the stratosphere, would be interested in my boring, *provincial* little life."

"Clare, I'm so sorry I said those things."

"I know. And I'm sorry for the stuff I said. But you know, Lexi, it was like you left the room and slammed the door in my face."

The singing wind shifted the clouds again, flickering shadows and light over Clare's face. Lexi thought she saw tears in Clare's eyes. Her own eyes stung in sympathy. How could she make this better? She couldn't do it by herself, that much she knew. "Clare . . ."

Clare shook her head. "Never mind. That's in the past. Done. Fast forward. Tell me why you're not still married."

"Oh, well." Lexi wasn't sure she could ever tell Clare the truth about her marriage. Just remembering made her burn with shame at her naïveté. So she flipped her hands out in a what-can-you-do kind of gesture. "I left him. To be honest, I don't think he was a very likable guy."

"Well, *hello*."

Lexi jumped up and looked out the window. "There's the ferry!" She whirled around, clapping her hands. "The moving van will be here any minute. All my stuff—tonight I'll have a bed! Clare, thanks for the coffee and the chocolate. Maybe we can—"

"That ferry will be at least fifteen more minutes getting to the dock." Clare stood, clamped her hands on her hips, and glared. "Is this the way you want it? Everything superficial, all air kisses and cotton candy friendship?"

Lexi flinched. "What do you mean?"

"For one thing," Clare counted on her fingers, "you were married to that man for ten years. Two, you're suddenly divorced. Three, you're moving back to the island. But you're not telling me why. If you're just going to give me a greeting card version of your life, fine. But don't expect anything more from me."

Lexi started to argue, then changed her mind. "I'm kind of out of the habit of exchanging confessions, Clare. I'd like to tell you everything, but it's all a bit, well, just *sad*. And I want to be happy right now. I want to be *jubilant*. I'm starting my life over, and I want to enjoy it, and you know what, I haven't even figured out where I want my furniture and stuff to be. I really do need to make some decisions before the movers get here."

Clare said, "Fine."

"Look—want to go out to dinner tonight? My treat."

Clare looked insulted. "You don't have to treat me. I make a perfectly good living—"

"Oh, stop it. I didn't mean it the way you're taking it. I just—You just gave me coffee and chocolates, why can't I treat you in return?"

But Clare was miffed. "I'm busy tonight. Jesse and I have plans."

"Another time, then?"

"Okay," Clare agreed grudgingly.

"Great. I'd better go get organized." Lexi hurried to the connecting door between their spaces. "Damn, I'd better change out of these boots before I fall and kill myself." She looked back at Clare, wondering if she could give her a hug. Clare was gathering up the coffee things, an obstinate expression Lexi knew so well on her face. "See you."

"See you," Clare echoed.

Lexi turned back from the door. "Clare, do you think Jesse could do some carpentry work for me? I need cubicles built downstairs for my shop, and a couple of counters."

Clare just looked at Lexi.

"I know Jesse doesn't like me," Lexi said, "but right now nobody here likes me, and if Jesse does the work, I'll know he'll do a good job and get it done on time, because you'll kill him if he won't."

Lexi's logic made Clare laugh. "I'll talk to Jesse."

"Thanks." Lexi waved, went through the door, and shut it behind her. Now she was in her own space, her unsullied, unmarked, starting-over-fresh place.

FOURTEEN

While the movers carried in Lexi's handsome furniture, Clare knelt by her window, hiding her face behind a curtain as she scanned the scene on the street below. She didn't want to seem curious. Or, Heaven forbid, fascinated, like some witless troll with nothing better to do than ogle the royalty. But she *was* fascinated, which made her so mad at herself she wanted to fling herself out the window onto the cobblestones.

At home that evening, after dinner, as they sat in companionable silence in the living room, Clare put her finger in her book to mark her place and told Jesse Lexi needed some carpentry work done in her new shop.

Jesse lounged on the sofa, his feet on the coffee table, engrossed in a handheld Nintendo DS electronic game. "I already have a job."

"It's April, Jesse," Clare reminded him. "You can take a few hours off whenever you want."

"Fine," Jesse grumbled, not looking up from his game.

Over the next week, whenever Clare went into her shop, she heard sounds of shoving and dragging from next door. Lexi was obviously getting her furniture in place. Clare considered knocking on the connecting door to ask if she'd like some help, but she couldn't quite bring herself to do that. Instead, she used her emotional energy as fuel while she cleaned up all the paperwork she'd let pile up on her desk.

A storm battered the Northeast, sending gale-force winds that stopped all ferries and planes to the island and kept everyone indoors. Clare spent the time folding the flats she'd ordered into handsome gift boxes. Usually her assistant, Marlene, helped her with this rather tedious work, but Marlene was down with the flu. Plump, uncomplicated Marlene was a great worker and a compulsive chatterer, currently obsessed with *Dancing with the Stars*. Whenever she had the opportunity, she'd regale Clare with descriptions of the dancers' costumes or intricate steps. Clare was sorry Marlene didn't feel well, but she was relieved not to have her there chattering away. Clare was quite content to sit in the quiet packaging room, a cup of cocoa by her side, folding and fixing Tab A into Slot B. Slowly the table grew with towers of handsome green boxes. She didn't even play a CD. She was too busy listening to the noises coming from the other side of the wall.

On the fourth day Clare heard the phone ring in Lexi's apartment. She heard Lexi's muffled voice as she spoke. Clare wondered who Lexi was talking with. An island person? Maybe her brother?

Maybe a museum curator or the conductor of a European orchestra.

You are going insane, Clare told herself. *Just call her.* But somehow she couldn't pick up the phone.

By Sunday afternoon the storm was over, the air was clear, and Clare was restless. Jesse had gone fishing in Maine with two buddies. Penny and her husband and baby had gone off-island to visit his brother and family.

She'd already started a rich beef stew simmering. It would be ready tonight for her to share with her father, and there was another depressing thought, being alone with her father. Clare had asked him to go with her to church that morning, but he'd refused, and she'd asked him if he wanted to attend the afternoon concert, and he'd refused. He was still in his pajamas and robe and it was two in the afternoon. Sometimes Clare felt as if she was in charge of a very large, very sulky child.

She could watch a DVD, or read one of the novels she'd brought home from the library. She wouldn't play around with chocolate today. She always tried to take Sunday completely off from work. She could clean out her closet—she'd been meaning to do that for *years*—

The phone rang. She nearly broke her neck getting to it.

Lexi said, "Clare? Hi, listen, I know this is very last moment, but I wonder if you'd like to go to the concert with me."

Clare hesitated.

"It's at four o'clock."

The thought of walking into the concert with Lexi made Clare feel just a little, well, actually, *glamorous*. "Yeah. Yeah, I'd like to go."

"Cool! I'll meet you at the bottom of Main Street."

Clare pulled out a crimson velvet shirt to wear with her jeans and added the garnet earrings she'd been saving for "good"—an occasion that so far hadn't arrived. All the red made her dark hair seem glossier, made her skin glow—or perhaps it wasn't the garnets that made her eyes as full of spice and mystery as her homemade chocolates.

FIFTEEN

When you're a six-foot-tall female, there's no way to be invisible. Lexi had certainly tried. Life with Ed had taught her to stand up straight, wear high heels, and flaunt her height and her skinny body, but here on Nantucket, Lexi panicked at the thought of walking into a crowded room. She'd stand out, as she always had, like a flamingo in a crowd of penguins.

Still, something in her, something she understood was probably perverse but had been bred into her probably defective genes, made her dress for the concert in her tightest, lowest-cut jeans, pink Uggs, a tight little pink cashmere sweater, and a leather jacket with brass studs on the cuffs, collar, and waist. She added her big fat diamond ear studs for the hell of it. She was who she was, and she had returned to Nantucket because she loved the island and everyone could just deal with it.

At least she was trying to think that way as she stood with Clare at the end of Winter Street, watching people walk through the wrought-iron gates and up the brick sidewalk to the dignified, forthright brick building that had been, long ago, the island school. Now it was the Egan Institute of Maritime Studies, with a collection of historical seascapes on the walls of the large assembly room used for concerts, lectures, and meetings.

Clare leaned close to Lexi and whispered, "Before we go in, can I say something?"

Lexi clenched her fists. "What?"

"You might want to take some deep breaths. You're hyperventilating."

Lexi glared at Clare, who looked as comely, wholesome, and natural as an apple. In comparison, Lexi felt like Carmen Miranda with an entire basket of bananas on her head. "I'm not hyperventilating. I have a slight cold."

Clare looked irritated. She opened her mouth, then closed it. "Look, Lexi. I know you're nervous about seeing everyone again."

"I'm not nervous."

"Well, you should be. It was a very big deal when you eloped with Ed Hardin. It was like you went off with, oh, I don't know, Osama bin Laden."

"Ed wasn't that bad."

"That's highly debatable, but we don't have time for that now. The point I'm trying to make is that we've all changed. Not just the kids we went to school with, but everyone. Like Penny—she never even spoke to me in high school, but now she's my best friend."

Lexi flinched. "Lucky you."

"Yes, lucky me. And it didn't happen overnight, believe me. We hadn't seen each other for years, not until I burned my hand when I was just starting up my business. I went to the ER and she was the nurse there, and she was so calm and confident; all those qualities she'd had in high school were just what anyone would want in a nurse, and I brought her chocolates later to thank her for . . ."

Lexi started walking. "It's lovely for me, hearing about your new best friend, but I don't want to be late for the concert."

"Fine. But get ready. People will stare. People will whisper. Remember, it's April. We don't have much to entertain us. My advice is, smile at people and say hello and forget high school and start fresh. Give everyone a chance."

"I intend to!"

"Then stop gritting your teeth and clenching your jaw and flaring your nostrils like some race-horse being dragged into a barn full of mules."

Lexi stopped walking. "That's how I look?"

"That's how you've always looked when you're out in public."

Lexi cast a desperate glance up at the heavens.

"Oh, cut it out," Clare chided. "This isn't surgery you're facing. Loosen up a bit. Think of something funny. Remember when Amber and Spring did karaoke night?"

Lexi smiled at the memory. She shook her arms out and stamped her feet and tossed her head. "Right. Okay, I'm ready now. Thanks."

The ticket table was at the front of the building, where the stage was also located. Clare's lecture and

Lexi's fidgeting had made them almost late, and as they gave the pretty teenage girl their ten dollars, they saw that the room was completely filled. The only empty seats left were either in the back row, or the front, and everyone was staring at them. The thought of all those eyes on her for the next hour gave Lexi the heebie-jeebies. "Back," she said tersely to Clare.

Lexi didn't feel like a flamingo now, she felt like a chicken, with the eyes of one hundred slavering foxes following her as she and Clare hurried to the last row and sat down. The few people who turned to mouth hello to Clare performed classic double takes when they spotted Lexi. In row after row heads bent to those next to them as the community went into a whisper-fest.

Patricia Moody, the chorus conductor, walked onto the stage and began her few announcements. The audience settled down. The concert began.

The program was an upbeat mixture of Gilbert and Sullivan, Broadway show tunes, and Cole Porter. As Lexi listened, she scanned the chorus for familiar faces. It took her brain a moment to adjust for the passing of the past ten years. Age, weight, wrinkles, gray hair, and glasses transfigured many of the older folk, while those who had been just kids when Lexi left now wore a look of authority and, in some cases, exhaustion. Lexi understood. Life was expensive here. People her age had to work two jobs to get by, and most of them lived with their parents because summer rents were impossibly high. Clare still lived with her father, and Lexi bet that when Jesse married Clare, he'd move into her parents' home. It was a nice, big old house with room enough for everyone. She spotted the Barbie Dolls in the front row of the audience. Amber Young and Spring Macmillan weren't related by blood, but in high school they'd been inseparable, rah-rah, gum-chewing cheerleaders who'd never been especially nice to Lexi—or especially mean, either. She was surprised at how pleased she was simply to see them again.

Old Marvin Meriweather was still singing. His rich baritone had been corrugated with age so that his voice vibrated like a galloping elephant's. Of course, Patricia Moody would not have asked Marvin to leave the chorus. That would have been too cruel, and this ensemble was about the community as much as it was about music.

Now Caitlin, whom Lexi and Clare had secretly nicknamed Queen of Sluts even before she dumped Adam to marry Corby Turner, opened her bright red lips and shrieked out a solo so truly off-key that a shiver of vengeful pleasure went down Lexi's spine. Clare elbowed her in the ribs. They exchanged glances and simultaneously bit their lips to keep from laughing. Seated here in the back row, they could see similar movements going on with the rest of the audience. In the front row, old Harsh Marsh dug a handkerchief out of her purse and noisily blew her nose. The only individual in the room who seemed to thrill to Caitlin's warbling was

Patricia Moody, Caitlin's proud mother.

Or maybe Caitlin's mother knew what she was doing, because after two more songs from the entire ensemble, the program ended with the audience applauding heartily. Whatever else was wrong with their lives, at least they hadn't made fools of themselves.

When the applause died down, Patricia Moody said, "Please join us for refreshments," and the crowd rose, glad to stretch and greet their neighbors to agree this had been the best concert ever, and, a kind of buzz swept the room, wasn't that Lexi Laney *Hardin* back there with Clare Hart?

"Let's go," Lexi hissed at Clare.

"No way. You are going to run this gauntlet, sport. You need to get it over with." As Clare spoke, she nodded and waved at friends in the audience.

Lexi grabbed her arm. "Then look at me," she hissed. "Talk to me. Pretend we're discussing something fascinating."

Clare linked her arm through Lexi's. "Okay, come on. Let's go get some hot apple cider. Close your mouth, you look like an idiot. Hmm, hot apple cider. What about apple cider chocolates? Not for the spring and summer, but maybe next fall? I might play around with that idea. Lexi, loosen up. They're not going to murder you."

"No, but they'll snub me. Or insult me."

"Then suck it up. *You* chose to come back here. Smile, or I'll pinch you."

145

Clare would, too. Lexi grinned and somehow managed not to trip over her own feet as Clare maneuvered her through the throng into the back room where the refreshments were set out. They joined the crowd reaching for cups, napkins, and cookies, then squeezed their way to the side of the room where they stood for a moment pretending to study an oil painting of Nantucket harbor in the whaling era.

"My goodness." The voice slicing through the air next to them was as familiar as an old nightmare. Harsh Marsh approached, older now, thinner, in a puce wool suit Lexi could have sworn she wore back when Lexi was in her sophomore English class. "If it isn't Lexi Laney. What causes you to grace our humble town?"

Lexi raised her chin defiantly. Was she imagining a sudden hush in the room? From the look on HM's face, it was obvious the older woman was eager to use her old powers to intimidate and judge. Lexi couldn't remember anyone ever liking HM. Gosh, maybe Lexi and HM could form their own club.

Clare kicked Lexi in the shin.

Lexi took a deep breath. "I've moved back to the island. I'm opening my own clothing shop. I'm divorced now, and I'm starting my life over, and this is the place I want to be."

Whispers flitted through the crowd.

HM looked smug. "The island's changed."

Lexi looked smug back. "So have I. Ten years

changes everyone. Are you *still* teaching?"

HM's mouth went prune-shape, always a bad sign.

"I like your jacket," a high sweet voice rang out. "I think it's quite felicitous to the eye."

A girl approached Lexi. Perhaps ten years old, her curly red hair framed an elfin face sprinkled with freckles. Behind tortoiseshell glasses, a pair of astute blue eyes gleamed. The girl wore cargo pants and a white sweater.

"Thank you," Lexi said. "I like your glasses."

The girl beamed. "They provide a useful contradiction to my name. *Jewel.* My mother was addicted to her music when she was pregnant with me. It could be worse. I could be named Snoop Dogg."

Lexi laughed, genuinely entertained. "What's your mother's name?"

Jewel rolled her eyes. "Bonnie Frost. My father's name is Tristram Chandler."

"Hey, I knew a Bonnie Lott in high school. And Tris Chandler was a friend of my brother's." Lexi smiled, remembering. "He was really cute."

Jewel nodded. "He's still cute. Also, he's available, if you're interested."

Startled and amused, Lexi faked a cough to hide a smile.

"My parents are divorced," Jewel explained coolly. "My mother has married again. My stepfather's name is Ken Frost. They have a new baby, a little boy. His name is Franklin Frost. Frankie for short."

"It must be fun, having a baby around."

"Sometimes." Jewel shrugged, so blasé. "I often find him a bit truculent." She changed the subject. "And are you Lexi Laney?"

"I am." It seemed only polite to offer her hand to Jewel in a polite handshake.

"I've heard about you," Jewel said cryptically.

"Is my daughter bothering you?" Bonnie Frost squeezed her way through the crowd. She wore her long chestnut curls caught up with combs to show off the enormous diamond studs in her ears. She was slightly plump with new baby weight and sleepless nights had brushed shadows under her eyes, but she was absolutely lovely. A baby—it must be the truculent one—lay in a kind of sling across Bonnie's body. "Oh, hi, Lexi, I heard you were back." Before Lexi could reply, the baby let out a long glass-shattering wail. Bonnie looked desperate. "I've got to go before everyone here kills me. Sorry about the noise," she apologized over the air-raid siren of her son's voice. "Nice to see you, Lexi. Jewel, honey, come on."

Bonnie grabbed Jewel's hand and towed her swiftly from the room. Jewel threw Lexi a see-what-I-mean look over her shoulder. Lexi waved at Jewel.

"Lexi Laney!" Patricia Moody, the choir director, put her hands on Lexi's shoulders and kissed her cheek. "I saw a picture of you last year in the *Globe*. You were at *Madame Butterfly*. Was it fabulous?"

Gradually the platters of brownies and small sandwiches set out on the long table emptied. A volunteer unplugged the heavy coffee urn and carried it off to the kitchen. People checked their watches or allowed themselves to be dragged away by fussy children. But the room was still fairly crowded when a teenage boy exploded in, his face glowing from exertion and excitement.

"Hey, parts of a Nantucket boat have washed up in Maine!"

"A Nantucket boat?" Marvin Meriweather's voice trembled. "I was down at Tris Chandler's boatyard just last week. Just gabbing, you know. He said he was going north this week, taking a boat up to a customer in Maine. I wonder if . . ."

"Nonsense!" Patricia Moody snapped. "Tris is an excellent sailor. It wouldn't be Tris."

"I don't know. These spring storms can come up so suddenly." Amber Young looked genuinely worried.

"Let's not be silly now," Harsh Marsh commanded. "We don't know that it was Tris's boat. No point getting upset for nothing."

Slowly, reassuring one another, the crowd dispersed, filing out of the building into the cool light of late afternoon.

"I'm glad Jewel didn't hear that," Clare told Lexi. "She's had a tough time with the divorce. She adores her father."

"She seems like an unusual child," Lexi mused. "I like her."

149

"Of course you do." Clare elbowed Lexi in the side. "She's going to set you up with your first crush. And you haven't seen Tris all grown up, Lexi. He is *fine*."

"I have no time for romantic fantasies," Lexi said firmly. "I've got a business to run."

SIXTEEN

Clare returned the tray of chocolates to the refrigerator. She had two refrigerators here at home, one for normal household use and one only for her chocolates. She liked being able to wander into the kitchen whenever inspiration hit. Often she'd wake up in the middle of the night thinking of a new kind of chocolate and she wouldn't be able to go back to sleep until she'd tiptoed downstairs and spent a few hours experimenting. She usually worked in the shop kitchen, especially once she had the recipe perfected. There was much more room.

Now she untied her apron. It was early afternoon. The windows bloomed with light. She opened the back door, and leaned against it, breathing in the fresh spring air. She'd work on the truffle later. After the long gray winter, this bright blue-sky day was too irresistible to resist. Maybe she'd go for a bike ride. The thought of whizzing along beneath the spring sun made her smile.

Her father was in the den, his eyes glassy as he stared at the television. It was after eleven in the morning, and he was still in his robe and slippers.

"Hey, Dad." Clare kissed the top of his balding head. "What's up?"

"Hello, sweetheart." He shifted around in his chair,

obviously making an attempt to prove he wasn't in another one of his grief-inspired comas. "Um, is Jesse coming over?"

"Tonight. He's coming for dinner. Actually, he's bringing dinner. He's got some kind of fish he caught up in Maine." When had her father last dressed, she wondered. "Hey, Dad, want to go for a walk? It's a nice day." If she could get him to dress for a walk, she could run his robe and pajamas through the wash.

Her father shook his head. "I don't think so, honey. I think I'll just watch this program."

The TV was tuned to ESPN, which was some kind of relief—Clare had seen her father sit through jewelry channel shows—but the program was about bowling, something they never did since there was no bowling alley on the island.

"Dad . . ."

"Maybe later." He waved his hand, as if swatting away a pesky fly.

"All righty then." Sometimes he seemed *determined* to be miserable. Often it was hard not to take his lethargy personally. She couldn't bring his wife back from the dead, but *she* was here, wasn't she? They'd never been close, but she was trying so hard, couldn't he try just a little, too? She was his daughter, after all.

Exasperated now, she tugged a wool hat on over her head, slipped into a down vest, and pulled on leather gloves. Her bike was in the garage. She wheeled it out through the side door, straddled it, and began to pedal.

As she zipped along the quiet streets, she decided she was being impatient with her father. She was in a more positive place these days, and she knew why, even though she didn't trust the reason. Lexi was back. And Lexi was just as much fun as she'd always been, and twice as fabulous. When they had walked into the concert, Clare had felt that old thrill from her high school days, to be seen in the company of such a dazzling creature. It was like showing up with a giraffe at her side, a really bewitching giraffe who could communicate only to Clare.

How could a friendship be explained? It was as mysterious as falling in love. Life seemed brighter, more fun, with Lexi back on the island. Clare couldn't wait to see the kinds of clothes she'd be selling. And Clare liked that something broken could be mended, especially something as mysterious and ineffable as a friendship. It made her feel optimistic—and all at once, as she spun past a yard where a man was throwing a Frisbee to his golden Lab, Clare thought: *I know what! I'll get Dad a dog!*

Recently, the MSPCA had been transformed by avid fundraisers from a storybook Hansel-and-Gretel cottage tucked away in the woods into a lavish multi-room palace with a huge parking lot and a reception area that rivaled the deck of the Starship *Enterprise*.

153

Clare had only been out here a few times in her life. Her father had always wanted a dog or cat, but her mother had been allergic, so Clare's trips had been as a companion to a friend taking a pet in for a checkup. She wondered whether Lexi had seen the new building yet. She wished she'd thought to phone Lexi to ask her to come with her. But no, Lexi's brother was the head vet out here; probably he'd already brought her out.

She was glad to see a familiar face. Helen Coffin, one of her mother's buddies, was seated behind the high curved counter, tapping away at a computer. Over her floral pantsuit, she wore a blue lab coat with *Helen* embroidered on the pocket.

"Clare! What brings you out here?"

"I'm thinking of adopting a dog for my father."

"What a good idea! Well, Jenny is our adoption officer, and she's gone to Jamaica for three weeks, but we do have some very cute little animals here, so let me get myself organized and I'll take you back myself. Paula's home sick with this cold that everyone's got, but fortunately we've got a quiet day." She clicked away at the computer, turning the screen into a series of starburst patterns, pushed back her chair, and took off her glasses, letting them fall to her impressive chest, where they dangled on a multicolored string of beads.

"I like your glasses chain," Clare told Helen as she led the way through the shining white halls to the adoption area.

"Why, thank you, so do I. I swear, by this time of year I'm so tired of all the gray and bleakness I pile on as much color as I can. Orvis is just grateful I haven't dyed my hair purple."

Laughing over her shoulder, Helen opened the door into a bright room full of clean, spacious cells inhabited by a number of sleeping dogs. At their entrance, the animals sprang to their feet and hurtled to the front of their cages, wagging their tails and barking.

"Oh, the poor things! I wish I could adopt them all." Clare walked from cage to cage, smiling and cooing and feeling like a fiend when she deserted one dog to look at another. Soon all the dogs were hurling themselves around their cages, barking, wagging their tails, wriggling all over with hope.

"Now this one is my favorite." Helen opened the door and lifted out a tiny bundle of white fur. "She doesn't have papers but I swear she's all shih tzu. Oh, give mama some love," Helen squealed as the little dog licked her face.

"Clare." A door swung open and Lexi's brother strode in, a white lab coat over his street clothes. "I thought I saw you come in."

"Adam!" Clare felt herself blush as he walked toward her. He was still handsome at six-foot-two, broad-shouldered, and much more serious-looking —he was a real man now. She couldn't stop smiling at him. "I saw the article in the paper about you. Welcome back."

"Thanks. I'm glad to be here. I really missed the island."

He smiled at her as if he found pleasure in just looking at her. Memories of her childhood crush flooded through her. She struggled for composure. "I, uh, I'm thinking of getting a dog for my father."

"I thought this little bundle of love might be just the ticket." Helen lifted the little dog and nuzzled its curly white head.

"I think *you're* the one who wants her, Helen." He smiled at Clare. "My opinion? Your father would be happier with a bigger dog."

Clare stopped at the last cage, where a medium-sized scrawny black-and-white long-haired mongrel with blue eyes and lopsided ears sat with her head cocked winsomely. "*She* looks pretty sweet."

Adam came to stand next to Clare. "She's very sweet. Just arrived. Want to meet her?"

"Well . . . okay."

"Oh, you're the cutest thing, but I already have a dog." Reluctantly Helen put the faux shih tzu back in its cage. "Is that the phone? I guess I'd better get back to the desk. It's nice seeing you, Clare."

Adam unlatched the cage door. Instead of dashing for freedom, the dog sat still, watching Adam carefully, her whole body quivering. All around them, envious dogs bayed and whined.

"Hello, girl." Adam entered the cage. He squatted down and held out his hand for the dog to sniff. "Aren't you a good girl." Very gently he stroked her head and back. "Come meet her," he said to Clare.

Clare felt like her very heart was breaking open as she knelt next to the dog. "We've never had a pet before," she told Adam. "My mother was allergic." She held out her hand. The dog sniffed it, then looked up at Clare with her odd blue eyes, and then, carefully, she licked Clare's hand. Then she scanned Clare's face for signs of approval. Clare rearranged herself into a sitting position. "Oh, aren't you pretty." She looked helplessly at Adam, who was seated now, too, leaning against the wall. "I want a dog for my father, not for me." But she petted the dog, all down her back. "Her fur feels like silk."

"You and your father could share," Adam suggested quietly.

In the other cages, most of the dogs were calming down, curling up to return to sleep.

"Well . . ." She couldn't take her hands off the dog, and the dog took a few cautious paces toward Clare, and then a few more, watching Clare's face carefully the whole time.

"Mutts make good pets," Adam told her. He put his arms around his knees so his big feet in their leather loafers stuck out and Clare saw that his socks didn't match. "They're not as high-strung as purebreds."

"How old is she?" Clare stroked the dog's big furry ears. One ear stuck straight up, the other flopped down over one eye. "Is this some kind of cute trick, this thing with your ears?" she asked the animal.

In reply, the animal inched closer to Clare. Her quivering had stopped, but her eyes were questioning.

"She's young, not more than eight months. She's had all her shots, she's been spayed, she's in good health."

"Do you think my father would like her?" Clare asked.

"Well, she's not so teeny-weeny he'd be embarrassed to take her for a walk, and she's not so big she'd be impossible for him to handle, and as you can see, she's a very amiable animal, so yes, I'd think your father would like her. Perhaps you should bring him out to see all the others first."

The dog was watching Clare as if her life depended on Clare's smile. "Oh, my," Clare sighed. "I think I'm in love."

The dog wagged her shaggy tail, and as if she understood Clare's words, she delicately stepped into Clare's lap, turned around twice, and lay down, nestling her chin on Clare's knee.

Clare looked over at Adam. He was as handsome a man as his sister was a beautiful woman, but his blond hair had darkened to brown, and unlike Lexi, he'd bulked up. He wasn't in the slightest bit fat, but he was . . . substantial. He looked so strong, and so gentle, so *right there* with her.

All at once Clare wanted to lean over the bundle

of dog in her lap and kiss Adam.

Adam looked back at her, not smiling now, very serious, so serious it made Clare shiver. What if she did lean forward and kiss him? What if she reached out and touched his hand?

The door flew open. Helen stuck her head in, beaded glasses swinging. "Dr. Laney, your eleven-thirty appointment is here."

Adam tore his gaze away. "Right. Thanks, Helen." He looked back at Clare. "What do you think?"

Clare could hardly breathe. "About what?"

Adam reached out his hand, and Clare's body zinged with so much desire she was surprised the current didn't frizz her hair, and the dog's, too. Adam stroked the dog's head, slowly, and the dog made a little happy moan. Somehow Adam managed to touch the dog in Clare's lap without touching her legs or her torso, but the nearness of his hand made Clare breathless.

"About the dog," Adam said. "Do you want to bring your father out here to see her?"

"No. I'll take her." She patted the dog's rump—a safe eight inches away from Adam's hand on the dog's head. As she did, the light caught her engagement ring.

Adam stood up. "Helen can help you with the paperwork. I'd better go see my eleven-thirty. You've made a good choice, Clare, I think that's a really nice dog." He walked away, stopping at the door to say over his shoulder, "Let me know how she works out."

He was giving her a reason to get in touch with him! "I will," she promised.

"And tell Jesse hello," Adam said, and left the room.

SEVENTEEN

During the month of May, the island slowly woke. The sun shone brighter, igniting the sea into a flashy, spangling blue, and the air was milder, enticing everyone outside, away from their dark sheltered lives. People tied back their curtains, washed windows, swept their porch corners free of the last of the pine needles fallen from Christmas wreaths, and hung baskets of faux flowers on their front doors. In town, the shopkeepers set out real pansies, daffodils, and crocuses in their window boxes, and the DPW street-sweeping machines, like humming robot house-wives, went up and down the main streets, whisking away all the sand spread over the once-icy roads, making each cobblestone shine like a polished gem.

It was the beginning of the magnificent party that was summer on Nantucket. Summer people arrived to open and air out their homes. Tourists came to stay in the inns and walk on the beach and dream of all they would do with their lives. Lexi's parents had always loved seeing their summer regulars return to shop in their store and to catch up on gossip—for Myrna and Fred it was almost as if their hundreds of children were home from college. The island was caught up in the excitement of some-thing—everything—beginning anew.

It was all so poignant to Lexi, so idyllic and hopeful, especially because she was back home. And she *was* back home. Every day she felt how people accepted her. Behind the post office counter, Martha Smith, who had dated Adam in high school, greeted her with a smile. At the grocery store, several people with familiar faces nodded and smiled at her as they steered their carts down the aisles, and Fred Carney, who now ran the meat department, actually stopped her to tell her that if she ever needed a special cut to ring the bell and ask for him. At the Main Street Pharmacy, Watson Lomax, who had begun his interest in drugs early in his teens, was now, amusingly, a pharmacist, who helped Lexi decide on which over-the-counter allergy medication to use. And Patricia Moody phoned to ask Lexi if she'd like to join the community chorus. Lexi thanked her for the invitation but declined, admitting she couldn't carry a tune.

Box by box, her merchandise arrived, trundled over the cobblestones by the UPS man and his dolly. The clothing was on the second floor, safely shrouded in dust-proof plastic, still in boxes, waiting to be ironed and hung on her padded silk hangers once the sawing, hammering, and painting were done. The racks were draped in protective plastic; the mirrors she'd ordered leaned against the walls in their cardboard boxes. The display cases for her jewelry and accessories had come, too, and sat in the middle of the shop floor covered with sheets. The walls were painted just as Lexi had dreamed they would be. She had done the work herself and she'd done a really amazing job. Her concept was clever, and she'd always been good at art, but this, well, this surprised her, how good it looked, just like her dreams. She had sheets of brown paper taped over the large front window so no one could see in until everything was perfect, and it couldn't be perfect until the cubicles were built.

Jesse hadn't come to build the dressing cubicles. Clare had promised he would, but he hadn't shown up, and she supposed it was no surprise. Why would he do her any favors?

She'd pored over the phone book, calling other carpenters, but all she'd gotten were answering machines. May was crazy busy on the island, Lexi knew that. Caretakers were running around turning on water and taking down shutters and repairing any damage the weather had done over the winter. Next door, Clare and her assistant Marlene were concocting and packaging chocolates from morning to night, so Clare was too busy to spend time with Lexi, and Lexi would be too busy, too, if she only had a couple of dressing rooms! But she had *no* dressing rooms!

What else could she do? Lexi looked around, her hands on her hips. Leaning against the wall were a group of photographs blown up to three feet by five and showcased in ornate frames. Each shot was of a tall, slender blonde walking on a stretch of beach.

They were pictures from her travels, but she didn't want these photos to be about her. She wanted them to be about the mystery and romance of walking on the sand by the water's edge. She wanted them to be mesmerizing, exotic, and dreamy. After hours of careful study she'd chosen six perfect shots with her back to the camera, then had them cropped so that she was to one side, in the shadow, or in the distance.

She couldn't hang them herself; they were too heavy. She would have to call her parents. They had invited her for Sunday dinner last week, and slowly the ice between them was thawing. Myrna was frankly curious about Lexi's merchandise and her father had offered his help with heavy lifting.

Just as she flipped open her cell phone, someone knocked on the door.

She pulled the door open. "Jesse!"

The sight of him knocked her breath right out of her lungs.

"Clare said you needed some work done."

Jesse wore work clothes—jeans and a blue denim shirt. His blond hair was pulled back in a pony-tail and a small gold hoop shone from one earlobe. He was slender and fit, his face already tanned, his eyebrows and lashes almost white. She'd always thought of him as the most laid-back boy she'd ever known, easy with his smile, lounging in his bones, always looking like he was about to start whistling. A sexual Huck Finn.

But right now—something about him sent her pulse racing. Suddenly her entire body seemed to *wake up*—she was uncomfortable and exhilarated at the same time, like a bird cracking open its shell. This was crazy. Lexi tore her gaze away from Jesse—that helped, to not look at him—and waved her hands around the room as she babbled.

"Oh, yes, Jesse, thank heavens you're here! I'm so grateful! Come in!"

Jesse came inside, looking around the room, and Lexi couldn't help it—she looked at Jesse. As if her gaze fell like heat on his skin, a flush spread up his neck. She wanted to seem natural. What would she say if Jesse was just another normal man? It wouldn't be so unusual to study a person you hadn't seen for years.

"You haven't changed one single bit," she told him truthfully.

"You have," he said, flashing her a sideways glance. "You're thinner, and honestly, I think you're taller."

"Ouch!" she responded, with a laugh, because this was Jesse, who never had a mean bone in him. "The main thing is, I think I'm smarter. At least I hope so."

He shot her another sideways glance. Their gazes connected and something flashed between them like an electric shock. Jesse walked to the other end of the room. Lexi stayed where she was, her heart fluttering, thinking, *What was that?*

"So what do you need?" Jesse asked. His voice was hoarse and as he heard his words, his blush deepened.

Oh, wow, Lexi thought, and knew she was blushing, too. When she spoke, her voice came out in a breathless mouse-squeak. "Two cubicles." She cleared her throat. "Two dressing rooms. I thought here, at the back. Just about six feet wide and deep, and I'll need these two mirrors mounted on the walls. I made sketches of what I want." Leaning against the display case where her various work papers were piled, she pulled out the drawings.

Jesse came to stand next to her. He picked up the papers. On his right wrist he wore a sterling-silver bracelet with a turquoise stone. How very Jesse. The turquoise was the same color as his eyes. He had a cut on one of his knuckles, and a long scar on his right palm. His hands and fingers were thick from working, the ends of his fingers callused from playing guitar. Did that mean his fingertips weren't sensitive to the touch?

". . . kind of wood?" Jesse asked.

Lexi's throat was dry. "It doesn't matter, just plywood, I'm going to paint it." Good grief, Jesse had always been a chick magnet in high school, but *she*'d never been susceptible to his power of attraction, perhaps because back then it took all her concentration simply to walk down the halls without tripping over her own big feet. But now! She felt like a raft at the edge of a whirlpool. This wasn't good.

Ripping her body away from the counter, she lurched back to where the cubicles would be. "And I thought curtains on rods, rather than doors. I mean, doors look more elegant, but they'd take longer to hang. I want to open as soon as possible."

Jesse put the papers down, carefully aligning them into neat piles. "You'd better get yourself another carpenter, then. I'm on Steve Sergeant's crew and we're stretched thin as it is."

"Oh, Jesse, I've tried to get someone else." *Oh great,* she thought, *insult the man.* Embarrassment washed over her. "Not that I didn't want you, I do want you!" Now Lexi knew she'd gone as red as a cooked lobster. "I mean, Clare, *Clare,*" yes, Clare was her life preserver here, "Clare said she'd ask you, and so I waited, and then you didn't come, so I thought I'd try someone else, but I can't get anyone else." She looked hopelessly at Jesse and felt her cheeks flame. The very sight of him did strange things to her belly.

"Watch out." Jesse's voice was low and warning.

"What?"

"You're about to knock over the paint."

Lexi clutched her head. "Oh, man, I'm such a *stork!*"

"Hey." Jesse stopped, attention caught by a picture learning against the wall. "Nice pix. Is that you?"

She focused. "That's me. That sarong I'm wearing? It's one that I designed myself."

But Jesse was looking at the beach. "Where is this?"

"Bali."

"Really? What's it like?"

"Oh, it's spectacular, Jesse. Enchanting, really. There's such a sense of peace and everything's *together,* animals, people, trees, the sand. It's like Heaven."

"Can I look at the others?"

"Sure." Lexi watched as Jesse knelt to sort through the pictures. The man was just drop-dead gorgeous. The years had added muscle and depth to him. He looked more adult. More powerful. She gave herself a mental slap and ordered her mind back to the pictures. "That's Maui. That's Nice. Rio, obviously."

Jesse gazed at the pictures with such an intensity Lexi knew he wanted to fade right through the glass, like Alice, and into that world. Her heart went out to him, spiraling back to memories of her own teenage days, when she'd yearned to travel, to leave this familiar place and see the world, the vast, romantic, mysterious world.

"I loved traveling," she said quietly. "It's the oddest thing, how seeing new places can open up vistas in yourself, places you never before even dreamed existed."

"Yeah," Jesse said, nodded. "I've been to the Caribbean a few times. But I'd like to go to Rio. Maui, too, someday. I'm not so sure about Nice; that might be too chi-chi for me."

"So go," Lexi told him.

Jesse snorted.

"Oh, come on, Jesse, carpenters make a killing on this island. You could afford a nice trip every so often."

Very gently, Jesse relinquished his hold on the picture of Maui, carefully leaning it against the wall. "Yeah, I suppose. I guess I've just been trying to save money to buy a house."

"But you'll have Clare's house, right?"

Jesse rose. "Clare's father's house. I can't plan to live my life out in another man's house."

"I can understand that," Lexi told him, but Jesse was heading toward the door, his back to her.

He turned, abruptly. "Look," Jesse said, his voice calm, but also angry, "I'll build your cubicles. I'll have to do it in the evenings. It won't take too long."

"Oh, Jesse! Thank you!" Impulsively, Lexi moved toward him, but stopped a few feet away, paralyzed. She felt like an adolescent in the presence of a rock idol. She hugged herself, simply to do something with her hands.

"Don't thank me," Jesse said hoarsely. "Thank Clare, I'm doing it because Clare asked me to."

"Yes, of course, I know that," Lexi babbled.

Jesse gave Lexi a look full of . . . she couldn't read it. Was it *disgust?* He looked so serious, not like Jesse at all. "I'll be here tomorrow about five-thirty," he told her, and strode away, out the door without a backward glance.

"Well," Lexi said out loud after he left, "that went well."

EIGHTEEN

Clare was in the kitchen, deeply involved in a complicated recipe for seafood pasta. She was chopping and boiling and peeling and stirring, each move a kind of ballet maneuver because Ralph bumbled around her feet, hoping for something to drop.

"Dad?" she yelled. "Dad? Could you take Ralph for her walk?"

No answer. She moved the saucepan off the burner, wiped her hands on her apron, and went into the den. Her father sat in his pajamas, staring at an old newspaper.

"Dad. Earth to Dad?"

Her father looked up, his gaze clouded with memories.

"Dad, I'm fixing dinner and Jesse should be here soon, and I'd love it if you'd take Ralph for a walk."

Her father nodded. "Well." He put the newspapers on the table next to him and pushed up with his hands from his chair. "Well, all right. How far should I take her?"

Clare sighed. So far the adoption of the dog had not morphed into the dream-come-true happy ending she'd hoped for. Her father seemed to like the dog, but in a passive way. He hadn't yet come to think of the animal as a creature with certain needs. Clare had encouraged her father to give the dog a name, and her father had stared at the amiable mutt who sat wagging her tail, ready for anything, and said, "Ralph."

"She's a female, Dad."

"Oh. Well, Ralphie? Or you can name her."

He wasn't connecting. "Oh, Ralph's a fine name, Dad. Kind of sounds like how dogs sound when they bark. Ralph! Ralph!" She'd thought she was pretty funny, and she did get a slender smile from her father. And he did bend to pet the dog, who shivered all over with pleasure.

Now Clare moved out to the hall, mentally tugging her father after her. "How about just around the block? Look, just put your raincoat on over your pajamas, no one will know. And here's her leash." Lifting it from the hook, she snapped it onto Ralph's collar, then took a plastic bag from the drawer. "And here's the bag in case she takes a dump. You remember the routine? Put it over your hand like a mitten, pick up the poop, then bring the top of the bag down like this and tie it, and voilà!"

Her father slipped his arms into his raincoat and dutifully accepted the paraphernalia. Together man and dog toddled out into the spring evening. It was almost eight o'clock, late for dinner, but Jesse was working at Lexi's and said he'd be home late, and her father didn't care when he ate or if he ate, for that matter. Clare stood at the door, enjoying the fresh air on her face and smiling. Okay, so it hadn't been love at first sight, her father hadn't leaped off the sofa and danced around the room with the dog in his arms, but he was out there walking, patiently waiting for Ralph to sniff messages off leaves and fences. It was more than he'd done for months.

Her father was moving very slowly. If he went at this pace around the entire block, they'd be eating dinner at midnight.

Really, she was tired. She'd been rising early the past few days, dressing and hurrying without breakfast or even a cup of coffee out to the wharf and into her shop. Marlene came in at nine and worked steadily alongside her, but always had to leave at five to fix dinner for her own family. Clare didn't have to come home and fix a proper meal. Jesse and her father were always perfectly happy with a pizza, but she wanted—subtly, even subconsciously—to reward Jesse for helping Lexi. It meant he worked extra hours in an already long day, plus he missed part of the televised Red Sox ball games. But it would only be for a few days; it was just a small job. She didn't understand why Jesse was being so sullen about it.

Back in the kitchen, she saw that the water had almost boiled out of the pasta pot. She refilled it and turned the heat to simmer. She poured herself a glass of red wine and carried it out to the back porch, sank onto a step, and leaned against the porch railing.

A winding slate path led from the house to the garage that had been transformed into her mother's studio. Now the building was dark. After her mother's death, Clare and her father had donated all her mother's art supplies—easels, pastels, oils, turps, and work tables—to the community school. So the room with its expanse of windows along the north and its glossy hardwood floor was bare. Perhaps they should turn it into a little apartment. The money from a rental would be helpful, especially now that her father had retired. Or perhaps, once she and Jesse were married and had a child or two, her father could live there. Not that she wanted to kick him out of his own house, but her parents had always told Clare they wanted to give her the house when she was older. Every now and then, during her twenties, she had rented her own little apartment in another part of town. A place of her own. She had loved the freedom to make each room look just the way she wanted it. But when her mother became ill, she'd moved back into the house to help, and since her mother's death it had seemed necessary for her to remain in the house to help her father. It wasn't such an odd situation she was in, living in her childhood home as an adult. Many of her friends were also doing it. Few people her age could afford to buy their own house on the island. Still, Clare felt like a snail grown too big for her shell. She wanted to move out, move on. Or stay, but make changes to reflect her own tastes and desires. Everything had gotten so drab and dusty in the house, but she couldn't yet broach the subject of changing a single thing, not with her father still in mourning for her mother.

Well, she could at least come out and clean up the flower beds, prune back the privet, and perhaps it wasn't too early to bring some of the lawn chairs out. She'd love to get over to the Cape to buy some new cushions for the wicker furniture on the back porch. She longed for deep pillowy cushions in pastel colors . . . she was in such a nesting mood these days. She and Jesse couldn't get married this summer, they'd both be working straight-out crazy insane hours. But if they married in the fall, she could have a baby next spring . . .

The front door slammed. She heard voices. Jesse and her dad were home. Back in the kitchen, she turned the heat up under the pasta pot and poured olive oil into the skillet. Ralph clicked into the room and stared at her with shy, hopeful eyes.

"Hi, sweetie." She bent to nuzzle and stroke the dog.

"I hope you're going to wash your hands before you touch the food." Jesse stood in the kitchen door. He had sawdust in his hair. He looked sexy and exhausted and cranky.

Clare made a face. "Hello to you, too, Sunshine. When did you get so frightened of dog germs? Don't answer that. Sit down. Have some wine." She washed her hands dutifully, poured him a glass of wine, and handed it to him. "Where's Dad?"

"I think he went into the den." Jesse collapsed in a chair and put his booted feet up on another chair. "I'm beat."

Clare began to stir-fry the veggies and scallops and fresh tuna. "You'll feel better soon. I'm making a yummy meal." She glanced over her shoulder. "How are the dressing rooms going?"

"I'll be through tomorrow night."

"So it's not such a big deal."

Jesse grunted.

Clare put the pasta in to cook, wondering what on earth was bugging Jesse. He was usually the sweetest man, patient, full of jokes and bonhomie. Perhaps it was just exhaustion, overwork, and the kind of psychological pressure every islander felt as the island population geared up to expand from the winter's nine thousand to twenty, then thirty, then, in August, fifty thousand residents. While the pasta boiled, Clare filled Ralph's bowl and set it down for her. She had planned to encourage her father to be responsible for the dog's meals, but it was still early. Her father had taken the dog for a walk; that was enough for today.

"I don't know why you got that thing," Jesse remarked, staring at Ralph, whose tail wagged happily as she wolfed down her food.

Surprised by the tone of his voice, Clare turned to look at Jesse. "Why, I told you. I think it will get my father out of his chair and out of the house."

"Yeah, if you nag him to do it. Be honest, Clare, you're going to be the one responsible for that animal. Which means you and I are going to be tied down even more than we already are."

"Tied down?" Clare's heart made funny jiggling movements.

"Yeah, like how can we travel?"

"Um, I didn't know we were planning to travel."

"You know I've always wanted to travel."

"True, but when we do get the chance to travel, well, by then Dad will be capable of caring for the dog."

"I'm not so sure."

The buzzer sounded. Clare poured the pasta into the colander to drain. "Jesse," she said over her shoulder, "what's up with you?"

Jesse looked away. His face was cloudy. "I just guess I wish you had consulted me before you went and got the dog. I mean, his presence changes my life as much as yours."

Clare's jaw dropped. "Oh, Jesse, you're right. I never really thought about that. I'm sorry, honey." On the stove, the sizzling oil made a crackling sound. Quickly she poured in the cream and stirred it with a wooden spoon. "Jesse, dinner's ready. Could you get Dad in here? And let's talk about the dog thing later, okay? I'm sorry, though, truly, if I seemed thoughtless."

"I'll get your father." Jesse rose and left the room.

Clare prepared a plate with pasta and the creamy

seafood sauce. As she carried it to the table, Ralph dashed between her legs so quickly she trod on one of the dog's feet and tripped, nearly sending the plate of food into the air. But she managed to keep her grip, and when she set the plate down safely on the table, she said to the dog in a very harsh voice, "No! Bad dog, Ralphie! Go lie down!"

Ralphie cringed at the sound of her voice.

Clare felt just completely miserable.

NINETEEN

At six o'clock on a windy spring evening, Jesse was at the back of Lexi's shop, hammering away. He'd been here for three hours, and so far Lexi had managed to act normal, or at least no more klutzy than usual. She had so much to do, she kept busy, zipping here and there around the shop, forcing her mind to focus on her work even though every cell in her body was tuned toward Jesse's presence. She turned up the volume on her radio, filling the room with sound so that she and Jesse didn't seem quite so very much alone here together.

She entered the far cubicle and sat down, trying out the corner bench Jesse had built. It was fine. She would put the first coat of paint on tonight.

"There," Jesse called over the dividing partition. "Done."

She stood, still planning. "Jesse, um, do you suppose you could come back tomorrow and do just a few more little bits? I'm so hopeless with a hammer."

Jesse came around the dividing wall and leaned on the open cubicle entrance. He smelled like new wood and soap and, just a little, of sweat. "What else?"

"I need the pictures hung up, and mirrors, one in

each cubicle and a couple out on the walls. And privacy curtains for the cubicles, so curtain rods should go up here and here—" She stretched to point to the places where the brackets should go on either side of the cubicle entrance. She felt her breasts rise as she raised her arms to touch the board running along the front. This brought her so close to Jesse, she was almost touching him. They were face to face, separated by only a few inches. "And hooks," she continued, backing up as she spoke. She was having trouble getting her breath. "Nice brass hooks here and here and here, for clothes."

Jesse entered the dressing room. It was a small space, meant for one woman and some light clothing. With two people, it was crowded, almost impossible to move. Jesse reached into his shirt pocket, then leaned forward. Lexi stepped back sharply, bumping into the wall. Jesse reached around her and made a mark on the wall with a pen. "Here?"

She nodded. She could smell him, she could feel the heat of his body. He put the pen in his pocket. He looked at her. Lexi felt something delicate and enormous approach, a shadowy and unexpected pressure, like the sand sharks that had brushed her legs when she swam at Steps Beach. Something frightening yet compelling, its presence an awesome, breathtaking gift.

"Jesse." She put her hand on the blue cotton of his shirt, just where it buttoned over his chest.

Jesse put his arms against the wall on either side of

her and pressed himself against her and brought his mouth to hers. She closed her eyes. His mouth was soft, his body hot. Sensations churned inside her. She had never felt this way before in her life, and she had no idea what to do, but she wanted this with every atom of her being. She wrapped her arms around him, pressing him closer. His erection was thick between them, so hard it almost hurt her. Sliding her hand down, she lay her palm on the bulge beneath the blue jeans.

He groaned, and pushed himself away from her. "We can't do this." He lunged into the other cubicle, grabbed up his tool belt, and strode across the shop to the front door. He slammed out the door, leaving Lexi alone, and trembling.

Brown paper still covered the two large plate-glass windows at the front of the shop while Lexi got it ready for its grand opening. She was glad for the privacy it provided. She walked to the front door and turned the latch. She walked to the radio on the counter and snapped it off.

Then she went back into the cubicle and pressed herself against the wall where Jesse had pressed her.

Never before had she felt so purely, physically, *alive*. The caressing heat of Maui, the perfumed air of Bali, the powerful surf on the New Zealand coast—none of that had awakened her like Jesse just had. She felt like Pinocchio transformed into a real person. Before she'd been wooden; now her body was supple and warm. And greedy.

Warning voices clamored, but she refused to hear them. Not just yet. For just a while more, she wanted to let her body soak in this extraordinary pleasure. Closing her eyes, she remembered Jesse's mouth on hers, his body pressing against hers. The soft warmth of his breath. The scratch of the bristles along his jaw.

And the way he looked at her. The look was so powerful, so intense, it was a kind of touching.

That hadn't been good ol' take-it-easy, laid-back, my-man Jesse who was with her just now. And there hadn't been a glimmer of the teasing, cocky, lady-killing Casanova, either. Jesse had looked worried. He'd looked desperate. He'd even looked just a little bit scared, and Lexi thought he'd been trembling, too.

Sinking down, Lexi folded up her knees and hugged them. She sat like that for a long time.

The spell didn't lift. Those few moments with Jesse buzzed around her like a hive of honeybees. All she knew was that she wanted Jesse to come back—now. She wanted him pressed against her, kissing her, touching; she wanted to run her hands over his warm, hard body—

—and that was something she could never have.

Jesse was engaged to marry Clare.

Clare had been her best friend, was still the best friend Lexi had.

What kind of person lets herself get sexually attracted to her best friend's man?

But what kind of relationship did Jesse and Clare have, if Jesse could act the way he had with Lexi?

No, not *act;* Lexi was sure that was no kind of an act. That was real.

Or maybe not. What did she know about the ways of men? Pathetically little.

Remember what you do know, she told herself. Remember your plans. Look around. Where are you now?

From the chaos and humiliation of her marriage and her divorce, she had gotten herself this far, *so* far. She'd made a plan, she'd worked as hard as she knew how, and she was trying to start her life over. She couldn't allow whatever had happened with Jesse to derail her new life. *Open your damn eyes,* she urged herself.

She opened her eyes. The cubicles were plywood. They needed to be painted. The rest of the shop gleamed with new, luminous color. She was creating more than a shop here; she was creating an entire world. She'd started her life fresh. She was friends with Clare.

She couldn't allow herself to be alone with Jesse ever again.

TWENTY

Jesse hadn't slept over, and as Clare stretched, warm and healthy in her bed, a piercing sadness, like resonant chords from an oboe, strummed through her. She'd been dreaming of babies, Penny's baby, the fantasy baby she and Jesse might have some day . . .

Closing her eyes, she rolled on her side, pulling the down comforter to her shoulders. It was still early. Could she fall back to sleep? Sensing something, she opened her eyes again and found herself staring right into Ralph's bright doggy eyes. Ralph saw Clare's gaze and sat up straight, quivering with her efforts to be patient. Clare was trying to make the animal belong to her father, but her father always shut Ralph out of his bedroom, so she slept in the hallway, tiptoeing into Clare's room at the first sound of Clare stirring. She was such a good-natured animal; she tried so hard not to pester Clare.

"Good morning, Ralphie." Clare reached out an arm and stroked the dog's head. "Okay. You're right. We should go to the beach."

Clare pulled on jeans and a long-sleeved tee, tied on sneakers, put Ralph in the van, and drove out to Fisherman's Beach. Her father was pretty good about walking Ralph twice a day, but no matter how Clare urged him to, he never took the dog out for a good run. Besides, she loved the deserted beach at this time of day; it was like the world was starting fresh, full of light and surging tide and spangling air. At eight o'clock, the beach would start filling up with swimmers and sunbathers who didn't welcome unleashed dogs. But this early in the morning, Ralph ran free.

She loved watching her. Ralph was fascinated and terrified by the ocean. She'd bark hysterically at it, all four legs nearly lifting off the ground in her excitement, and when a wave receded, she'd chase after it, triumphantly wagging her tail, nearly yodeling with exultation. When the waves came surging back in, Ralph always stood frozen for a moment, puzzling over this rebound of bravery on the sea's part, but when the cold water touched her paws, she'd turn and race up the shore toward Clare, and she'd actually try to hide behind Clare's legs. Clare would bend to pet her and reassure her, and Ralph would shake out her coat and go into an "I'm just walking here" act, strolling along next to Clare, eyeing the perplexing surf, until optimism once again overcame her and she rushed out to chase another wave back to its place.

Farther down the beach a man was walking, accompanied by a couple of dogs. After a moment, Ralphie spotted them, too, and immediately she bounded toward the dogs, wagging her tail so heartily her entire body undulated.

"Good morning, Clare!" Adam Laney waved at her. "What a day!" He wore swim trunks and a T-shirt and his honey-brown hair was wet.

"Hi, Adam. Don't tell me you've been swimming. Isn't the water too cold?"

"I like it this way. It's refreshing." Adam gestured toward the dogs. They were tearing into a clump of seaweed, lured by the various smelly bits caught inside. "They're going to need baths."

"Baths?" Clare echoed in consternation. "Gad. I don't know if I can manage that before I get to work." She thought of dog hair in the bathtub, smelly towels on the floor.

"I just aim the garden hose at them and soak them down. Gets the salt off their coats, too. Leave them in the backyard to dry off in the sun."

"Ah. Thanks for the tip." She smiled up at him.

"So your father likes his dog?"

"Ralph. He named her Ralph." They both laughed. "I can't say he's wild about her, but he is dutiful. He feeds her and takes her out twice a day. And she hangs out with him when I'm at work, so I know he has some kind of company."

The dogs were on their backs, rolling in the seaweed. "That's enough, you jokers." Adam whistled and clapped his hands. His dogs immediately sprang to attention. Ralph looked up, curious. "Let's walk," he urged the dogs.

Clare matched her gait to Adam's as they continued along the beach. The dogs raced around, bumping into Clare and Adam's legs, chasing one another, tails wagging, ears flapping, tongues flying.

"Life is so simple for them," Clare said musingly.

"And not for you?"

She felt Adam's gaze on her face. All her senses flipped to red alert. The space between her arm and his as they walked seemed glittery with the electricity of attraction. "Well . . ."

Adam asked, "I've got a thermos of coffee up by the dune. Want to share it?"

"Great!"

They sat cross-legged on the sand, side by side, looking out at the ocean. Adam unscrewed the plastic top, poured the cup full, and offered it to Clare.

As she took it from him, their arms bumped. Clare felt herself flush. She brought the cup to her mouth, remembering all those years ago, when just the possession of an apple his lips had touched made her pulse race.

"You were saying . . ." Adam prompted.

"Oh, well, Adam . . . I guess I keep thinking about family. My parents were both so cerebral I'm surprised they managed to keep me alive through infancy."

Adam laughed. "Your father was a great teacher. Your mother was a fine artist. And you turned out pretty well, in spite of everything."

She looked at him. "Thanks." She met his eyes. His gaze was gentle. "I want a lot of children," she confessed, then immediately felt surprised at herself and flustered by the way she blurted out such an intimate thought. She lifted sand in the palms of her hands and let it run through her fingers. "I mean, I want to have children and be a better parent to them than my parents were to me."

"Does Jesse want children?" Adam asked. He stared out at the horizon.

Clare chuckled. "I'm not sure Jesse's through being a child himself."

"But you believe he will be, one day."

Clare traced her fingers in the sand. "Honestly? I don't know." Guilt flooded her. She felt as if she were betraying Jesse, talking about him this way. She changed the course of the conversation. "Do *you* want children?"

Again, Adam remained silent instead of answering. Clare looked over at him. His profile was strong, his nose broken from a football injury, his lashes long and dark.

"I don't know, Clare. I suppose if I met the right woman."

"What about Melanie Clark?" Clare asked, and she could tell she was turning beet red at her intrusiveness.

"What about her?"

"Well, you're dating her . . ."

"Not anymore." He didn't explain, but tilted the cup, sipped more coffee, then handed it to her. "You can have the rest." He rose, brushed sand off his shorts, and walked down to the water's edge, whistling to the dogs. He threw sticks into the water for them. They plunged ecstatically into the waves, lunging back out with sticks in their mouths, while Ralphie stayed on the shore, jumping up and down in her odd four-legged way and barking.

He's certainly good with dogs, Clare thought. He's made himself a kind of family already with his dogs. And he's not dating Melanie anymore. She wondered what that was about.

And why did she care?

A few hundred yards away, a group of energetic early-morning swimmers stalked through the sand to the sea. Clare downed the last sip of coffee, screwed the lid back on the thermos, and rose. She walked down to join Adam.

"I've got to get back," she told him.

"Mmm, me too." His legs were muscular, hairy, freckled with sand. The wet dogs shook themselves, spraying Adam and Clare with drops of cold water. "Now we'll both need showers."

Clare thought of him in the shower. Naked. She thought of them both in the shower, together, naked.

"I, um, my car's parked up that way."

He pointed in the other direction. "My car's up that way."

"Well, thanks for the coffee." Why was she finding it so hard to pull herself away? "Maybe if you're here tomorrow, I could bring coffee . . ." She wasn't quite sure what she was talking about, what she was offering or what she wanted.

His eyes were calm on her face. "Or not. It's nice just to walk with you."

What if I jumped on you, wrapped my legs around you, and kissed you, would *that* be nice? Clare thought. Being in his presence was like being caught up in an undertow; it was taking all she had simply to breathe. "Okay, then," she managed to say. Ralphie slammed into her legs, nearly knocking her over. She was grateful for the interruption.

"Come on, Ralphie," she said, and bent to clip the leash on her collar. "So, well, bye." She didn't quite meet Adam's eyes. No more intense mutual gazes if she was going to walk off this beach.

"Bye, Clare." He clapped his hands and his dogs came to heel.

Clare watched him for a moment. She felt unaccountably buoyed up. "Come on, Ralphie," she urged, and ran along the beach, in and out of the waves, as if she were a child, and Ralphie, emboldened by Clare's company, jumped and barked and ran next to her, bounding with joy.

TWENTY-ONE

In Lexi's dreams, a man was kissing her. In the irrational way of dreams, the man was both Jesse and not Jesse. The kiss was compelling, intoxicating, surrounding her in an endless warm sea of pleasurable sensation.

She woke, feeling relaxed and supple in her limbs. She stretched luxuriously, allowing herself to take her time rising up out of the dream. For a while she lay on her side, gazing at the strip of sun falling across the pine floor. She allowed herself to sense the day—it would be a good day, windless, bright, and sunny.

Suddenly she was full of energy and plans. In a flash she was out of bed, pulling on her painting clothes. She made coffee and carried a mug downstairs, where she set it on a counter and began to organize herself to paint the cubicles. She taped plastic over the wood floors, pried the lid off the paint can with a screwdriver, set up her little aluminum ladder, and picked up her brush. Hours later, she remembered her coffee.

By noon she'd finished painting. Her wrists and back ached from crouching and stretching to reach all the corners. She had to get out into the fresh day. Pulling on a sweater, she drifted out her back door.

The bright light of the late-spring sun on the blue waters dazzled her, almost made her dizzy. She took a deep breath of the salty air. The tide was in, lapping gently at the rocky bulkhead. A pair of mallards floated idly past, and across the way, on one of the stanchions at the town pier, a cormorant stood with his wings spread. The tide had washed a line of dark seaweed up along the curve of beach. Several gulls waddled along, inspecting the tangled mass for any live shellfish. A man in a brilliantly colored wet suit paddled a kayak away from shore. She shivered. He'd be cold out on the water.

A small figure sat very still on the end of the town pier, arms hugging her knees to her chest, facing out steadily toward the Brant Point lighthouse and the channel opening to the Sound. She seemed forlorn. Lexi walked over the low shelf of pebbles until she reached the beach, then she squelched her way over the sodden sand toward the town pier. The old weathered boards made a knocking noise as she went down the pier, passing rowboats, sailboats, and launches, all tied up, resting in the quiet water.

When she reached the end, she saw that the girl was Jewel Chandler, the precocious child who had spoken to her at the concert.

"Jewel?"

The girl turned. An attempt had been made to tame her curly red hair into braids tied with green tartan ribbons. She wore cargo pants, a green sweater, and a fleece jacket.

"Oh. Hello, Miss Laney." She didn't smile. Behind her tortoiseshell glasses, her eyes were very serious.

"Mind if I join you?"

"Okay." Jewel looked back toward the water.

Lexi sat on the cool splintery boards, folding her long legs Indian-style. "School's out?"

"Teacher's meeting."

"Ah. So you're here . . ."

"I'm waiting for my father."

Jewel's father—Tristram Chandler. The newspapers had reported that identifying numbers had confirmed that the boat washed up on a Maine shore was the one Tris was sailing. So far there had been no sign of the man's body.

"Jewel, I'm so sorry."

"You don't need to be. I know he'll come back. That's why I'm here. Waiting for him." The girl kept her eyes on the horizon.

Lexi studied the girl's face. "Does your mother know you're here?"

Jewel flashed a quick, impatient glance at Lexi. "Of course."

"And she doesn't mind? I suppose you know how to swim. I mean, what if you fell in?"

"I'm an excellent swimmer. And I have no intention of falling in."

"How long will you sit here?"

"Till dark. Then Mom says I have to go home."

"Won't you get bored?"

"Bored?" Jewel sounded incredulous. "No, I won't get bored." Her shoulders slumped. "I do get tired. I didn't know that hoping was such hard work."

Oh, dear, Lexi thought, hadn't anyone explained to the child how little chance there was that her father was still alive? "But it's spring," Lexi said softly. "Don't you have things to do?"

Jewel gave Lexi an indulgent glance. "I'm a child, not a brain surgeon."

Lexi grinned. "Still. Don't you want to, oh, ride your bike? Build sand castles? Eat ice cream cones?"

Jewel gave this some thought. "Yes. I would like to do all those things. But this is more important. When my dad comes home, I want him to see me waiting here. I want him to know we've always been waiting for him, every minute."

Admiration and pity twisted Lexi's heart. "Well, do you like to read?"

Jewel nodded, the first sign she'd shown of eagerness. "I love to."

"What are your favorite books?"

"Harry Potter, of course. And anything by Madeleine L'Engle. And I know it's light, but I do enjoy Nancy Drew."

"Oh, I loved Nancy Drew!"

Jewel nodded. "I guess I could bring a book. I guess that would be okay." She sounded as old and jaded as Dorothy Parker. "I'll have to think about it. I wouldn't want to not be hoping."

The child was so vulnerable, so determined. Such a little girl, facing the mysteries of the sea. "Maybe I could help you hope."

Jewel looked surprised. "Really? That would be cool. I mean, my mom isn't hoping, why should she, she's got a new husband and baby." She gave Lexi an assessing stare. "I don't discuss this with just anyone."

Lexi bit her tongue to keep from smiling at the child's solemnity. "I understand."

"It would be nice if you helped," Jewel decided. She stared back at the water. "You could visit me now and then."

Lexi was flattered. "I could bring you an ice cream cone."

"Really? That would be awesome." For just a moment, Jewel sounded like a child.

A Boston Whaler chugged in toward the pier. A fisherman clad in waders waved at Jewel. So everyone knows about Jewel's vigil, Lexi thought. Everyone will help look after her.

"I've got to get back to work. My shop is right over there. Come by if you need anything."

Jewel nodded. "Thank you."

Lexi pushed herself to her feet. "I'll see you soon." She strode away, then turned back. "Good luck!"

"Thank you," Jewel said, tossing a smile over her shoulder.

Lexi wandered away, down toward the salt

marshes where the harbor dwindled into creeks and sandy beaches. Had she done the wrong thing, she wondered, offering to help hope that Jewel's father was alive? Jewel was old enough to know about death. She was old enough to know about probabilities. She'd grown up on the island; she had to know that people drowned, that the sea was cruel and careless, that nature had no interest in any child's hopes.

And yet, how does anyone live without hope? Jewel was hoping for her father; Lexi was hoping to someday meet the love of her life. Would they be happier if they believed neither man would ever appear? The sea was cruel and careless, true, but it also was full of miracles. Sometimes, Lexi thought, you had to take a stand. Reality or hope. For today at least, she chose hope.

TWENTY-TWO

As Clare and the dog cut through the sand dunes along the path to the beach, the sun was rising. On this calm June morning she could feel the night's chill vanish like popped bubbles as the sun warmed the air. The water rolled sleepily toward the shore, its lacework waves whispering "sea."

Clare sank down on the sand to enjoy the sky unfolding its colors, from dove gray to fire opal to a profound shining endless azure, the lavish, spendthrift blue of summer. She pulled her sweatshirt off over her head. No one else was around. Ralph was down at the water's edge, frightening the waves.

Carelessly, she palmed a handful of sand, enjoying the tickle as it trickled through her fingers until she was left holding only a small moon shell. This clever spiral calcium structure had once been home to a simple, rather unattractive creature, a gelatinous creeping mass. Who could explain why the whorls and stripes were so intricately, carefully, and exquisitely marked?

She and Lexi had named "their" beach "Moon Shell Beach" because of the abundance of moon shells on the sand, but Jetties Beach had many more moon shells, and "their" beach had many other kinds of shells—periwinkles, scallops, razor clams, mussels. She supposed it was the romance of the word *moon* that entranced them. Back then, everything romantic, enchanted, and dreamy had seemed to be located far away, on another sphere completely from their common, infuriating homes.

How fascinating that Lexi had traveled so far and chosen to return to the island. Somehow it made Clare feel just a bit better about her own decision to live here. She'd lived off-island during college and visited friends on the West Coast, but she'd never seriously considered living anywhere else. She loved Nantucket. She wasn't crazy about living with her father in the house she'd grown up in, but rentals on the island were insanely expensive; she couldn't have opened her shop if she hadn't lived at home. And since her mother's death, she'd been glad, for her father's sake, that she still lived at home. She could only imagine what a wreck he and the house would have been without her.

In the distance, a dog barked. Instantly, Ralph took off running down the beach toward the approaching figures. Adam, Lucky, and Bella. She rose and walked toward them. She was beginning to count on these casual morning meetings. Somehow they made her more optimistic about the future.

But why, she wondered, did such a thought even occur? Did she need assistance being optimistic? She stamped on the vacant shell of a spider crab, pleased with the crunching noise. Adam strolled toward her, his family of dogs playing around his legs, and Clare thought how grown-up he seemed, so reliably connected to the world. In contrast, Jesse was about as stable as a windsurfer. His light-heartedness had always been one of Jesse's charms, but sometimes Clare thought that asking Jesse to settle down and be part of a family was like cutting a bird's wings. The creature would be alive, but the mysterious, essential self would be lost forever.

That was the romantic way to look at the problem. A more realistic way, and one that she hated, was how often Clare felt as if she was more Jesse's mother than his beloved.

When she first fell in love with Jesse, back in high school, she'd been crazy for his good looks, but more than that, she'd been fascinated by his playful recklessness. It had appealed to her secret love of outlaws and rebels. Not that Jesse had ever been outright rebellious. He'd never been serious enough about any idea or cause to fight for it. He hadn't cut classes or battled with his teachers or coaches or other guys. He just loped along through his days, having a good time, too relaxed and happy to remember to do his homework or study for a test. His grades had been abysmal. Obviously a smart kid, he could make the teachers smile even as he gave the wrong answer, and scraped through high school on his good nature. Which had been fine. He hadn't wanted to go to college. For a while he was almost serious about getting together a bluegrass band, but even for that he couldn't find the discipline to make himself show up at every practice.

Now they were both adults, engaged to be married, ready to start a family, and Clare could sense a kind of tension in Jesse, an anxiety. In the past few weeks, he'd been more restless and ill-tempered than she could remember him ever being. One evening they'd had dinner at Penny and Mike's, and Jesse had been as twitchy as if he'd just come down with a bad case of poison ivy. He'd held little Mikey and said all the right things about what a cute baby he was, but Clare noticed how quickly Jesse handed the infant back to his mother. He didn't share a look with Clare; he didn't say, "We should get one of these." She'd been hoping he would say that—how could anyone hold little Mikey and not want a baby?—but not then, or later as they drove home, did Jesse initiate the subject of a family.

That didn't mean Jesse didn't want a family. And Jesse loved her. She knew that. She just had to go ahead into the future she wanted, and sort of seduce—or drag—Jesse along with her.

And sometimes that seemed like a lot of work.

"Everyone is eccentric," her mother had advised her once, when Clare was feeling especially hopeless about Jesse. "Look at your father and me. We're hardly normal, and yet we muddle along."

Clare's mother had adored Jesse. He had always

been able to make Ellen laugh. He often flirted with her openly and honestly, even occasionally causing her to blush. She had told Clare over and over again, *Jesse's a good man. Just give him time.*

She had given him time. She was still giving him time. But recently she was frustrated, thinking, why did she have to be the one to give him anything? Why did she have to be the one waiting patiently at home with milk and cookies for the errant wild child to return, abashed, even if charmingly abashed? So many times, especially after one of his episodes of straying, Jesse had told her, as they made love, that Clare brought out the best in him, that she made him "work," that without her he was lost. She'd grown accustomed to the idea of being not just the woman who waited at home for him, but being his home itself.

And just how would that work when they had a family? It seemed to Clare that the most magical thing on the planet was what everyone else called an ordinary family, and that was what she wanted. She wanted a chaotic kitchen with children covered with flour as they made birthday cookies, and a big fat SUV full of baby seats, violin cases, and hockey sticks. She wanted to attend baseball games and swim meets, but first she wanted—oh, how she wanted!—to sing lullabies.

"Good morning!" Adam held up two thick paper cups. "Lattes from Fast Forward!"

"My hero!" Clare laughed. She accepted one, lifted

the lid, and took a long sip of the sweet, hot, powerful beverage. "Wow. That's the way to start the day."

They walked slowly down the beach, the three dogs chasing one another into the sand dunes and back down to the water's edge.

"How's business?" Adam asked companionably.

"Good. Really good. Not so many drop-ins—that will come in July and August—but lots of special orders. I've got Marlene on full-time now and two part-time girls, and this is the only time of the day I'm not moving as fast as I can." She looked up at Adam. "You must be busy."

"We are. Summer residents are arriving with their pets, and tourists on mopeds are bringing in injured 'bunnies' they've found on the side of the road, and we have to educate them about contagious diseases from rabbits. We've got a new vet to help us out over the busy season."

"Oh? Where's he from?"

"She. Miranda's from Georgia. She's just out of school, and she's got a delightful southern accent that charms all the patients and their owners." He chuckled.

Does she charm all the *vets,* too? Clare wondered, surprised as an unexpected blaze of jealousy shot through her. "Miranda," she said. "Pretty name."

Adam nodded. "Pretty woman."

Clare spotted another crab shell and stamped on it with extra force. "I like to hear them crunch," she explained to Adam. "It's like eating popcorn."

He laughed. "Popcorn. My summer sustenance." Clare glanced up at him quizzically.

Adam explained, "Now that the town's so crowded, I forget to buy groceries, and when I do remember to buy them, I'm standing in front of an empty refrigerator, too exhausted to consider making a trip to the grocery store. Plus, the thought of sitting in traffic after working all day makes me so tired I end up making do with a bag of microwave popcorn and a couple of beers."

"I know what you mean," Clare agreed. "Although I bought a Crock-Pot last summer, and that's been helpful. I just fill it up and turn it on in the morning and dinner's ready whenever I get home at night."

"Good idea. Does your dad do the grocery shopping?"

Clare snorted. "I wish. No, he's not reliable. Even when I give him a list, he forgets to take it, or forgets to get all the items."

"Does Jesse shop?"

"Not usually. He's living in the garage apartment at his parents' house, so some nights he eats dinner over there. But I don't mind shopping. I like to look over the food, especially the produce. I love this time of year, with fresh asparagus and new potatoes and fresh strawberries. You should come over sometime when I've been out to Moors End Farm. I make the best strawberry shortcake."

Adam bent, picked up a piece of driftwood, and

threw it into the ocean. His two dogs went scrambling, head over heels, into the surf. Lucky captured the stick and brought it back to Adam, wriggling with pride. Adam threw the stick again.

Clare moved up the beach and sat down with her back to a sand dune. Thank heavens for the animals, Clare thought. They were great buffers, providing time for her face to cool down—she was sure it was crimson. What had she just done? Invited Adam over to her house for dinner? Oh, that would be a congenial group, her father, her, Adam, and Jesse. Not that Jesse disliked Adam; he liked Adam just fine, although Adam was two years older and had always seemed a decade older than Jesse, if not from a different species. Or Adam could come over some night when Jesse played poker or ate at his parents'. Now there was a bright idea. It made Clare tingle all over with embarrassment and a warm, delicious feeling she didn't dare investigate or even name.

Ralph rushed up to her, tongue hanging out, tail wagging, spraying sand on Clare's legs as she settled on the sand to watch the other two animals brave the ocean.

"Good girl," Clare told Ralph, petting her.

Adam threw the stick one more time, then walked up to the dune and joined Clare. His dogs began a fierce game of tug-of-war with the stick, stealing it from each other, accidentally bopping each other on the head with it, or tripping themselves.

"What a pair of clowns," Adam said.

"Ralph's afraid of the water," Clare told him. "She's fascinated by it, but too scared to go in."

"Smart dog. The undertow here is pretty bad." Adam squinted as he stared out to sea. "Look at it. Shining and calm. Makes you forget how dangerous it is."

"I know. Every summer someone gets swept up and thrown down by the undertow—broken leg or arm. Remember the summer David Sutton broke his neck?"

"And now we've lost Tris," Adam murmured.

"Well, we don't know for certain about Tris . . ."

"It's been three weeks. Bobbie wants to hold a memorial service. Tris wouldn't be gone so long without letting someone know he was still alive. He wouldn't do that to his daughter." Adam's voice broke. He looked away, blinking back tears.

Clare protested, "But Tris is an ace sailor."

"And the sea is full of peril." Adam crushed his cup in his hand. Abruptly, he rose, stalking over the sand to stand just at the water's edge. Clare could tell he needed this moment alone.

Shouts sounded from down the shore. She turned and saw four teenage boys racing toward the waves, carrying surfboards. Adam watched them, too, for a while, then came back to stand by Clare.

"I haven't surfed for years," Clare remarked.

"I haven't, either." Adam kept his gaze on the boys. After a moment, casually, he said, "I've seen Jesse surfing."

"Oh, yes. He windsurfs, too."

"Without a life jacket."

"I know, I know. I'm always nagging him about it. He's hopeless. But he loves the water."

"And being Jesse, he'll probably be just fine. He's kind of like the guy in the wrecked car who's so drunk he doesn't break a bone."

Clare laughed. "Yeah, that's Jesse, all right." She quickly added, "Jesse's not a drunk, Adam."

"I know that, Clare. He's just one of those guys who's naturally stoned on life. I envy him. I wish I could be just a little more relaxed."

"I think you're *perfect* just the way you are, Adam," Clare assured him, then immediately got flustered at her words and the heat with which she'd spoken.

Adam smiled when he said, "That's because you don't know me very well, Clare." He looked down, meeting her eyes.

For a long moment, they held their gaze, their connection.

"Adam . . ."

"Time I headed to work." He held out his hand. Clare took it, and he pulled her to her feet. Excited, Ralph bumped into her legs, and Adam kept hold of her hand as she steadied herself. Then he dropped her hand.

"Thanks for the coffee," Clare said. "I'll bring it tomorrow."

"See you then." Adam tossed the words over his

shoulder as he ran down the beach, his dogs at heel.

Clare watched him go, bringing the hand he had held to her mouth. She smelled salt, and the sea, and sunshine.

TWENTY-THREE

Lexi and Clare were at Fifty-Six Union, leaning toward each other over a crisp white tablecloth. A spring storm slashed the windows with rain and blew cold wet gusts through the door when anyone entered or left. Inside was all warmth, delicious smells, murmurs of conversation.

"So Jesse's done your work?" Clare asked.

Lexi made a face. "Most of it. But I'm not ready to open yet, even if Jesse has finished with the cubicles. I've got a lot of inventory to unpack and some hasn't even arrived yet. As long as I'm open by the Fourth of July, I'll be happy."

"Yeah, the island doesn't really start hopping until then." Clare lowered her voice and leaned over her plate. "Lexi, I want to ask you something. You've seen Jesse a few times now. Tell me, what do you think about him?"

Lexi took a sip of wine. "Jesse?"

"I mean, how do you think he *feels?*"

"What do you mean?"

"I mean, do you think he's happy? Do you think he's *content?* He seems so restless these days. I think maybe he regrets asking me to marry him."

Lexi chose her words carefully. "I know he wants to travel, Clare. He did talk about that. When he saw my pictures of the different beaches, he said he'd like to go there, to Bali, and Rio."

"He's traveled!" Clare retorted, defensively. "He's been to Jamaica and Costa Rica and Tortola."

"I didn't mean to make you angry, Clare."

"I'm not angry at you." But Clare put her fork down and leaned her elbows on the table and rested her chin in her hands, thinking. "Maybe I'm angry at Jesse. Maybe I'm really angry at myself. Lexi, aren't you just *dying* to have children? Why *didn't* you have children?"

A half-smile twisted Lexi's mouth. "So you want a baby?"

"You have no idea." Clare sipped her wine. "Or maybe you do."

"Yes . . ." How much should she tell Clare? Just thinking about it made her melancholy, and tonight was meant to be fun.

Clare persisted. "You and Ed didn't want children?"

Lexi ran her fingertip around the rim of her wineglass. "Oh, yes. I wanted children. But Ed already had children, so he was sort of through with that phase of his life." She forced a smile. "He turned out to be such a Prince of Darkness, I guess I'm glad we didn't have children together."

Clare nodded thoughtfully. "Well, Lexi, I'm not sure Jesse has what it takes to be a father. At least not for a few more decades."

Lexi grinned. "He is a boy."

"He is. Peter Pan." Clare hesitated, then let it all spill out. "Lex, I've run into Adam several times, walking on the beach with Ralphie, and he's so nice, he's so stable and kind and so *grown up*."

"Yeah, Clare, but you don't want to be with someone just because they're stable."

"I know, I know. I'm not saying this right. Maybe I'm not even thinking this right just yet, and please don't say anything about it to Adam, promise?"

Lexi nodded. "Of course."

"I . . . I think I'm kind of attracted to Adam, Lex. Sometimes I even think I'm kind of in love with him."

"But you're engaged to Jesse."

"I know!"

The waitress appeared and whisked away their salad plates and set their entrees in front of them.

"Um, smells divine." Clare leaned over her spicy shrimp-studded fried rice and inhaled. The moment the waitress left, she made hair-pulling motions. "I'm going nuts, Lex! Sometimes I think my love for Jesse has become five percent affection and ninety-five percent pure stubbornness. Sometimes I wonder whether I'm going to make him marry me just because I want to prove to him and to myself and to the town that I've won. Do you see what I mean?"

Lexi nodded. "I do."

"But when I'm with Adam—" Clare broke off, considering her words. "I really like being with

209

Adam." She grinned wickedly. "Plus, he's really hot."

Lexi narrowed her eyes. "Don't you dare break his heart."

"No, it's not like that, Lexi. I mean I wouldn't just sleep with him and still be with Jesse." She waved her hands. "Oh, I don't know! I'm just confused. Don't pay any attention to me. Tell me about you, Lexi. Have you met anyone you want to date?"

Lexi shook her head. "All I've been doing is working, day and night. It's like Noah's ark is about to land. I remember how it was with my parents' shop in the good days. One moment life is organized and the next there are hundreds of wild animals thundering around and it's all you can do to keep them fed and stabled."

Clare laughed. "You're so funny, Lex." She reached across the table and took her friend's hand. "I'm so glad you're home."

TWENTY-FOUR

Dawn was breaking as Clare biked down to Swain's Wharf. She wore mittens, a wool cap, and a vest because these spring mornings and evenings were still cold. During the day, especially working like a maniac in her shop, she was warm enough in jeans and a long-sleeved tee. Her assistant, Marlene, wasn't coming in until nine, when they would open the shop together, but there was still so much work waiting to be done, Clare had hardly slept for thinking about it. She assured herself that with older, plumper, cheerful Marlene bustling around, they'd get it all done.

Her bike bounced when she hit the Belgian blocks of Commercial Street. She braked to a halt, crossed the narrow lane to Sweet Hart's, wheeled her bike around to the back, and locked it up. Just a few feet away, the water of the harbor sparkled as the sun and wind stirred it. Boats bobbed along the town pier, small motorboats, fishing boats, pleasure boats. Mallards paddled near the curve of beach and herring gulls dropped sand crabs on the wooden boards of the pier, then dove down to tease out their breakfast from the cracked shells.

As she unlocked the back door of her shop, she saw that the lights were on next door. So Lexi was

211

here early, too, but of course, all Lexi had to do was to walk downstairs from her little apartment. She hoped Lexi would be ready to open tomorrow. When she asked Jesse how the work for Lexi was going, he'd been abrupt, said he'd gotten a good start but had to go back. Brown paper still covered the shop windows and no sign hung above the front door.

She was so curious about the kinds of things Lexi was selling. Impulsively, she rapped on the shop's back door.

A moment later, Lexi opened the door just wide enough to peer out. She wore black leggings and a long white shirt covered with paint splotches. Her hair was messily clipped back and she had circles under her eyes.

"Clare!" Lexi wandered outside, yawning and rubbing her eyes. "I've worked all night long, can you believe it?"

"Are you going to be able to open today?"

"No, not until tomorrow, but that's okay, most people don't start arriving until Friday, right? I've got a few more finishing touches." She looked shyly at Clare. "Want to see it?"

"I'm dying to see it!"

Lexi hugged herself and did a little jog in place. "Oh, I'm so nervous, so excited! Come around to the front door. I want you to see it the way a customer would." Lexi went back into the shop and Clare went around to the front.

Lexi held the door wide. "Ta-da!"

Clare walked inside. Her jaw dropped. "Wow."

It was a dreamy summer paradise. Painted over all the walls were dreamy scenes of azure and turquoise water, golden sand, pale blue sky. Wind chimes and seashells dangled from the ceiling, gently spinning in the breeze from the open door. Racks of clothing along the two longer walls held garments in myriad shades of blue, and in the middle of the shop were curved display cases glittering with jewelry like a pirate's trove. A tall wicker shelf held pashminas, silk scarves, clever purses, sparkling belts, and hair accessories. Scattered over the walls were gold-framed photos of beaches, the sand of each beach a slightly different shade of gold or white. A lone woman stood on the beach, draped in loose, dreamy turquoise or indigo silk.

Clare clasped her hands to her chest. "Lexi! How fabulous! So magical!"

"I'm so glad you feel that way! I want it to feel magic. And look!"

Lexi reached behind the counter at the front and brought out her shop's sign, a quarter board carved in an elongated spiral. Against a cream background, gold letters read: *Moon Shell Beach*. "It's heavy. I've got to have Jesse hang it for me."

Clare said, "Moon Shell Beach?"

"Yes! Don't you love it? Everything here is totally Moon Shell Beach. All the garments—the sarongs, beach cover-ups, little tops, long skirts, everything. Not only are they beachy colors, but look what I've done!" Lexi held up a turquoise skirt with a gauze lavender overlay hemmed with tinkling beaded silver shells. "Every single item from this shop has a sterling silver moon shell on it somewhere." She picked up a lace cami from the wicker shelf. Tied to the left strap by a thin silk ribbon was a tiny silver shell.

Numbly, Clare fingered the white price tag on the camisole. "One hundred fifty dollars?" she squeaked.

Lexi carefully folded the camisole and returned it to its place. "Yeah, everything here is special, Clare. Made from the finest fabrics, with lots of hand-sewing. And of course the silver shells."

Clare pulled out a caftan hanging from a rack. It was a swirl of blues, embroidered lavishly with silver threads, the neckline adorned with a rainbow of beads, stones, and shells. The price tag said a thousand dollars. "You're kidding."

"Clare, most of the women who come here for the summer can pay this kind of money. And for everyone else, I have so many little things—that beach bag is only fifty dollars. And look, for thirty dollars, you can buy these little blue silk boxes with a sterling silver shell on top. I mean, that's not much to pay for a memento to take home, or to give to friends."

Clare looked at the box. It could hold a roll of stamps. Running her fingertips over a Moroccan-inspired beaded skirt, she said, "I can't believe you

214

named your shop Moon Shell Beach." She glared at Lexi. "What a crappy thing to do."

Lexi looked as if she'd just been slapped. "You don't like it?"

"Lexi, it was the name of *our private beach*. Our childhood secret place. It was *our* name, yours and mine, our *private* name." She shook her head angrily. "I can't believe you just claimed it for yourself alone. Or perhaps I should believe it, that's the kind of thing you do now."

"But Clare, don't you see? I meant it as a kind of . . . homage—" Lexi pronounced it the French way, *o*mage, "to our friendship. To our perfect sunny summers, and freedom, and laughter!"

Clare wanted to tell Lexi just where she could shove her *homage*. "Really, Lexi, how can you not get this? I feel so *violated*. You've taken something precious and private and used it as a kind of gimmick! And for what? To make money! It's just so, so *smarmy* of you!"

Lexi's eyes were filled with tears. "Oh, Clare, I never meant that. I thought you'd be pleased. Honestly, I thought you'd be so pleased."

Clare glared. "Pleased that you would capitalize on a private childhood memory."

"Well, it's *my* memory, too!" Lexi protested.

"Right. Well, Lexi, it's *all* yours now. Good luck with it."

Clare whirled around and stormed out the front door. With shaking hands, she unlocked the front door of her own shop, her little shop that shared a wall with fucking Moon Shell Beach, her little shop where the average transaction was thirty dollars. Lexi could make more in her shop selling one over-priced caftan than Clare could make in a day's work. But it wasn't the money that burned Clare, it was the *concept*. It was the selfish appropriation of one of her most dearly prized memories; it was like stealing an entire phase of her childhood.

Stomping up the stairs to her kitchen, Clare fought back tears. Automatically she began preparations for work, washing her hands, setting out sugar. Glancing at the recipe she'd perfected, she tried to focus on her work, but she was shaking, and she couldn't concentrate.

Moon Shell Beach.

She stopped, staring into space, thinking. What a clever concept, really. That shop was an entire world. Just entering it was like a mini-vacation from reality. Why had she responded so childishly? Okay, she admitted to herself, perhaps she was shocked at the sheer scope of Lexi's creativity. Certainly she'd been surprised at the ambience of the shop. But was she jealous? No, not jealous. Perhaps a bit intimidated. The clothing was so expensive, way past her budget. But it wasn't just the money. She really did feel violated by Lexi appropriating their secret name. And yet a memory could not be owned.

Irritated with her thoughts, Clare picked up her cell phone and punched in Penny's number. When her friend answered, Clare said, "Hey, I'm just calling to chat. How's Mikey?"

"Oh, Clare, we can't talk now, we're getting dressed up for play group." In the background, Mikey was babbling.

"Play group? How can he *play?* He's eight months old!"

"Mostly they just lie on blankets and look at each other, but Mikey loves seeing little people like himself. And there's this one little girl, she's a year old and can reach out to touch him, and he just squeals with ecstasy whenever he sees her. Anyway, I'll call you later." Penny clicked off.

Clare forced herself to work, trying to calm herself with the familiar and engrossing motions of pouring and stirring, but she still felt rattled and uncomfortable with herself. She was glad to hear the door slam and Marlene tromping up the stairs.

TWENCY-FIVE

"Hey ho!" Marlene clattered in, bringing in a gust of fresh air and her own cheerful energy. "Hey, look at you! What's up? Got a cold?"

Clare ran her hands through her hair, scrubbing her scalp, trying to jolt her mind into the present. "Hi, Marlene. I'm fine. Just having a little brain stall."

Marlene hung her jacket on a hook. At the sink, she washed her hands. "So what's on the agenda for today?"

"More truffles, to start with." Clare forced herself to focus. It helped that Marlene was around. Together they went into automatic work mode, working with the ganache they'd made from cream and chocolate.

For a few hours, work required her complete concentration. By late afternoon, though, Clare felt wired and slightly anxious, as if she were infected with a fever. Several times she looked at Marlene, wanting to talk things over with her, but Marlene was a compulsive gossiper, and Clare didn't want her private musings shared with the entire town.

"Let's stop for the day," she told her employee. "You go on home. I'll clean up."

"Sure?" Marlene asked.

"Yeah. It's fine. I'll see you tomorrow."

"Great. Thanks! It's so nice out, I can't wait to get outside."

It was nice out? Clare realized she'd been so engrossed in her own thoughts she hadn't even looked out the window. Now she did, and she saw how the day glowed. Pulling on her sweater, she hurried out into the sunny afternoon. She paused by the door to Lexi's store.

Moon Shell Beach. That shop was an entire dream world.

Shoving her hands in her pants pockets, she ambled over the cobblestones toward the beach, trying to understand her emotions. She felt as if Lexi had stolen something from her. Had cared so little for their sacred fantasy that she was carelessly selling it to the world. Yet Clare had been the one, years ago, who had first grown up and away from their little beach.

She arrived at the town pier, and stood on it a moment, looking around. A few sailboats drifted on the horizon and a fisherman motored steadily from the Sound toward the harbor. From Tris Chandler's boatyard came the sound of voices and the revving of engines. *Tris*. She hoped he was all right. Somehow all right. Miracles did happen, men did wake up from amnesia, or from comas. It was possible that Tris had been injured when his boat sank and was now lying in a hospital, gradually healing.

Clare whispered a prayer for Tris, and for Jewel.

Jewel Chandler sat at the end of the pier, a small brave figure with her glowing red hair. Lexi sat next to her—they were playing cards. Jewel shouted triumphantly and Lexi laughed in response. It was so nice of Lexi to spend time with Jewel, Clare thought, and suddenly she was wistful. Why was Lexi doing this, spending time sitting on the end of a pier with a child, waiting for the impossible, for a man who was almost definitely lost to the sea to come sailing home? Was Lexi kinder than Clare? Or just most *hopeful?*

She walked on, her thoughts churning. It had taken a certain kind of courage for Lexi to leave the island to marry Ed Hardin, and it had taken more courage for her to return to the island to start her business. It was like leaving the safety of shore and swimming into the ocean, hoping it wouldn't take you under, hoping for that phenomenal lift and ride the waves gave, that breathtaking experience nothing else could provide. To throw yourself in wholeheartedly, surrendering to the waves, was always a bit of a risk.

Somehow Lexi could do that in her life. Could Clare?

Could *she* leave Jesse?

Jesse had a sweetness about him that he would carry throughout his life. She did love him. But over the past few years that love had changed. Jesse had become a challenge for her, a contest. When he slept with someone else, she was betrayed. When he returned, she was triumphant. How sad, really. She didn't want to live that way for the rest of her life.

But she was almost thirty. She had invested so much time, emotion, and patience in sexy Jesse Gray, and they were both getting older. It was time to settle down and have children. Any baby of Jesse's would be the cutest infant on the planet! All right, she was getting nesty like all her friends this age, but she was so close to marrying Jesse, so close to having his baby, could she really give that up?

She didn't want to hurt Jesse. But in her heart, she suspected that if she left him, he might not be destroyed. After his dramatic proposal of marriage almost two years ago, he had not suggested a wedding date, and he practically broke out in a rash when she mentioned children. Jesse was like a child himself, depending on her to keep him on the straight and narrow. He was like a caged beast, and she was his trainer, and if he purred under her gentle touch, still in his deepest nature, didn't he yearn to range free? What would be the best for Jesse?

And now, Adam. When she was with Jesse, she was always just a little anxious, trying to guess in advance what would make him happy, what would keep him with her. But with Adam, she felt so completely at home.

Could that be because she'd had her first girlish

crush on Adam? Was she simply revisiting old emotions?

No. No, the way her body came alive when she looked at Adam, when she heard his voice, the way her breath caught in her throat when his hand touched hers—that was no childish memory. That was fiercely in the present, and completely transfixing.

Clare gazed out at the harbor shimmering beneath the sun. She felt the same fierce physical tug on her body when she was with Adam that she thought the oceans felt from the moon. But there was more. Adam was the sensual pull of the tides, but he was also the safety of the waiting shore.

In comparison, Jesse was a heron, a sleek free spirit, too wild to rest on the land, too restless to stay in one place.

Perhaps Adam was not in love with her. But perhaps he was, and perhaps she could set Jesse free, and free herself as well.

TWENTY-SIX

Jesse folded his napkin, leaned back in his chair, and patted his stomach. "Baby, you grill a mean steak." Stretching out his lanky form, he lifted his legs, rested his feet on a chair, and yawned.

Clare smiled. It had been such an odd couple of hours, eating dinner with this man, knowing that when the last bite was taken, she was going to say what she now said: "Thanks, Jesse. I'm glad you liked it. I have something to tell you, and I wanted you to be . . . comfortable while we talk."

"Oh, man." Jesse looked wary. "Now what?"

Her hands were shaking. When she returned from the beach, she wanted to do it right away—it was almost as if she'd already done it, and she wanted to move on, but she owed Jesse the dignity of a serious conversation. Her father was happily ensconced in front of a long PBS show. The door into the living room was shut. Ralphie lay next to Clare's chair.

She removed her engagement ring and set it on the kitchen table. "Jesse, I'm breaking off our engagement."

Jesse stared at her as if she'd just put the toaster on her head. "Excuse me?"

"I'm breaking off with you, Jesse. For good. I

don't want to marry you, and I don't want to be engaged to you, and I hope we'll be friends, but—"

Jesse's feet thudded to the floor as he straightened. "Clare! What are you even talking about? I haven't fooled around since we got engaged!" His tone was indignant.

Softly, Clare said, "Oh, honey, this isn't about you fooling around. This is about me, and how I feel about you. How I feel about *us*. Jesse, I love you—"

"Then what's the problem?"

"—but I've realized I've come to love you as if you were, oh, my brother, or a friend."

"A friend who can make you scream in bed."

"Yes, that's true. But I want more than that for a marriage, Jesse. I want a nice, solid, boring marriage with a couple of kids and no dramas. And you want, well, for one thing, you want to travel."

"Oh. Right. I get it. You've been talking to Lexi." Jesse balled up his paper napkin and threw it on the table. "Lexi's got you all stirred up."

"Jesse, this has nothing in any way to do with Lexi. You told me yourself you didn't want a dog because it would tie you down, keep you from traveling."

"Oh, hell, Clare, a man can have his dreams, can't he?"

"Absolutely, and I want you to *have* your dreams, Jesse. I *want* you to travel. But I want to stay here, and get married, and have children. And that's not your dream. It's never been your dream."

Jesse frowned and rubbed his forehead hard. "Well, Clare . . ." He struggled to express himself. "I love you. We've been together our entire adult lives."

Clare nodded. "Yes, that's true. If you don't count the weeks—the months—when you've been screwing someone else."

"I'm over that now. You know I am. I thought you understood that. I don't know what I have to do to convince you that I'm through playing around, Clare. I can't erase the past. I can't undo what I've done. I can't—" Jesse squirmed, agitated.

"Jesse, calm down. I'm not talking about the past. I'm not even talking about sex. I'm talking about what I want out of life. *What I want for the rest of my life.*"

The starch in her voice made Jesse take a deep breath. He studied her face. "You're saying I'm not what you want for the rest of your life."

He looked like a little boy now, a sweet, innocent, sensitive little boy who couldn't understand why he couldn't have a puppy.

"Yes, Jesse. I'm saying that. You're not what I want for the rest of my life. I don't want to be married to you."

"You don't want to have children with me."

She caught her breath. Of course Jesse knew her most vulnerable point. His child, that darling tender blue-eyed baby, floated just beyond her vision, a dream she had had for more years than she could remember. "Oh, Jesse." This was the hardest thing to surrender, the image she'd cherished for so many years, of Jesse's baby in her arms, and her eyes filled with tears.

Jesse jumped up from his chair, came around the table, and knelt next to Clare, putting his arm around her back. Next to him, Ralphie sat up, alert and worried, watching Clare with her wide, anxious doggie eyes.

"Clare." Jesse almost shook Clare in his desperation. "Clare. Look. Let's go in the bedroom and get you pregnant right now."

She gulped. "Jesse, sweetie, no." It was like she was explaining basic mathematics to a two-year-old. "If we had wanted to have a baby or get married and have a life together, we would have done it before now, and we just haven't."

"Because we've been saving money!"

She continued as if he hadn't spoken. "And it's a good thing we haven't, it's all right, because we love each other, we care for each other, but we're not meant to be married to each other."

Jesse stood up and paced around the kitchen, stomping in frustration. "You just said we love each other!"

"We do, Jesse. That doesn't mean we want to be married to each other. Think about it now, come on. *Think.*"

"You know what I *think,* Clare? I think you've gone crazy."

She blew her nose and shoved her hair away from her face and pushed back her chair and stood. She took hold of Jesse and held him at arm's length. "Look at me, Jesse Gray. I am sober and I am sane. I love you like a dear dear friend. But I know I'm not the right woman for you to marry, and I know you're not the right man for me."

Jesse studied her face. He was all there, concentrated on her. Tears welled in his blue eyes. "Well, hell, Clare, this is just awful. This is just, well, it's *confusing*."

She stroked his face tenderly, knowing it was probably the last time she'd touch him this intimately. "I know, honey. But you can figure it out. We can figure it out. It's going to be fine. Better than fine. When you wake up tomorrow morning, you'll feel set free."

He shook his head, then dipped his jaw so that his mouth was touching the palm of her hand. He kissed her hand. She let him, for a moment, looking at his familiar face with bittersweet affection.

Jesse said, "Want to go to bed?"

She threw back her head and laughed. "Jesse, you are hopeless!"

"Does that mean you don't want to go to bed?"

She moved away from him, laughing. "I don't want to go to bed."

He put his hands on his hips, glaring at her. "You're sleeping with someone else."

"I swear, Jesse. I'm not."

"Well, *hell*." He shocked her when he turned suddenly and slammed his fist into the wall. Coffee cups and spoons jangled all over the kitchen. "Just how do we go on from here, Clare?"

She shrugged. "You go to your house, I'll stay here. We sleep. Tomorrow you can come over when I'm gone and get your things. I'll work. You'll work. By tomorrow evening you'll have fifteen women lined up to console you in bed."

"I don't want fifteen other women. I want you, Clare."

"I know that's what you think, Jesse. But give yourself some time. This is the right choice for both of us. At least, I'm sure it's the right choice for me."

Ralphie trailed nervously after her as she ushered Jesse to the door. Clare thought she would be exhausted, but she was weirdly charged up. Now that she had broken off with Jesse, she felt impatient. She wanted him gone.

"I'm phoning you tomorrow, Clare, to see if you've changed your mind," Jesse said.

"I'm not changing my mind, Jesse." She almost had to shove him out the door.

CWENCY-SEVEN

The phone rang just as Lexi came out of the shower. She considered not answering. It was late, and she was exhausted. Still . . . she picked up the phone.

"Hey, Lexi, can I come over? I've got news." Clare's voice was warm, friendly, even exuberant.

Lexi was confused. "Well, I don't know what to say, Clare . . ."

"Oh, Lexi, I'm so sorry about freaking out this morning, it was unforgivable of me, although I hope you'll forgive me, of course. Listen, I love the name of your shop. That's not what I want to talk about."

Warily, Lexi asked, "What *do* you want to talk about?"

"Oh, Lexi, please just let me come over!"

"All right. Come over. I'll put some coffee on."

"No. I'll bring champagne."

"You're pregnant."

"Ha! Not even close." Clare's laugh was musical.

"You and Jesse eloped." Lexi found herself smiling in response to Clare's enthusiasm, and this conversation reminded her of childhood phone calls when they had so much to say they couldn't seem to hang up in order to meet somewhere.

"Colder and colder. No more guesses. I'm on my way!"

Lexi pulled on a long-sleeved white T-shirt and a pair of plaid men's boxer shorts. She spent a few moments trying to straighten her immensely chaotic living/office/warehouse space and finally settled on removing a box of padded hangers from one of the two armchairs by the window. Outside, darkness had fallen, and stars shone down like lighthouses in an unimaginably vast ocean. She couldn't imagine what Clare had to say but the happiness in her voice was contagious.

She saw Clare's Sweet Hart's van slam to a halt on the cobblestones and hurried down her back stairs to reach the door just as Clare knocked.

Lexi held the door wide. "Come in."

Clare didn't waste a glance on the store, but raced up the stairs to Lexi's living quarters. She wore khaki shorts and a chocolate-spotted white shirt and carried a bottle of champagne with her. "Glasses?" she asked.

Lexi gestured around the room. "Juice glasses will have to do. I haven't gotten around to unpacking things like crystal."

"Perfect. Fine." Clare popped the cork, then hurried to hold the bottle over the sink as the bubbly liquid fizzed over the neck.

Lexi gawked. If she hadn't seen Clare in her extravagant states before, she'd worry about her now in this manic mood. She held out two glasses and waited.

Clare poured the champagne. She held up her glass

in a toast. "I've broken off with Jesse."

Lexi nearly fell over. "I don't believe it."

"Believe it. I did. And Lexi . . . I feel so happy! So *free!*"

Lexi bit the inside of her lip. "What caused this breakup?"

"I don't know, Lexi. All sorts of things, I guess. Adam, certainly—and I swear on my life, if you mention this to Adam, I'll truly never speak to you again—whatever happens between Adam and me is hands off to you, Lexi, okay?"

Lexi leaned back against the kitchen counter. "Of course. I won't say a thing to him."

"Okay, first, I guess, is Adam. I am just experiencing the most wonderful sensations, emotions— such clarity, such pleasure—when I'm with him. And maybe nothing will happen between the two of us, or maybe something will, but it made me realize how muddy and tired things had gotten between me and Jesse. How my whole spirit seemed to ache from holding on so tight, keeping Jesse on some kind of leash, and that was just so wrong for Jesse and wrong for me." Clare couldn't stand still; she gestured and turned and walked away and came back to face Lexi. "And you coming back. I don't know, it could be that seeing you back here, knowing you got divorced and you're happy and optimistic and starting over and oh, I don't know, just *throwing* yourself onto Fate . . . well, I can do that, too! I *want* to do that."

"It might get lonely," Lexi warned.

"I know that. But it will be more genuine, Lexi. I won't be living my life trying to force Jesse into a role he doesn't want to play."

"So you've told him?"

"Just tonight. After dinner."

"How did he take it?"

"He was surprised, of course. Confused and kind of angry. He kept thinking I suspected him of sleeping with someone else."

Lexi bent down to pick up a loose bit of the foil from the bottle. "*Is* he sleeping with someone else?" Guiltily, she remembered Jesse's kisses, and her own response.

"He swears he isn't, but that doesn't even matter now, Lexi. That's not why I broke off with him."

Lexi straightened so she could watch Clare's face. "But Clare, you know how Jesse is. How are you going to feel when he does sleep with someone else? When he gets engaged to someone else? When he marries someone else and you all live on this island and see each other every day?" *What if Jesse and I got together,* she wondered, but forced that thought aside. This wasn't the right time to think about that.

Clare was bubbling. "Honestly, Lexi, I'll feel fine about it. I can't explain it, it's like they say about having a veil lifted from your vision, or in this case more like a weight lifted off my shoulders. I want Jesse to be happy. I don't hate him, I don't wish him ill. I know he'll find someone else and marry someone else, and even if I end up a spinster living with a dog and eating too many of my chocolates, I'd rather do that than be with him."

Lexi reminded her vaguely, "Spinsters live with cats."

"Right!" Clare lifted her glass. "Guess that means I won't be a spinster."

"No." She chose her words carefully. "Perhaps you should wait a few days to celebrate. Let your emotions settle. Maybe you'll realize how much you miss him. How much you love him."

"Oh, Lexi, I know exactly how I feel! I'm happy. I'm free. I'm starting over."

"Well, it's very brave of you. But go slowly," Lexi advised. "You seem a little . . . *volatile* these days."

"Oh, Lexi!" Clare stomped her foot impatiently. "Come on, drink with me." Clare clinked her glass against Lexi's. "Here's to the future."

Lexi said quietly, "Right. Here's to the future."

TWENTY-EIGHT

Lexi woke with a hangover. It had been after midnight when Clare finally wound down and went laughing off down the stairs and into the night. Lexi had collapsed on her bed with all her clothes on, and now the sun was glaring in the windows like an irate timekeeper. It was after ten o'clock. She took a long and extremely hot shower, letting the water pound away her slight headache, flashing back on Clare's visit. Clare had been so happy, almost bored with the whole subject of Jesse, and somehow they'd gotten onto remembering their childhood, laughing like girls while they drank the entire bottle of champagne.

Remember when we pretended to be in the CIA and left notes for each other in the books at the library? Remember the time we Super Glued Harsh Marsh's desk drawer shut?

She rubbed her scalp hard as she toweled her hair dry. She drank two cups of strong coffee and ate a piece of toast with peanut butter. No chance she could open today; there were too many things left undone. She found her list and scanned it. Hooks had to be hung in the cubicles—four in each. And brackets for the curtain rods and holders for the tiebacks. Would she be able to mount the hardware herself? In her own home, she would trust her work, but she wanted everything in Moon Shell Beach to be perfect. Plus, she needed the quarter board with the shop's name mounted above the front door and that was one thing she really couldn't do herself. Jesse had said he'd come back to finish the work . . . should she call him? He would assume Clare had told him about their break-up . . .

She caught herself staring off into space. There were a million other things that had to be done. She would not stand here thinking about Jesse Gray.

All day she unpacked, checked inventories, ironed, sewed, and stacked. Now and then she noticed people entering Sweet Hart's, and she smiled, imagining Clare flying around the shop on her newfound high.

She wasn't even thinking about Jesse when her phone rang and Jesse said, "I'm downstairs at your door."

It was late afternoon. Jesse looked rough, his shirt stained with sweat, his work boots covered with sawdust, and dark circles under his eyes. One look at him, and Lexi knew to focus on the shop, not on personal matters.

"Oh, Jesse, thanks for coming. I need the sign mounted, and some hooks put on the walls, and the curtain brackets. It shouldn't take you too long."

Jesse nodded without speaking and headed to the back of the shop. He had already marked the spots for the hooks, and in only a few minutes he had them securely fastened. Wrestling Lexi's footstool around, he stood on it to nail in the brackets. Then he took the sign outside and hung it above the door: *Moon Shell Beach.*

Lexi and Jesse stood side by side on the cobblestones, looking up at it.

"Looks good," Jesse said gruffly.

"It really does." This was a huge moment for Lexi, and she was disconcerted to find her attention distracted from her shop to the simple fact of the handsome man standing next to her. The man just radiated sex. It had to be a chemical thing.

"Want to share a celebratory drink with me?" she asked lightly, wincing at the very thought of putting alcohol into her system after last night.

Jesse shook his head. "Thanks anyway." He headed back into the shop and picked up his toolbox.

"Well, Jesse, let me pay you before you go."

"I'll send you a bill."

"Oh, right, sure, of course." Lexi flapped her hands. "Jesse . . . Jesse, Clare told me you two have broken up."

Jesse didn't look at Lexi and his voice was low. "I'm sure she did."

"I just, well, if you ever . . ." She didn't even know what she wanted to offer. Consolation? A shoulder to cry on? Sex?

"I've gotta go, Lexi." Jesse's shoulder brushed hers as he passed her on his way out the door.

It was quiet after Jesse left. Lexi stepped back out into the cobblestone lane to gaze at her sign. Next door, Sweet Hart's was empty; the *Closed* sign hung on the door. Tomorrow was not Lexi's official Grand Opening Day—that would be on Saturday, and she'd put an ad in the paper announcing it. But tomorrow, Friday, she would open. In the morning there would be plenty of time to hang the lavender and blue panels of raw silk she would use for privacy curtains on the cubicles. She went through her shop and out the back door.

For a moment, she stood just looking out at the harbor. In the strong, late-afternoon light, the water was darker, and the wind had picked up, making waves swell and retreat against the sandy curve of beach. The tide was coming in. The herring gulls were still at it, screaming and dropping shells on the town pier, then dive-bombing down to eat the tender meat inside. She wondered what Clare was doing. She wondered what Jesse was doing. She saw Jewel sitting at the end of the pier, with the sun blazing down on her.

Grabbing up a tube of sunblock, she closed the door behind her and walked over the beach to the town pier.

"Hey, Jewel."

The child's face lit up. "Hi, Ms. Laney!"

"Mind if I join you?"

"That would be excellent."

Lexi dropped down onto the warm boards next

to the girl. "Look what I've brought you." She held out a tube of sunblock.

"Thank you, Miss Laney. But I have my sunhat." Jewel tapped the floppy straw hat on top of her head.

"True, but what about your arms and legs?" She was not going to lecture the child about skin cancer. Surely Bonnie Frost lathered her daughter up with sunblock each morning. Lexi just wanted to be sure.

Jewel looked down at her scrawny girl legs protruding from yellow shorts. They were brown, with a glow of burn along the tops. "Well, I suppose it's a good idea. Thank you." Taking the tube, she smeared sunblock on her legs. "Feels good," she said. "Cool."

Lexi stretched out beside Jewel. "Might be wise to do your arms, too."

Jewel complied. "You aren't very tanned," she noted.

"True. I'm always working. No time for play."

"That's what my mother said about my father."

Lexi hid a smile. Of course the girl wanted to talk about her father. "I knew your father when I was in school. Well, I'm two years younger than Tris, so I hardly knew him. He was so old and sophisticated." Lexi smiled, thinking how from her vantage point, a teenage boy was *so* not sophisticated, but she saw the way Jewel nodded, her gaze growing dreamy, and of course from the girl's point of view, a teenage boy was a creature of infinite mystery.

"He was a friend of my brother's, Adam Laney, you know him, the veterinarian. He was really nice to little kids. I mean your father and my brother. They were the coolest guys in the school, and they weren't ever mean or snobby. They both worked in the summer, but on their time off they were always at the beach with a whole gang of boys." Lexi closed her eyes, remembering those long-ago summer days, the heat and glare and salt spray, how she and Clare spread their striped beach towels on the sand close enough to watch the guys as they body surfed or played Frisbee on the beach. The popular older girls would saunter by in their bikinis, striking poses to attract the guys, and the guys were attracted, no doubt about it. They'd yell at the girls, or chase them into the ocean, their bodies brown and slippery as seals.

"Everyone thought your father was cute," Lexi continued. "We didn't call guys handsome then. We called them cute or hunky. Whenever they could, my brother would go out with your father on Tris's sunfish. They loved capsizing—" Lexi stopped a moment, wondering if this would frighten Jewel, then continued. "They thought capsizing was the best fun. Sometimes they were real goofs in the water. My parents got mad when they heard about it, but Tris and Adam were ace swimmers, they were like dolphins." She remembered watching them from shore. She could hear their raucous nutty boy laughter all the way across from Monomoy. When they reached the town pier, they'd fall backward into the water, splashing like drunken whales. They waded up onto the beach, dripping water off their muscular sunburned shoulders, their bodies as powerful as gods as they dismantled the sunfish and hefted the rudder and sail in their arms.

"I know," Jewel said, nodding. "My dad's second home is the water. I know he's fine, I know he's somewhere, I know he'll come home."

"I hope you're right," Lexi said. She wrapped her arm around Jewel, hugging her tightly. She didn't come here to help the girl, she realized; she came here for herself. Jewel was so good at hoping, and Lexi wanted to be good at that, too.

TWENTY-NINE

By the end of the day, Clare's hangover headache had disappeared. When she arrived home after closing her shop, she felt clean and oddly virtuous. It had been a perfect day at Sweet Hart's, busy but not insane, and she'd had a chance to chat with some of the returning summer people she enjoyed. She found herself singing as she made a light meal of pasta and salad for herself and her father. After dinner, she phoned Penny to tell her the news, longing to discuss her feelings for Adam with her sensible friend, but baby Mikey was down with a summer cold. He wasn't ill, Penny assured Clare, just snotty and coughing and uncomfortable, and in addition, he was cutting two teeth, so he was thoroughly cranky.

Over the sounds made by the fussing baby, Penny said, "You did the right thing, breaking off with Jesse. I'm proud of you!" Mikey sneezed. "Gotta go!"

Light lingered high in the sky, the air was fresh, and Clare couldn't sit still. She clipped on Ralphie's leash and took her out for a walk around the block. She felt so new, and so intelligent, and somehow in control of her life. As she strolled down the street, she was content to let Ralphie "read the newspaper" on all the bushes she could find, while she meditated upon the right time to tell Adam that she'd broken off with Jesse.

It would only be mature to wait a couple of weeks after breaking off with one man to start a relationship with another, wouldn't it?

On the other hand, she'd told Marlene today that she'd broken off with Jesse, so the island gossip line would be scorching as the news was passed along. Wouldn't it be better if Clare told Adam herself, before he heard it from someone else? Perhaps tomorrow morning she could take Ralphie for a walk on the beach, and if she happened to run into Adam there . . .

Suddenly she couldn't wait another minute.

"Come on, Ralphie, let's run!" She turned sharply, yanked Ralphie's leash, and sprinted back up the street toward her house. Ralphie galloped along beside her, tongue lolling out of her mouth, a smile on her doggie face. She liked this game.

The moment they were home, Clare unsnapped the leash and led the dog into the living room. "Here, Ralphie, good girl." She took a rawhide bone from the shelf and handed it to Ralphie, who dropped to the floor, held it between her two front paws, and gnawed blissfully. "Dad, I might not be home tonight. Will you remember to take Ralphie out before you go to bed?"

Her father was engrossed in *Jeopardy!*, but he nodded.

"Thanks." Clare bent over to smack a kiss on his bald head, then grabbed up her purse and hurried out to her car. Radio blasting, she drove as fast as she dared through the town and out Madaket Road and over to Crooked Lane.

Clare pulled into the drive of Adam's cottage and threw herself out of her car almost before she'd turned the engine off. As the white crushed shells crunched beneath her feet, she could hear Adam's dogs barking like maniacs. A light by the front door came on, and before she could knock, the door opened, and there stood Adam.

He was in jeans and a flannel shirt. He was barefoot and his hair was rumpled. He had a beer in one hand. "Clare?"

"Adam." Her heart was ticking over so fast she was afraid she was going to faint. "Can I come in? I have to tell you something."

He looked puzzled. "Sure." He held the door open for her.

She entered his house. Lucky and Bella immediately twined around her ankles, wagging their tails, sniffing, whining for attention.

"What's going on?" Adam asked.

"This," Clare said, and launched herself at him.

She grabbed his face with both hands, pulled his head down, and smashed her lips into his mouth. Her haste, her desire, made her clumsy. They both staggered until Adam ended up with a wall at his back. She pressed her body against his.

Adam pulled his mouth away. "Hey, hey, hang on a minute. Clare, you're engaged to Jesse!"

"Not anymore. And never again."

He pushed her away so he could see her face. "Seriously?"

"Seriously." She was running her hands over his shoulders and arms and chest; she wanted to touch him all over at once. She moved her hips against his and felt his hardness beneath the denim. "Oh, Adam, I want to go to bed with you."

Adam looked wary. "What, is this rebound sex?" Before she could answer, he said, "Oh, what the hell do I care?" and picked her up in his arms and carried her into the bedroom.

Clare wrapped her arms around his neck and kissed his face as he walked. He fell onto the bed with her and put both hands on her shoulders. "Slow down. Slow down."

"Can't," she gasped, trying to unzip his jeans. "Need . . ."

They struggled against one another on the bed. In her hurry to get her tee off, she knocked him in the nose with her elbow. He yanked off her jeans and panties. He pulled down his jeans and boxers. She kicked her sandals across the room. They hit the wall with a thud.

The dogs whimpered and panted around the bed, curious and slightly alarmed. Adam wrenched himself away from Clare's arms and strode across the room, naked. Clare stared at his erect penis and nearly swooned.

"Out," Adam said firmly. The dogs shuffled out into the hall. He slammed the door. He returned to the bed and paused to stare down at Clare, lying naked on top of his duvet. "My God, you're beautiful."

In one quick movement, Clare was on her knees. She pressed herself against Adam, nuzzling the brown hair on his belly, running her hands down his strong muscular thighs.

Adam groaned and took her by the shoulders and lay her back on the bed, then pushed his knees against her knees, spreading her legs apart. He ran his hand over her body from shoulder to breast to belly to groin, and cupped her crotch with his hand and curled his fingers in the hair between her legs.

Clare grabbed his shoulders. She kissed his neck, his collarbone, and then he entered her, and she let her head fall back, her eyes closed, as she felt his length and width and heat press into her. She wrapped her legs around his back, she wrapped her arms around his chest, she turned her head to the side and burrowed her mouth against his arm, biting it slightly as she moaned.

They could not slow down. His thrusts were rapid, hot, hard, almost painful, but she responded in kind, tilting her hips for better leverage, clutching him with her arms and legs as if she were drowning and he was everything that could save her. He shuddered against her, climaxing, and she came, too, in such an intense orgasm she felt like an animal, a beast, a sea creature squeezing out of its shell, expanding into a world of sensation.

"Wow." Adam fell next to her, catching his breath.

She turned on her side and nestled her face in his chest, inhaling his strong, fabulously male scent. She couldn't stand to be even this separate from him, so she rolled on top of him and aligned her bare legs to his so she could feel his movements as he caught his breath. She pressed her lips against his neck. He wrapped his arms around her, holding her tight. Skin to skin, they lay together, clamped, locked, sweaty, dazed.

At two in the morning, Clare and Adam sat in his kitchen, voraciously eating bacon-and-tomato sandwiches, the bread smothered with mayo. They were both still naked. They'd made love again and again, until they were exhausted. Now they chewed and swallowed and chased the food down with beers in silence, their bodies demanding fuel.

Clare finished inhaling her food and licked her fingertips.

Adam handed her a paper napkin. "Want another one?"

She shook her head. "That was heavenly, thanks."

He took her hand and pulled her up. "Let's get back in bed." He laughed at her expression. "I have to lie down before I fall down, that's all."

They snuggled together, spoon style, sated in all ways, the duvet warming them in the cool night.

Bella and Lucky curled up on the rug next to the bed, and soon their snores filled the room.

"That was a rather Cro-Magnon experience," Adam said to Clare, smoothing her hair down so it didn't tickle his nose.

Clare chuckled. "It was." She maneuvered her body even closer to his, her bum resting against his groin.

"Want to talk?"

She closed her eyes. "If I can. I'm so sleepy . . ."

"Then sleep," Adam said. "We can talk in the morning."

But in the morning when they woke to find each other naked in the bed, they made love again, and then they both had to shower and dress and hurry off to work.

It was a glorious day. Clare unlocked the door of Sweet Hart's and went around her shop, raising the blinds, organizing the cash register, getting things ready for the day. She moved in a kind of suspended bubble, performing ordinary duties without really thinking about them. She had a thousand things she needed to do. Instead she perched on the tall stool behind the counter, tucked her chin into her hands, and thought about Adam.

The phone rang.

"Hey," Adam said. "I miss you."

"Ooh, I miss you, too."

"Let me take you out to dinner tonight."

"I've got a better idea. Let's take a picnic to the beach."

"Good thinking. Shall we bring the dogs?"

"Sure." They settled on a time and place, and Adam said he had to go deal with his first patient, an obese cat, and Clare laughed and they said good-bye. She didn't think she'd ever been happier in her life.

ᴛᕼᓮᖇᴛY

Moon Shell Beach opened. The first day, a few women drifted in, curious and idly gazing, and some of them gasped at the price tags, shot Lexi a look, and left, but many more smiled as they touched the fine material of the clothing and held it against them while they stared in a mirror. The next day was her Grand Opening. Clare brought in an opulent congratulatory arrangement of calla lilies and bird of paradise. Adam and their parents sent a huge vase of roses. Perfume drifted lushly through the air. Lexi offered her customers small cups of champagne or seltzer water. They sipped, and shopped, and bought, sometimes so infatuated with a scarf or bracelet that they wore it right out of the store. After that, word of mouth drew people to the shop, and Lexi had no time to think of anything but work.

She could tell that Clare was busy, too, by the amount of foot traffic passing her window. She'd assumed there would be enough of a lull in every day to sit out back sipping coffee and relaxing, comparing notes with Clare, but she discovered she couldn't leave her shop alone for a moment. There was simply too much to do.

At the end of the week, she locked her door just before five and ran next door to Sweet Hart's.

"Clare, can you give me a minute? I need your advice."

Clare was flushed and rumpled from moving as fast as she could. "Come upstairs and help me fold boxes while we talk." She locked her door, turned her sign to *Closed*, and led the way to her second floor. She threw herself into a chair and waved at the refrigerator. "Diet Coke or water if you want it," she offered.

"How are you?" Lexi pulled out a chair, moved a pile of flats waiting to become boxes off the chair, and collapsed in it.

"Busy. Really busy. Which is good. But I haven't had time to think. Every year I forget how crazy summer gets."

"So you haven't seen Jesse?"

"Nope." A smile lit her face. "But I've seen Adam."

Lexi stared. "Get *out*. Clare!"

Clare hugged herself. "Oh, Lexi. It's all so new, and I'm so much in love it's scary. But we're trying to be adults about it. I'm trying to take it slow . . ."

"I'm surprised I haven't heard about this from someone. At least Mom and Dad should have told me."

Clare shook her head. "We haven't been out in public together yet." She blushed deeply. "Haven't been out of bed yet, really."

"Are you talking about marriage?"

"No, no, no, Lexi. Back up! We haven't even talked about seeing a movie together. I'm just feeling very teenage right now, like a girl with my first adolescent crush."

"Appropriate, since Adam *was* your first adolescent crush."

"I know. But it's still so raw—I'm a little scared, Lexi. I don't know if I can trust my emotions, they're so intense." She gave herself a shake. "Let's talk about something else. How are you? How's the shop?"

"It's great, Clare. I'm really doing well. But I'm barely keeping up with it all. And yesterday I had a shoplifter!"

"What happened?"

"Someone was asking me to show her one of the more expensive necklaces from the display case, and both dressing rooms were full, and people were going in and out like crazy. I just had a moment to glance toward the pashminas, and I saw a really chic older woman looking at them, she had a hyacinth-colored shawl in her hand, and I took the necklace out for my jewelry customer and when I looked back, the woman had gone, and so had the hyacinth pashmina."

"A moment is all it takes," Clare told her. "You're going to have to hire some staff."

"But my shop is so small! And that means I have to pay someone . . ."

"Would your mother want to work for you? She has retail experience."

"No. I wouldn't ask her. She loves being retired."

"Then hire two or three people part-time. Either that, or watch your merchandise walk out the door. How much did that pashmina go for?"

"Four-fifty." Lexi smiled apologetically at Clare, because Clare was so touchy about money. "Four hundred fifty dollars."

"Ouch." Clare shot Lexi a serious look. "You're going to have to call the Merchants Association and get added to the shoplifting phone list. If any merchant spots a shoplifter, he phones three people and describes her or him and they phone three people, and right away all the other merchants know who to watch out for."

"I can't believe the people who come to Nantucket for vacation would *steal*."

"Why? Because they're rich?" Clare snorted. "How do you think they got that way? Case in point —your ex-husband." She shook her head. "Sorry, Lex. That was mean."

Lexi smiled. "Yes, mean . . . but true." She tapped her fingers on the table as she thought. "Okay, how do I find decent part-time help?"

"You can advertise, but maybe you don't have to. There's a community of Russian women on the island, good-looking, hardworking, honest, with good English. And they're all drop-dead gorgeous. They'd be perfect for your shop. I know they're all looking for work. Do you know Sophia who runs the lunch counter at Congdon's Pharmacy? Talk to her. She knows everyone."

Two days later, Lexi had her first employee, Oksana Volnapova. Almost six feet tall, Oksana had auburn hair streaked with magenta and green eyes slanted like a cat's. If Moon Shell Beach was a dream universe, Oksana was the dream resident. "This will be for you," she would say to a customer, holding up a swirl of silk, and you believed her, because she looked as if she'd just arrived from the Winter Palace where she lived with her lover the tsar, and their minions.

That was not the reality. When Lexi had asked her what her parents did, she'd replied, "My mother is a nurse. My father is a shoemaker. Where I lived, we did not throw away our shoes." But Oksana didn't make Lexi feel any obscene-American-consumer guilt. She loved clothing, admired Lexi's creations, and knew how to show them off. Every day she wore clothing the store sold, and she was the perfect walking advertisement, so willowy and graceful and striking, she enhanced anything she put on. She complimented Lexi on her garments; she rubbed the fabric between her fingers, nodding, saying, "Very nice." Other times, after an especially trying customer had pulled all the pashminas off the shelves only to desert them in a wadded pile in another part of the store, Oksana would mutter under her breath: *"Durak."* When Lexi asked her to translate, Oksana told her it meant "stupid." After that, if a customer annoyed Lexi, she'd mutter *"durak,"* and catch Oksana's eye, and they'd grin.

Lexi's mother wandered in occasionally, and Lexi grabbed a moment to go outside and catch her breath. They didn't discuss Adam and Clare. They didn't discuss anything but casual subjects, the weather, local gossip. They knew they'd be interrupted by walk-in customers, and they always were. Some evenings Lexi drove over to visit her parents, and to indulge in one of the meals Myrna kept ready, in case Lexi visited. Then they would talk about her shop, but often they simply relaxed in front of the television, watching a Red Sox game. With every passing day, Lexi felt more and more at home on the island.

CHIRCY-ONE

Rain pattered against the roof like a volley of spilled beads or clicked against the windowpanes when the wind gusted it sideways. Moon Shell Beach was crowded all day long with shoppers more bored with the weather than seriously looking. Lexi and Oksana were busy helping customers and discreetly mopping up the rain people tracked into the store. They didn't have time for lunch, they scarcely had time to run to the bathroom.

Late in the afternoon the clouds rolled away, taking the wind with them, and the sun broke out. The evening was radiant, fresh-washed, and warm. Suddenly no one was in the shop. Everyone was out enjoying the sunshine, and Lexi was glad. This gave her and Oksana a chance to tidy the shop and restock the shelves and racks. Oksana sang a light Russian folk song as she worked. Lexi couldn't understand the words, but the tune was cheerful. At seven, they put the *Closed* sign on the door and dimmed the lights. Oksana strode off to meet her friends, and Lexi went upstairs to her living quarters to catch her breath.

She'd been on her feet all day, but even though she felt like falling flat on her bed and never moving again, an evening like this was too good to waste.

She tossed her dress on her bed and pulled on shorts and a T-shirt, stuck her feet into thongs, and grabbed up a beach bag into which she tossed a bottle of red wine, a glass, an opener, a box of crackers, a package of cheddar, and an apple, and hurried down to the street and her car.

She set out driving without a clear idea of where she wanted to go. She only knew she needed to be away from town with its clusters of people. She needed some time alone with the sand, sea, and sky, so she steered toward Surfside Beach on the south side of the island. It wouldn't have been busy today, not with the storm.

Several cars were already in the parking lot. Standing at the top of the hill, she scanned the beach and saw the sand curve emptily toward the west. She sauntered down between the dunes and turned, strolling along the shore away from the few beach-combers. The surf pounded dramatically, driven by the day's wind, the whitecaps blazing like jewels in the sun's light. She took a long, deep breath of the fresh salt air. The crazy froth of the leaping waves excited her. She wanted to run into the cold surf, to dance in the waves, to be knocked over, drenched and dragged by the ocean. But she knew the undertow was dangerous here, so she resisted the urge.

One lone figure rode the waves on his surfboard, the crimson and black of his wet suit flashing in and out of the turquoise water like flying fish. Lexi found shelter between the dunes, spread her beach blanket, and settled down to watch. She'd never surfed, she'd always been afraid to, especially out here where the undertow was so strong, but she loved watching others ride the waves like mythical half-fish, half-human creatures.

Sitting cross-legged, she opened the wine and poured herself a glass. Except for the occasional cry of a gull, the only noise was the seething of the surf. She felt her shoulders relax and her heartbeat slow.

And then the surfer came out of the waves, carrying his surfboard, and her heart jumped like a dolphin surfacing because it was Jesse who was walking up the shore toward her.

"Hey," he said. "I thought that was you."

His blond hair, darkened by the water, was plastered around his face and the wet suit displayed the strong lean lines of his body with perfect clarity.

Could he tell how she couldn't tear her eyes away from him? "Hi, Jesse. Good surf?"

He nodded. "The best. The wind came from the right direction today to get it going just right."

Suddenly Lexi felt lit up, vividly alive, like an Alice in Wonderland who'd just drunk a magic potion and walked through a shining glass into another world. This world was all summer sky and sea, and Jesse, Jesse wet and masculine. "I . . . I'd offer you some wine, but I only brought one glass."

"No problem. I'll drink from the bottle. Just let me get out of this." He nodded toward the east.

"I'll grab my stuff." Dropping the surfboard, he sprinted away, sand flying up from his feet.

In a few moments he was back, carrying a towel and a sweatshirt.

"What a day," he said as he unzipped his wet suit and pulled it away from him. Lexi couldn't tear her eyes away from his lean body as it emerged, one arm, another arm, his slender back, his muscular chest with swirls of hair matted between his nipples, twisting down past his belly button to the top of his swim trunks. He tossed the suit aside like a husk, yanked the sweatshirt on over his head, then dropped down next to Lexi.

"Mind?" he asked, gesturing toward the bottle.

"Help yourself." She was overwhelmed by his presence. His legs, furred with blond hair, seemed so physical, so naked; his bony, sand-encrusted feet so masculine and somehow primitive.

Jesse took a swig of wine, then accepted the cheese and bread she held out. "Thanks. Come here often?"

It sounded like such a pickup line, they both laughed. "Actually, no. I've been too busy getting the shop up and running to enjoy myself."

"I know what you mean. Well, everyone who works in the summer knows. But I decided a long time ago I was going to enjoy myself."

"I'm so surprised," Lexi said with obvious sarcasm.

"Hey." Jesse punched her shoulder softly.

"Ow." Impulsively, Lexi grabbed his fist.

Jesse unfolded his fist and slid his palm against hers, slipping his fingers around hers, so that a delicate sexual heat rose against their skin.

"Life is short," Jesse said. "I can't let it be all about money."

"Of course not," she answered, glad her voice worked.

"You were brave, Lex. You got to *live* your life."

She was shaking now. She pulled her hand away. "You mean when I married Ed? Well, I got to travel, that's for sure. But I wouldn't say it was exactly living."

"Why not?" Jesse tilted the bottle again. Lexi watched his mouth circle the bottle's rim. She saw his throat work as the liquid slid down.

"Because I didn't love Ed. And he didn't love me."

Jesse stared at Lexi. "How could any man not love you?"

She felt his eyes on her, a steady gaze. Her heartbeat tripled. "Well, love is pretty complicated."

"I've always thought it was pretty easy," Jesse said quietly.

"Easy," she echoed. What she wanted was as easy as her dreams.

"Life can be just about the moment," Jesse told her. "Just about now. The beach, the sun on our skin."

She tried to joke. "Now you're getting philosophical on me."

"No," Jesse told her. "Just the opposite. I'm getting physical on you."

With one strong movement, Jesse shoved the bottle of wine so that it stood anchored in the sand. He took Lexi's wineglass from her and laid it in the wicker basket next to the bread and cheese. Gripping her shoulders, he pressed her firmly onto the ground. She was aware of the shifting pockets of sand beneath her, the cotton towel beneath her legs. Jesse stretched out next to her, lying not quite on top of her, and very intently, as if he were about to give CPR, he stroked her hair away from her face and brought his mouth down on hers. His breath was sweet, his lips slightly chapped, and strands of his hair tickled her face. His kiss was soft, his tongue salty. He lifted himself so she could get her arms around him, and he slowly drew his fingers over her face, and chin, and neck, and then he touched her breasts.

A low moan moved through her. Her body arched up, seeking his. His fingers fumbled for the zipper on her shorts. The sun had moved toward the horizon, and shadows from the dune draped them in an indigo blue. Jesse tugged off her shorts. Slowly, he slid his fingertips along the line of her jaw, around her neck, over her collarbone, over her breasts.

Jesse moved his hand down and down, over her belly, over her pubic hair, and then, with such languor, he parted her legs. A sweetness surged through her like she'd never known before. She had never known a man could be so gentle. It was as if Jesse were hypnotizing her, and as he stroked her, she sensed the delicacy of her skin as everything once dormant and cringing awakened with delight.

The dunes rose around them, enclosing them, and the light of day softened, sheltering them, and the sand beneath her surged into little hills and valleys, supporting her body as Jesse circled his fingertips and slipped his fingers against the silk of her skin, and like a magician, conjured up a rich cream between her legs that had never been there before. Gulls sang out as they flew overhead. She spread her legs and arched her hips, and Jesse moved down inside the V she made.

He thrust inside her. She felt a pressure, a deep internal shifting, like a bolt of liquid silk uncoiling within. Jesse's face was next to her ear, his breath warm and labored. He lifted himself up to give himself leverage as he shoved himself deeper into her. She closed her eyes, abandoning herself to sensation, as her body allowed itself to be a cup, a channel, a basin, flooded and foaming with plea-sure. Still he pressed into her, like a creature forcing his way home. Something broke off inside her, something was unlatched and unleashed. Pleasure spilled through her like the sea breaking through the jetties, tumbling, frothing, undeniable.

Jesse lifted himself off her. She was shivering, and he covered her with the towel, and laid his sweatshirt across her legs. Lying on his side, he held her close to him, and stroked her hair, and whispered, "Sssh."

But tears filled Lexi's eyes and dripped down her face, and she couldn't stop them. Half-laughing, she admitted in a choked, embarrassed voice, "I don't even know why I'm crying."

Jesse kissed her forehead. "It's all right," Jesse said, and his voice sounded so tender. "It's good to cry."

"Oh, Jesse." Rolling sideways, she buried her face in his chest.

He held her against him. She could feel her heart and his both subsiding from their pounding. Her blood spun a warm mist of ease through her limbs. A kind of happiness she'd never known before enfolded her in the softest arms. Perhaps she drifted into a kind of sleep.

After awhile she opened her eyes and looked up at Jesse. "Could we do that again?"

"Of course," Jesse said.

Darkness was falling. The breeze off the water chilled their skin, so they'd pulled on their clothing and huddled together, with the beach towel over their legs like a blanket. Sitting cross-legged, side by side, they faced the ocean, and though they couldn't see it, they could hear it surging and plowing toward them.

Lexi's body felt heavy, drugged, and sated, but her mind was waking up.

"Clare," she murmured.

Jesse snorted. "I was wondering how long it would take for you to bring her up."

"Well, Jesse, you were engaged to her. I'm one of her oldest friends."

"I know, babe," Jesse agreed. "You're right."

"Oh, Jesse." Lexi ran her hands through her hair. "Now I feel terrible."

Jesse wrapped a comforting arm around her shoulders and pulled her to him. "Hey, it's not the end of the world we're talking about here." He nuzzled his mouth into the top of her head, and she could feel his words come out against her skin like warmth. "I think this was a good thing, what happened between us just now, Lexi."

She lifted her head and looked at him, stunned. "You do?"

"What? You think I'm so trigger-happy I would have jumped anyone?" He kept his arm around her shoulder, but his voice was angry.

"I . . . I don't know what I thought, Jesse." Reaching out, she drew her fingers gently along his face. Just looking at him made her smile. "I don't think I was exactly *thinking*."

He smiled and brought his forehead to meet hers. "We're a pair of brain surgeons, aren't we?" He kissed the tip of her nose, her cheeks, her chin, her mouth. "I'll tell you this much, whatever happened between us just now, I want more of it."

A thrill streaked through Lexi at his words.

Jesse drew back a little, so he could look Lexi right in the eyes. "And of course you should tell Clare. She won't mind. She broke off with me, remember? And if rumor's right, she's got something going with your brother."

"Incestuous little island, isn't it?" Lexi mused.

"Look, tell Clare," Jesse said. "That's all I want to say about her. I don't particularly want to talk about her, and I certainly don't want what's between you and me to be about Clare in any way."

Lexi was surprised. She wished she'd been the one to say that. Had she assumed he didn't run so deep, wasn't quite so perceptive? "I know," she agreed quietly. "You're absolutely right."

He reached out his hand. "Come on. It's getting chilly, and we've both got to work tomorrow."

Lexi set the wine bottle and glass into the basket and folded her towel over her arm. The waves sighed like the breath of a watching creature as they walked barefoot through the sand along the ocean's edge and up between the dunes to the parking lot.

Jesse walked Lexi to her Range Rover, like a gentleman seeing his date home, waiting patiently as she stowed her sandy picnic gear in the back. He opened the door for her and watched her settle in. "I'll call you," he promised. "I don't know how soon, but I'll call you."

Lexi nodded. Jesse gently closed the door and walked across the lot to his truck.

As she turned the key in the ignition and steered

the car onto Surfside Road, she realized she was shaking all over. The sea breeze chilled her, but it wasn't only the temperature that had her trembling. She hit the heater onto high and a blast of warm air roared into the car. She felt so . . . so *everything*. Happy, but kind of guilty. Astonished, and terrified. Hopeful, and frightened. She wanted to push back all the other thoughts, just for a moment, just for one brief moment, and allow herself to indulge in a pure hit of joy. Making love with Jesse had been a revelation. His mouth, his arms, his body—she nearly swerved off the road, remembering.

THIRTY-TWO

Marlene was at the dentist, so Clare was in Sweet Hart's by herself. Usually mornings were slow, so she hoped to get some special orders filled while she was behind the counter waiting for walk-in business. When the phone rang, she answered it absent-mindedly, searching the desk behind the counter for her favorite pen.

"Clare?" It was Lexi.

"Lexi, hey, listen, I'm busy—"

"I know, Clare, but we have to talk." Lexi's voice was shaky. "Look, I'm coming over right now." The phone went dead.

The door opened and a young mother with a little boy wandered into Sweet Hart's. The child's eyes grew large at the sight of a chocolate whale.

"Whatever you want, Forest," the mother said, dreamily eyeing the delicacies.

Lexi burst in the door. She wore a tiny gold tank top and a gauzy full skirt embroidered with beads. Her blond hair was pulled back into a sweeping ponytail and her arms were ringed with gold bracelets. She looked like a goddess.

"Clare! Listen, I've got to—" She went quiet when she noticed the mother and child.

The little boy lifted up a chocolate whale wrapped

in plastic while his mother studied a box of almond crunch.

More calmly, Lexi said, "Listen, Clare, I can't stay, I have to open my shop, but I didn't want you to hear it from anyone else . . ."

Clare had childproofed her shop as well as possible, but the child clutched another chocolate whale, and another, while the mother meandered obliviously off to the other end of the shop. "Hear what?" she asked, only half listening.

Lexi slid behind the counter and stood close to Clare. "Clare." She touched Clare's arm. Leaning close, she whispered, "Clare, last night I slept with Jesse."

"What?" She stared at Lexi, whose words didn't seem to make any sense.

"On the beach. I ran into him. He was surfing. I was having some wine. We just—It just happened. And maybe, well, maybe I'll see him again . . ."

"Cool!" The little boy dropped the chocolate whales on the floor as he spotted a bag of gold-foil-wrapped chocolate pennies. He stood on his toes but couldn't quite reach it, so he jumped, grabbing out, and knocked a pyramid display of boxed chocolate truffles onto the floor.

"Careful," Clare cautioned, zipping around the counter. She took the boy gently by the hand and pulled him back. "Better not step on any of the boxes."

The mother turned and looked at the mess her child

had made. "Oh, Forest, you've dropped your whales. Now they won't be pretty anymore. Silly boy." She took her son's hand and led him out of the shop.

"Well, that was nice." Lexi bent, almost knocking heads with Clare as they gathered up the fallen candies. "These boxes look okay, Clare, they aren't dented or anything."

"Thanks, Lexi." Clare rearranged the display, focusing on the material objects, which seemed much easier to arrange than the emotions colliding within her.

"I don't want you to be mad, Clare." Lexi wrung her hands nervously.

"I'm not mad, Lexi." Clare put her hand to her forehead. "I actually don't know what I am right now."

"Then stop messing with those boxes and look at me," Lexi begged. "If you want me to stop seeing Jesse, tell me now."

Clare frowned. "*Seeing* Jesse?"

"Well, you know . . ."

"I'm not sure I do. Do you mean dating Jesse? Sleeping with Jesse? Getting serious with Jesse?"

"I guess I mean that. All of those. I mean, I don't know yet, Clare. I'm not sure of my feelings and I certainly don't have a clue about Jesse's." Moving closer, she put her hand on Clare's arm. "What I do know is that I don't want to lose your friendship again. So if you don't want me to see Jesse, I won't."

"I wouldn't ask that of you, Lexi. You should do

what you want. I'm over Jesse. Completely, so don't worry about that. But still, it just seems . . . so *weird*. I mean, if you do keep 'seeing' Jesse, I don't want to know all the intimate stuff. It's just too strange . . ."

Two women in floral Capris carrying capacious beach bags entered the store, laughing and gesturing and swooping down on the merchandise with cries of delight.

"Can we talk later, Clare?" Lexi asked.

"Sure," Clare agreed, and it was with relief that she turned her attention to her customers.

THIRTY-THREE

"Hey, babe."

"Hi, Jesse." Lexi clutched the phone between her neck and shoulder as she talked. She was wrapping a sarong for one customer while keeping a watchful eye on a pair of giggling teenage girls who were clearly using the shop to play dress-up. "How are you?"

"Tired. How are you?"

"I—" Her attention was pulled in several directions at once. She wanted to soak in the sensuality of Jesse's voice, but the teens were slithering toward the front door. One had a silk scarf still draped around her neck.

"Hang on, Jesse!" Lexi dropped the phone. "Girls!"

They kept on walking. Clearly their wealth entitled them to the privilege of rudeness. The truth was, Lexi didn't want to offend them because they looked as if they could easily spend a lot of money in this store.

In three long strides, Lexi had her hand on the scarf. "I think you forgot to take this off." Gently she lifted it away from the girl's neck.

"Oh, *merde!*" The girls sniggered, pushed at each other, and tottered in their high-heeled sandals out into the sunshine.

Returning to the counter, Lexi picked up the phone. "Sorry, Jesse. Customers."

"How about dinner tonight?" Jesse asked.

"Oh, yes, that would be great!"

"I'll be at your place about eight. And don't worry, I'll eat anything. See ya."

She stared at the phone, stunned. She'd assumed Jesse was offering to take her out to dinner.

Now, as whenever Lexi had a moment to catch her breath, she stepped out her back door into the fresh air. She scanned the horizon, admired the new yachts floating in the harbor, and let her eyes rest on Jewel Chandler, neatly settled with her back to one of the stanchions. She sat cross-legged, head bowed, and Lexi was certain Jewel was saying a prayer. She stared out toward the opening of the harbor or pulled something out of her backpack and bent over it, sporadically lifting her head to scan the horizon.

Lexi wondered where Tris was. She hoped he was alive somewhere, safe somewhere. Often she said a little prayer for him. She remembered how infatuated she'd been with him as a girl.

And now, was she only infatuated with Jesse? Was she *in love* with Jesse? Was he in love with her? Would they get married, have children, and live on the island happily ever after? That wasn't a vision that came clear for her. It was so odd to be back on the island, with so many intimate connections with so many people. Only now was she *really* getting it, how warped her marriage to Ed had been. So empty. No passion in all those years.

She closed her shop at five. She thought perhaps Clare might stop in, or phone, but she glimpsed Clare hurrying out to straddle her bike, and soon she had pedaled away. Lexi yawned, and stretched, and climbed to her crowded apartment on the second floor. More work here. More work constantly. Lexi unpacked the day's deliveries with rapid movements. She set up her iron and prepared the new garments, and pinned on the price tags. Draping them over her arms, she carried them down to the shop, taking care not to tread on the delicate fabrics. Back up the stairs she went to prepare more merchandise, and when that was done, she broke down the cardboard boxes and carried them down, tucking them neatly into the small area hidden by a trellised rose-covered fence where her garbage cans and recyclables waited for the trash removal.

The work was engrossing. She had to inspect each garment for flaws, rips, and irregularities, and she was glad for this; it made it impossible for her to think about Jesse and Clare. In fact, when he knocked on the back door, it took her a moment to think who it could be.

"Hey, babe." He had showered, and his blond hair was darkened by water.

"Oh, Jesse!" She glanced at her watch. "I lost track of the time. Um . . . come in."

Jesse followed her up the stairs to her apartment. He wound his way through the chaos of boxes and supplies until he stood at the window looking over the harbor. "Nice view."

She studied Jesse, gauging her own responses to his presence. No doubt about it, the man was gorgeous. She could easily imagine the body beneath his jeans and blue button-down shirt, and she appreciated that he'd worn a nice shirt for her.

Then he turned and looked at her, and the sexual attraction shot through her.

"Wine?" she offered. "I don't have any beer."

"Wine would be good." He collapsed on a chair.

Lexi poured the wine and brought the glass to him. She sank into a chair across from him. "Jesse, I told Clare that . . . we're seeing each other."

"Oh, yeah?" His voice was light, but he dropped his eyes.

"She wasn't mad, or upset, but I think she feels a little funny about it all."

"So do I," Jesse said honestly.

They sipped their wine at the exact same moment, then laughed at how self-conscious they were.

"It's all right." Lexi reached a comforting hand across to hold his hand. Touching him made her entire body go warm. She felt a blush rise from her chest up her neck, into her cheeks. "We don't have to be serious, Jesse. We don't have to talk about love or the future."

"How 'bout we don't talk at all." Jesse set his glass

on the table and rose. He pulled her up next to him. They stood kissing slowly, and she touched Jesse's handsome face and he ran his hands down her back and slid them into her waistband and down her buttocks, his bare palms against her bare flesh. They moved to her bed, stripped off their clothes, and lay together, making love slowly, in an almost thoughtful, melancholy way, pausing to gaze at each other, looking at each other steadily, as if trying to prove to themselves that they knew who they were with, that this was personal, and not just a matter of lust.

Afterward, they lay watching the light slowly drain from the sky. Jesse's stomach growled. "I've got to eat something."

They lay side by side, flat on their backs. Lexi stirred slightly. "My cupboards are really bare." She lifted herself on one elbow. "We could go out."

He was quiet for a while. "No. No, I don't think we should show up in public just yet. You know what this town is like. I feel sort of like I owe it to Clare, and to you and me, to wait a while before we show up anywhere as a couple."

"You're right." Lexi rose and walked naked through the apartment to the refrigerator. "I've got some old brie and crackers . . ."

"I think I'll go home, Lex. My mom's always got some kind of casserole in the fridge for me to heat up."

"That's fine," Lexi said, but she sort of wished

he'd thought of Lexi, of her hunger and her needs right now.

Jesse dressed and came to hold Lexi against him for a moment. "I'll call you tomorrow. I don't know when, I'm working about eighteen hours a day."

"Don't worry, Jesse," Lexi told him, then grinned at her own words. As if Jesse would ever worry about her!

part four

CHIRCY-FOUR

Summer deepened. The days were hot and humid, the nights cooler, the air drifting with evening mist. Lexi was always in a rush, too busy to eat, too wired to sleep, too preoccupied to think about love. She remembered now that it was just completely impossible to have much of a personal life if you owned a shop on Nantucket in the summer.

All the stores stayed open until ten, so people could wander in after a movie or dinner to toy with a scarf or a bracelet. They swept in on a tide of lightheartedness, dropped money like seashells, and swept away, on to another store.

Two or three times a week, her mother called to invite her to dinner, and Lexi went, glad to get a nice big home-cooked meal. She hoped she'd see Adam, or even Adam and Clare, but he was never there, and when she tried to maneuver her parents into discussing her brother's love life, they always managed to avoid the topic, maneuvering her in turn into a discussion of town politics or local news.

Lexi managed to get about five hours of sleep each night. The rest of the time she was running, up and down the stairs to unpack the new goods UPS brought from New York and off to the bank with her money bag to make deposits. At ten, after she closed the shop, she spent an hour cleaning, re-arranging, polishing her display cases and windows. She'd asked Oksana to give her more hours, so the other woman worked every day from one until nine, and took Sundays off. Lexi didn't take any day off.

She was glad to have Oksana working for her. The exotic Russian moved smoothly, swiftly, catching garments from customers before they hit the floor, easing them back onto their hangers. She had special sensors for shoplifters, too, and Lexi always knew something was up when Oksana glided over to the front door. When she spoke, she sounded like a leather-clad dominatrix, low and sultry, so it was a surprise to hear her sweet, angelic singing voice. During rainy periods when the shop was empty, she would sing, winging the exotic folk melodies through the air.

Jesse was working hard, too. These were the days when he could work eighteen hours for time and overtime, exhausted, but happy to be making serious additions to his savings account. He phoned Lexi every day, and sometimes she was able to talk, and sometimes she had to say "Sorry. Busy. Later," and close her phone, knowing Jesse understood exactly.

On stormy days, Jesse would come into the shop, his blond hair plastered to his handsome face, his body shrouded by a yellow rain poncho. The rain gave Lexi and Jesse their most relaxed times together. Few customers would leave the coziness

280

of a restaurant or home to explore the shops. As the rain pattered against the windows and the wind whipped the harbor waters into dancing triangles, Oksana and Lexi and Jesse relaxed a bit to compare notes on their days. Much of the talk was about the complications of simply driving on the island with its narrow roads and avenues built for simple Quaker carts and now congested with Hummers and the world's most expensive SUVs. People shouted at each other at intersections. The parking lots of the grocery stores never had empty spaces, forcing customers to drive around and around and around, until they were ready to ram into another car out of sheer frustration. Aisles at grocery stores weren't wide enough for all the carts. Clumps of tourists planted themselves on the sidewalks, forcing others to walk in the street. Horns honked. The summer days were long and hot and the tempers grew short.

Perhaps once a week Jesse spent the night with Lexi in her apartment above the shop. They made love, or had sex, Lexi wasn't sure which, and she didn't want to try to figure it out, not now. She'd learned by growing up on the island never to make an important decision in July or August. No one was sane then. Anyway, it was easy, being in the now with Jesse. It was soothing. No pressure. No future. Just today.

On the other side of the wall, she knew that Sweet Hart's was busy, too. If Lexi ran into Clare on the street, they flashed friendly smiles, perhaps exchanged a few chatty words—"Business good?" "Fabulous." "I know! Me too!" But Lexi sensed that Clare had raised a kind of wall around her. She clearly didn't want to discuss Jesse, didn't want to know about Lexi and Jesse, and for the time that was fine with Lexi. She didn't exactly know what the hell she and Jesse were doing.

Still, Lexi couldn't help but be aware of the moment every morning when Clare wheeled up on her bike and opened the store. Customers with sand crusted on their ankles and sunburned noses drifted from Lexi's shop into Clare's and back again, and occasionally Marlene would rush into Moon Shell Beach, breathlessly begging for change for the till. Chubby Marlene and willowy Oksana gradually became friendly as they took breaks during a lull to drink an iced coffee while dangling their feet over the seawall. Soon Marlene was asking Oksana and Lexi if they wanted a sandwich because she was off to Provisions to buy lunch, and by the end of July, Marlene was bringing chocolates over every day for Lexi and Oksana. "To keep up your strength," Marlene told them.

Lexi never saw her brother come down the wharf and wander into Sweet Hart's. She wasn't surprised. The MSPCA was in another part of town, and with all the pets of the summer residents, Adam was just as insanely busy as everyone else.

As often as possible, if the shop was quiet, Lexi would leave it in Oksana's capable hands and stroll out to the town pier to visit Jewel. The girl still came every day to sit at the end, facing the opening of the harbor. She brought her lunch box, and she carried books in her backpack, and crayons and paper. She was such an odd, solitary child, and she always managed to bring their conversation around to her father. Lexi could mention penguins or Harry Potter and Jewel would find a way to mention her father. She didn't mind. She liked hearing about Tristram. She liked telling Jewel that she'd known him when he was just a teenager. Jewel often asked her to talk about him, and when Lexi reminded her she'd already told her, Jewel would say, "But I want to hear it again." It was becoming a ritual, a magic rite, a charm. Lexi pitied her a bit, but she also admired her, and thought that if they'd been the same age, they'd be close friends.

CHIRCY-FIVE

"Good grief," Marlene whispered. "It's the Barbie Dolls. They've never set foot in Sweet Hart's in all the years you've owned it. You ought to change lovers more often."

Clare grinned. "Oh, stop it," she told Marlene. *I hope I never change lovers for the rest of my life,* she thought silently.

"Hi, Clare!"

"Hieeee, Clareee."

Spring Macmillan and Amber Young, onetime high school beauties and teenage snots, giggled their way into the store. They were both married now, and they'd kept their looks, one brunette, the other blond, with a baby doll prettiness they accentuated with pastels and with clothes really too young for their ages.

"Hi, Spring. Hi, Amber." Clare nodded a silent message to Marlene to carry on rearranging a display case Clare had been working on. *She* was the exhibit these two had come to see.

"I can't believe we've never been in your store before, it's so *darling!*" Spring cooed.

"I've been meaning to come in," Amber simpered, "but I'm always on a diet. Got to keep my girlish figure."

"You both look nineteen," Clare dutifully responded.

"So do you!" Amber cried. "I don't think I've ever seen you looking so good, Clare."

"Thanks." Clare couldn't help smiling. She knew it was true. Happiness was making her glow.

"I think I'll have some of those chocolate truffles." Spring pointed, then shrieked. "Oooh! I didn't realize they were so expensive! Well, just give me one."

"Would you like it in a box?" Clare asked.

Spring glanced at Clare to see if she was being snide. "No. No, I'll just eat it here." She paid for the candy, then nibbled on it as she looked around the shop.

"I'll take some of the chocolate blueberries," Amber decided. As Clare exchanged the pretty polka-dot bag for Amber's money, Amber said, casually, "So, rumor has it that you and Jesse have broken off."

"Rumor's right," Clare admitted with a smile.

The two women swarmed up to Clare. Spring asked, "And you're dating Adam Laney?"

"I am."

"Ooh, he's really buff," Amber said. "Lucky you." She tilted her head, trying to look innocent. "But what about Jesse?"

Clare knew what they wanted. They were like persistent rats who would nibble nibble nibble at her until she broke open and spilled the news. "I think Jesse's dating Lexi. You know her new shop is just next door. You should check it out. Moon Shell Beach. It's fabulous."

That threw them off kilter. She could see the cogs turning: Would Clare recommend Lexi's shop if Lexi had stolen Jesse from her? Were Clare and Lexi still friends? Who had left whom, Jesse for Lexi or Clare for Adam? Spring and Amber were practically drooling, and it wasn't over the chocolates. She really couldn't blame them. Well, she was so happy these days she seemed to look at everything with a forgiving eye.

"So, you, um, you see a lot of Lexi?" Spring couldn't quite get up the nerve to ask if Clare was mad at Lexi for being with Jesse, if Jesse in fact was *with* Lexi.

"Hard not to," Clare responded ambiguously, "when our shops are right next door. Really, you should see the clothing she's got in there. It's from heaven."

"Oh, okay . . ." Spring and Amber fluttered their fingers at Clare and left.

Clare could hear them entering Moon Shell Beach. The exact words were muffled, muted by the wall between, but their inane giggles came through. Oksana's sultry tones floated through in reply. Clare wondered vaguely where Lexi was.

Sometimes during a lull in business, Clare went outside to gaze at the water and catch her breath, and she would hear Lexi and Oksana talking, Lexi's familiar voice murmuring, Oksana answering in her low tones, and then laughter would ride out into the air like music. Clare would feel jealous, and curious. What were they laughing about? She was fond of Marlene, who was a great worker, but who never had the sense of style or the sense of humor Lexi had.

Occasionally, on a rainy day, she caught sight of Jesse ambling down the wharf. He'd duck into Moon Shell Beach, and Oksana would cry, "Don't drip on the merchandise!" in her sexy dominatrix voice, and soon Clare would hear all three of them laughing together.

The weird thing was that she didn't miss Jesse as much as she missed Lexi, yet together, they made her feel left out. When she was with Adam, she never thought of Jesse, but alone, or in her shop, she wondered whether her renewed friendship with Lexi could survive if Lexi and Jesse got serious. How would she feel if Lexi purred about Jesse's lovemaking? How would she feel if Lexi got engaged to Jesse!? What if Jesse *married* Lexi? But did she want Jesse to break Lexi's heart?

Bonnie Frost strode into Sweet Hart's, little Frankie bobbing along in a back carrier.

"Oh, what a cutie pie!" Clare came around the counter to stroke the baby's velvet cheek. "How are you, Bonnie?"

"I'm fine." Bonnie looked frazzled but lovely. "Actually, it's your friend I wanted to see."

"My friend?"

Bonnie strode across the room to stand at the window looking out at the harbor. "Lexi. *There.* There she is with Jewel. I want you to stop her, Clare."

Clare joined Bonnie looking across the blue expanse of water. At the end of the pier sat Jewel, and Lexi sat next to her. Their heads were bent together.

Bonnie said, "Lexi gave Jewel a bead kit. They're making some kind of bracelet."

"Well, what's wrong with that, Bonnie?"

"What's wrong is that Lexi's encouraging my daughter to have false hope!" Tears suddenly glittered in Bonnie's eyes. "Jewel will have a hard enough time dealing with Tris's loss without Lexi building up her expectations! For God's sake, parts of his boat washed up in Maine! Jewel has to face the truth!"

"I doubt that Lexi is telling Jewel that Tris is alive," Clare said softly. "I'm sure she's just letting Jewel talk about Tris. That's a good way to learn to let him go."

"But she's *not* letting him go! Why else would she insist on sitting out on that dock every damned day! When Lexi joins her, it makes it seem like a *reasonable* thing to do! Jewel should be playing with friends like a normal child!"

Clare backed away from the blast of Bonnie's anger. "It's Lexi you should talk to about this, surely."

"Right," Bonnie sneered. "Right. And sooner or later Lexi will tell Jewel that I'm the reason she's not joining Lexi, and then Jewel can blame *me* for keeping my daughter away from everyone she loves." She pulled a tissue from her shorts' pocket and blew her nose. "Jewel always loved her father best. She behaves like the most demonic brat around Ken, she won't even give him a chance. She's just *perverse*."

"She's a child," Clare said quietly.

"Oh, right, right, make *me* the monster. Everyone already thinks I am, leaving the sainted Tris. But I had to! I don't regret it one iota! You grew up here, Clare, you know what it's like to feel like some poor little peasant while everyone else is royalty! Tris would come home with grease on his hands, and I couldn't get it all out of his clothes—" Bonnie flung her arms around. "You have your shop, I'll bet you're making a ton of money. And Lexi! Well now, Lexi struck it rich all right, marrying Ed Hardin. She swans around like a princess and I look like a drone!"

Clare came to Lexi's defense. "Lexi works, Bonnie. I know, because I'm right next to her. She's working seven days a week in her shop—"

"Yes, and have you seen what she sells? I can't afford clothes like that! Can you? She's going to give Jewel a taste for the kind of life Ken and I can't possibly afford."

"Has Lexi been giving Jewel expensive gifts?"

Thwarted, Bonnie strode back across the store. "No," she admitted. "Just that bead kit. And a couple of books. Oh, come on, Clare, talk to Lexi for me, won't you?" A strange expression crossed her face. "Or aren't you talking to Lexi anymore?"

Oh, good grief, Clare thought, putting her hands on her hips. Would Bonnie go through this bizarre charade just to get the latest gossip? She had never been a close friend of Bonnie's. Bonnie had always been irrational and cranky and spoiled.

"You should take your concerns to Lexi." Clare's voice was cool. "Now, if you'll excuse me, I've got to get back to work."

CHIRCY-SIX

Clare felt so *new* with Adam.

Adam was taller, wider, and more massive than Jesse. Next to him, Clare felt petite and somehow younger, more delicate. Adam touched her more than Jesse had—he kissed her passionately in the morning, he rubbed her feet at night, sending her into swoons of delight, and when they watched TV, he pulled her against him, so that she nestled between his arm and his chest.

He talked to her more than Jesse did, too. He had opinions about national and town politics. He regaled her with humorous anecdotes about his furry and feathery patients. He asked her about her day, and he paid attention, he listened, he remembered. He said, "So did the chocolate baskets sell as well as you'd hoped?" It was lovely to have a man care so much about what she did and said.

He spent almost every night at her house. Her father liked him, and Ralphie adored him, and Clare loved seeing him at her table. Some nights he brought take-out so she didn't have to cook; he never expected her to cook. He brought her little gifts from time to time—roses, or a good bottle of wine, or a bit of costume jewelry that caught his eye in a shop window.

When they went to bed, the exhaustion and petty worries of the day vanished as they explored each other's bodies. Clare felt new with Adam as his larger hands learned her curves and contours, her silky spots, the places that made her gasp. Her own hands felt new, her fingertips reborn as she drew them through his thick chest hair, down to the curly thatch of fur around his groin. She knelt over him on hot summer nights, her naked body sleek with sweat as she drew her tongue over his long muscular back and his enormous long limbs, as she softly sucked on his muscles, ligaments, tendons, knuckles, earlobes, the pads of his fingers and hand, the hard ropes of his veins. She wanted to ingest him. She wanted to pull all of him inside her. He would flip her onto her back and shove his penis into her, filling her, and she would lie very still, not moving, not wanting to send either of them off on that spiraling explosion of pleasure; she would lie so still she didn't breathe, feeling the heat and width and length of him wedged into her so tightly it almost hurt.

Then he would move his hips, slightly. He'd shove himself in even further. And she was gone.

The summer days rolled on like the tides. Regular customers, renting on the island for the summer, dropped in for their daily treats. Day-trippers wandered in, went wild over Clare's truffles, and went out with their totes filled with Sweet Hart's boxes.

Occasionally a friend would enter the shop, sample a chocolate-covered blueberry, then ask, "So, how's Jesse?"

"I'm dating someone else," she'd reply. "Someone very different from Jesse, an island man . . . it's all very brand-new, I can hardly talk about it yet." And saying even this much about Adam lifted her away from the confusion that had been her life with Jesse into a clear shining bell of happiness.

Most nights Adam slept over. Clare would curl next to him like a cub nestling up to a big protective bear. They would lie in bed, wrapped around each other, skin to skin, resting after sex. Clare held Adam's limp, exhausted penis in her hand. She couldn't not be touching it.

One night Adam murmured into her ear, "I think I've always been a little bit in love with you."

Her heart thumped. *Love.* Such an enormous word. She knew she loved Adam, too. But then what had that been with Jesse? Clare shifted on the bed to look up at him. From here she could see the whiskers he'd missed under his chin when he shaved that morning. "Even when I was a snotty little kid?"

He ran his hand down her back and over her hips. "You were a cute little kid."

"Oh, come on, you didn't notice me. Lexi and I were always spying on you and your friends. All you cared about was football, baseball, sailing, and fishing."

"So, *you* noticed *me*."

"Oh, Adam, I always had a crush on you." She twined herself even closer, kissing his chest, his muscular bicep, his neck. "And now . . ." She wanted to tell him she loved him, but would he believe her, so soon after Jesse? Could she mean it?

Adam rescued her. "You don't have to say it. And I don't need to hear it. This summer's been confusing and dramatic enough already. I don't want you to make any promises to me until you're sure you can keep them. It's enough, for now, to be with you, like this."

She nuzzled against him. "I know, I know, Adam. But sometime I guess we should talk about the future . . ."

"If you don't stop that, I won't be able to talk at all," Adam said, and rolled her onto her back, lifting himself up over her.

The island sweltered beneath a constant August sun. Everyone had sunburns, or went around with white cream slathered on their noses, and women didn't leave the house without wide-brimmed sun hats. Now business fell into a predictable pattern. Mornings were busy as women walked around town organizing themselves for the rest of the day, buying chocolates for the guest room or birthday parties, ordering special boxes for anniversaries. At lunch, a lull fell. It was too hot to be anywhere except the beach or a backyard hammock. Around four, freshly showered and ready for a long leisurely summer evening, people crowded back into town, refreshed, ready for the divertissement of delicious chocolates, eye-catching clothes.

At home, Clare's father was perking up. He was always shaved, clean, and dressed these days, he talked to Adam at dinner, he watched the Red Sox with Adam, and sometimes the two men went together to take Ralphie for her evening walk. Clare couldn't figure out why her father was getting better. Was he relieved to have Jesse out of their lives? She'd always known her father wasn't crazy about Jesse, and she could understand that. How could a parent trust a man who had made his daughter cry so many times? Or perhaps her father was happy because Clare was so obviously happy, and life seemed so positive, so forward-going. For whatever reason, she was grateful.

THIRTY-SEVEN

Along the southern coast of the continent, hurricanes began to brew, spinning their ghostly white whorls like mythical furies. Some days stiff breezes rose, sending papers skipping across the cobblestones and clattering rose branches against the walls. The stores were busy those days, when the sand blew into children's eyes or stung against ankles. Chocolate sales went way up, as people flocked in to buy the comfort and tranquillity contained in chocolate's chemicals.

Clare got to work early. There was so much to do. She was just lifting a tray of new Nantucket Nuggets into the display case and sliding the glass door shut, when the phone rang. She snatched it up with one hand as she opened the next display case with the other hand. "Sweet Hart's."

"Clare, it's Lexi."

"Oh, Lexi, I'm straight out busy."

"I am, too. But I *have* to talk to you. Could you meet me at Moon Shell Beach tonight? After ten tonight?"

"Lexi—"

"Clare, this can't wait."

"All right, but why do we have to go all the way out to Moon Shell Beach? We're grown-ups now. Let's just have a drink."

"You'll know why when I tell you. I really need to tell you this at Moon Shell Beach."

"Miss?" Two women stuck their heads in the door. "Are you open yet?"

"Fine," Clare snapped. "Ten-fifteen."

Clare arrived at the marsh to find Lexi's Range Rover already parked on the side of the road. She found the entrance to the path and impatiently shoved her way through the thickets. She'd phoned Adam to tell him she couldn't see him tonight, and she was tired and cranky, so she crashed along, smashing grasses and mosses beneath her sandals, and came out onto the beach to find Lexi already there, pacing on the sand.

Late-summer light, moonlight, and lights from all the boats in the harbor lit their beach in a cool blue glow. A breeze ruffled the waters and made the tide splash onto the sand.

Lexi's white-blond hair was twisted high at the back of her head, held with a clip. She wore a short-sleeved white tee with a dramatically swirling peach and ivory skirt.

"Clare! Thank you for coming. It's really good of you. I know you must be exhausted—"

"I *am* exhausted. You must be, too. So what's up?"

Lexi looked anguished. She hugged herself, then flapped her hands in the helpless gesture Clare had seen all her life.

"Oh, stop it, Lexi!" Clare snapped impatiently.

"Clare, I'm *pregnant!*" Lexi snapped back.

Clare gawked. "What?"

"Just a month, but I had to tell you."

"It's Jesse's?"

Lexi nodded.

A gull flew overhead, silent except for the flap of its wings.

"Well, *damn,* Lexi. Didn't you use birth control?" Jesse had been a fanatic about birth control with Clare. She'd been on the Pill for years. That meant that Jesse was either so much in love with Lexi or so driven by uncontrollable passion that he hadn't used a condom.

Lexi looked away, embarrassed. "Not the first time."

That stung. As if trying to walk away from her emotions, Clare strode past Lexi down the small beach, until she was at the water's edge. A cloud drifted over the moon. Shadows caught, then vanished. Clare tried to still her racing heart. She thought of Adam. That helped. She thought of Lexi, pregnant. Turning, she asked, "What are you going to do?"

Lexi's voice was low. "Clare, listen. I got pregnant three times when I was married to Ed. And I had three miscarriages."

Clare's hand went to her heart. "Oh, Lexi. I'm sorry."

"So I want to try to keep this baby, Clare."

Jesse's baby, Clare thought. Clare's dream baby . . . in Lexi's arms. A kind of panic struck her. "Lexi, you know what? I can't do this."

"Clare—"

"I'm sorry. I'm not in love with Jesse anymore, and I wish you well, but I just can't—I can't be here right now." Abruptly, she turned back to the path.

"Clare!" Lexi followed. "Clare, please."

Clare kept walking, and the sharp-edged grasses lashed her bare skin. She wanted to run.

Behind her, Lexi yelled, "Clare, stop. Clare, you are my best friend, you've always been my only best friend. *I need you now.*"

Clare stopped. She turned to look at Lexi.

Lexi stood with her hands on her waist. "Clare," she said softly. "A *baby.*"

Clare remembered being a little girl with Lexi, carrying their dolls swaddled in blankets, solemnly discussing bottles and diapers as they held their babies close, patting their backs, rocking them. Clare thought of Penny's baby, Mikey. The snuggling weight. The trusting eyes. The gleeful laugh. She felt tears well in her eyes.

"Gosh, Lexi, it will be so beautiful."

Lexi's mouth trembled. "You think?"

Stepping forward, Clare put her hand on Lexi's belly. For a moment they both were very still, listening, waiting. Then Clare laughed. "Flat as a board, as always."

Together they walked back to the beach and settled down on the sand, side by side, their arms wrapped around their knees, looking out at the water.

"Does Jesse know?" Clare asked.

"No, I haven't told him yet. Haven't told anyone but you. I want to wait at least another month. I mean, I've miscarried before in the first or second months."

"Maybe it was Ed's sperm causing the miscarriages," Clare suggested.

"Oh, I hope so." Lexi put her hands on the sand as she leaned back. "I don't know what Jesse will do. I don't even know what I want him to do."

"He's not Mr. Reliability."

"I know. This might completely freak him out."

"Or not. He might be in love with you."

"I don't think so."

"Are you in love with him?"

Lexi was quiet. "I'm attracted to him. He makes me laugh. They always say you should marry a man who makes you laugh."

"Have you talked about marriage?"

"Ha. Are you kidding? Jesse has trouble committing to dinner."

"He was always that way," Clare said.

"So I know I can't count on him," Lexi mused. "But I've got my parents."

Clare took a deep breath. "And you've got me." She wrapped an arm around Lexi. "I can't say it's going to be easy for me, Lexi. I've wanted Jesse's

300

baby for years. A baby, a sweet little baby, with white-blond hair and blue eyes. And *you've* got it. No matter what else happens in my life, you'll have Jesse's baby. And I just don't know how gracious I'm going to be able to be about it. So give me some time, okay?"

"We've got time," Lexi said.

Thirty-Eight

Some August days shone like pure gold. On those days the humidity lifted just a little, so that the sky was clearer, the air purer, and everyone was in a better mood. The merchants were swelling their bank accounts, foreseeing a pleasant, even lavish, winter ahead. They'd be able to take their families to Costa Rica for school vacation, perhaps even add that second bathroom. The institutions—the library, historical association, science museum—found their coffers filling as relaxed billionaires happily presented checks and started endowment funds in their names. Blue, red, and white sails zipped across the horizon during the day, and at night the island's restaurants were all booked, table after table of rested, tanned, happy patrons enjoying the ruby tomatoes from Moors End and Bartlett's Farm, or the delicate perfection of rococo desserts.

As Labor Day grew closer, more women crowded into Moon Shell Beach, wanting to buy souvenirs of their summer, wanting to take some of the radiance of Lexi's clothing home with them, like taking a suitcase full of glittering sun into the coming fall.

Lexi's morning was too busy for thought. At noon, there was a lull.

"Oksana, I've got to go to the bank. And I'll bring back some lunch. Want anything?"

Oksana was in a cubicle, gathering clothing. She emerged, drawing aside the curtain. "Some noodles from Even Keel and an iced coffee. Thanks."

As Lexi walked past the boat basin and up Main Street, she felt better, not so nauseous, and stronger. The sun on her shoulders relaxed her. She knew she looked great in her cocoa slip dress and beaded sandals. Could she trust her stomach to accept a nice big iced chocolate coffee? That might clear her brain. She might be able to think more than an hour into the future. She might be able to clear up her confusion about Jesse.

"Hi, Lexi," Mimi called from the bookstore.

Smiling, Lexi waved back. She was home, after all. She'd been in worse places in her life, that was for sure. She could be optimistic.

Someone grabbed her shoulder—hard. Someone yanked her so that she spun sideways, nearly losing her balance.

"I need to talk to you." Bonnie Frost stood there, looking strained. Stuffed into his little backpack, her son gnawed on his fist, grizzling and drooling, red-faced, rashy.

"Hi, Bonnie! Hi, baby!" Lexi put her finger up to stroke the baby, but Bonnie jerked away from her as if she were poison.

Bonnie's face was dark with anger. "I thought I made it clear I want you to stop visiting Jewel on the pier!"

Lexi took a deep breath and tried to keep her tone placating. "Look, Bonnie. I'm not *making* her sit there. I'm not encouraging her. I'm just keeping Jewel company. She seems so *lonely.*"

"Don't you dare tell me about my own child! You have no idea what is best for her. I'm her *mother.* I know what's going on in her mind, and I'm worried sick!"

Bonnie didn't seem to be aware that she was shouting. Passing shoppers stifled embarrassed grins and some just stopped on the sidewalk, frankly staring at the two women as if they were another of Nantucket's entertainments.

"Bonnie, let's sit down." Lexi put her hand on the other woman's arm, intending to lead her to one of the wooden benches.

Bonnie jerked herself away. "Take your hands off me! And *listen.* I'm not kidding! I'm going to go to court and get you served with a restraining order if you don't stay away from Jewel."

Lexi was appalled. "Bonnie, that's way over the top! I'm not hurting Jewel."

"You're giving her hope that her father's alive!"

"Well, maybe he is!" Lexi shot back. "Maybe he's not conveniently dead just because *you want* him to be."

Bonnie slapped Lexi hard on the face.

Lexi gasped. Her hand flew to her cheek as sudden tears sprang into her eyes.

"You have no right to judge me," Bonnie hissed.

"I'm trying to protect Jewel from getting her heart broken worse than it already is. You have no right to encourage her to hope for the impossible!"

Lexi was hyperaware now, as if she were both in her body and outside it, looking down at herself with her bright red cheek and Bonnie with her angry face and the sidewalk crammed with people gawking with concern and delight.

She was aware of Bonnie's baby grabbing Bonnie's hair and trying to get it in his mouth.

She was aware of her own baby, floating peacefully in her belly.

"Bonnie," she said very quietly, "sometimes it's okay to believe in the impossible. Sometimes miracles happen."

"Don't be such a fool," Bonnie snapped. "Tris is dead, and I'm telling you once and for all, you crazy bitch, leave my daughter alone." She strode away.

By late afternoon everyone in town had heard about Bonnie Frost slapping Lexi. People took sides, arguing over the phone, over drinks, over dinner. Some thought Lexi was meddling in matters she should leave alone. Others thought Bonnie had been neglecting Jewel ever since she started her affair with Ken Frost, and it was a good thing *someone* was paying attention to the child.

As Clare waited on customers and settled chocolates into their ruffled paper cups and rang up sales, she overheard people gossiping, but she didn't join in. Lexi, it seemed to Clare, was not doing anything wrong. Jewel was a good kid, too precocious for her own good, and obviously an independent thinker, a bit of a loner—someone Clare and Lexi would have hung out with if they were all the same age. All Bonnie and Ken thought about was money, and more money. Clare sympathized with Jewel, and with Lexi.

Then she remembered that Lexi was pregnant with Jesse's child and a lightning bolt of jealousy speared through her. Maybe the baby would be a little girl like Lexi. Or a boy who looked just like Jesse. She squeezed her eyes shut, warding off the pain. *Not now. Not now.* She had to work. Thank goodness for work.

CHIRTY-NINE

This Sunday morning with its heavy fug of humidity had an almost Louisiana lethargy about it. The harbor was as still and flat as a sheet of glass and few boats had their sails up.

Lexi turned the air conditioners onto high. Heat made her drowsy, and the cool dryness seemed to alleviate the worst of the nausea. She'd thrown up that morning, and now her stomach growled hungrily.

She strolled around the shop, straightening and double checking her inventory. A frantic customer rushed in and bought ten small boxes for party favors. A man came in to buy a necklace his girlfriend had admired, and while Lexi wrapped it in a gift box, five women off a tour boat clustered in, chattering and bumping into the display cases, lifting shawls and skirts and letting them fall. Lexi glanced at her watch. Where was Oksana?

Finally all the customers were gone. Lexi wondered if she had time to rush upstairs to grab a peach.

The door opened.

"Busy morning?" Lexi's mother came in. Myrna looked good these days, tanned and rested and cute in white clam diggers and a striped top.

"Pretty busy. And Oksana hasn't shown up yet. And I'm starving."

"Well, you'll be glad I came in." Myrna lifted a thermos and a box from her woven basket. "Iced tiramisu coffee and some homemade blueberry muffins. Thought you could use a little picker-upper."

"Gosh, Mom, thanks!" Lexi grabbed a muffin and munched ravenously. How cool it was, having her mother here like this. She wanted to tell her mother she was pregnant, but not yet. And not here, where a customer could walk in. "Delicious."

"Good." Myrna looked around the shop. "I remember when Dad and I ran our store, our summer help was usually college kids. They always partied too hard on Saturday nights and showed up late on Sundays or came in with hangovers."

"Oksana's not like that." Lexi drank the iced coffee carefully. Her stomach seemed ready to accept it. "She's never done this before. I hope she's not sick."

The store phone rang.

"That's probably her right now," Myrna said.

"Moon Shell Beach, Lexi speaking."

"Hi, Lexi," a man growled. "Clyde Thompson here. Have you seen Jesse?"

"No . . ."

"He didn't show up for work today. I'm short-handed as it is."

Last night Jesse had stayed at his parents' house,

308

claiming exhaustion, but this was more information than Clyde Thompson needed. "Look, I'll phone you if I hear from him—" All at once Lexi's heart thudded. "Oh, Clyde." She dropped the phone, reaching for the stability of the countertop.

"What's wrong?" Myrna grabbed up the phone. "Hello? This is Myrna Laney. Can I help you?"

"Hi, Myrna, it's Clyde Thompson. I'm looking for Jesse. He didn't show up for work today."

"I see." Myrna studied Lexi's face.

"Is there something going on I should know about?" the contractor demanded.

"I don't know, Clyde."

Lexi raised her head. "Just tell him I'll call him back as soon as I know anything."

FORTY

Lexi thought she might faint. She swallowed bile, steadying herself against the counter.

Her throat was dry when she said, "Mom, will you watch the shop? I'm going up to the pharmacy —the one where the Russian women work. They might know something about Oksana."

"Of course," Myrna said. "Go ahead. Take your time. I'll be fine."

"Thanks. I'll be back as soon as I can."

She hurried into the heart of the town, tripping over cobblestones and bricks, stumbling like someone lost. She didn't feel the shade from the green arch of the trees above her. She didn't see the fabulous merchandise in all the shop windows she passed. Her mind would not articulate her fears; instead it played a frantic loop that had her muttering as she walked.

"He *wouldn't,* he wouldn't, he wouldn't just go without a word . . ."

Occasionally a tourist would glance at her quizzically, but she didn't care, she was caught up in the pounding of her heart and the thudding of her sandals against the pavement, they were like drum rolls, and she burst into the pharmacy like a mother throwing open the door to a room where her kid sat smoking pot.

Several people were at the counter having coffee and chatting. Behind the counter was the lovely, tall, blond Sophia, adding whipped cream to a hot fudge sundae. Lexi was trembling as she approached the counter.

Sophia wiped her hands on the apron around her waist. "May I help you?"

"Sophia, we've met before, I'm Lexi Laney, I own Moon Shell Beach where Oksana works." The words came tumbling out fast. "I'm sorry to bother you, but I need to know, you're a friend of Oksana's, and she didn't show up for work today. I was wondering whether you might know where she is."

Sophie smiled nervously. "Yes, I have something for you."

Lexi felt the atmosphere change in the pharmacy. Silence fell as the pharmacists and customers went silent, straining to listen.

Sophia reached under the counter. "Oksana left this for you."

Lexi took the white envelope, so innocent and pristine-looking, with *Lexi* scrawled on it in curly script. Her heart raced, her fingertips felt cold.

"Thank you, Sophia," she said quietly.

Somehow she managed to leave the store and walk through town back to her shop. The summer sun burned down on her, but she was icy with dread.

When she got to Moon Shell Beach, she didn't enter the shop but went around to the back to sit on the bulkhead. The ocean lapped musically against the shore. Sails cut back and forth on the blue water. A gull screeched overhead. Lexi opened the envelope.

Two pieces of paper were inside. Lexi unfolded them.

The first, in curly script, said only, "Lexi, I am sorry. Forgive me. I fell in love."

The other piece of paper was covered in Jesse's sideways, nearly illegible scrawl.

"Lexi, I'm sorry, but somehow I think you'll understand. Oksana and I are leaving the island. We're going to get married as soon as possible, and then we're going to her hometown. Labinsk— you can find it on the map—is in the middle of Russia. I'll be able to travel everywhere. With my savings I'll be able to buy a little shop for me and Oksana. I know this seems awful of me, to just leave like this, but the truth is, it's like in the *Wizard of Oz*, where the black-and-white world becomes Technicolor. For the first time in my life I know exactly what I want to do. I never meant to hurt you. But I know you don't love me, not really. We had a good time together, the two of us. I hope your future life is as happy as mine. Fondly, Jesse."

Fondly? The casual indifference of the word stabbed Lexi hard. She made two fists, crumpling the notes in her hands as if she could destroy the words.

"Lexi?" Her mother stuck her head out the back door. "You have a customer . . ."

"Thanks, Mom." She could not break down right now. She would not. She pushed herself up. She entered the shop. She handed the notes to her mother.

The interior of Moon Shell Beach was cool and dry and calm and fragrant, a tranquil oasis against the summer heat. A woman in a tennis dress stood in the shop, holding one of Lexi's caftans. Lexi had work to do, and that grounded her for now. She took a deep breath. "How may I help you?" she asked.

FORTY-ONE

"Good afternoon, ladies." Clare was still in a luxurious state of honey-drugged indolence. As she moved around the shop, restocking the shelves, tweaking the bows on the boxes, her light summer dress floated around her and her beaded bracelets clicked musically on her wrists. She was so much in love she was even glad to see the Barbie Dolls when they wandered into her shop.

"We're just looking," Amber cooed. "My mother-in-law's birthday is next Saturday . . ."

Clare squinted at them. Something more than a birthday was going on. "How about this box? It's assorted chocolates."

Amber and Spring were eyeing her carefully, trying to read her mood.

"Oh, come on," Clare laughed indulgently. "What's up with you two?"

Amber pounced. "Have you talked to Lexi today?"

Clare looked wary. "No."

"Gosh," Spring giggled. "She's right next door and you don't even know."

"Know what?" Clare wanted to shake them. They were such little teases, the only way she could get them to spill would be to act as if she weren't interested, so she turned her back on them and began to polish the glass of the display case.

Amber couldn't wait. "Jesse's gone. Oksana, too."

Clare went still. "What?"

"My brother, Hank?" Spring exploded with the news. "He was in the pharmacy this morning when Lexi came in. He heard Lexi telling Sophia that Oksana hadn't shown up for work, and he saw Sophie hand Lexi an envelope she said was from Oksana."

Amber had to get in on this. Eagerly, she continued, "Hank knows Jesse's been dating Lexi, so he phoned Gordie Evans, who runs a contracting business, and Gordie phoned Clyde Thompson, who heads up the crew Jesse works for, and Clyde said Jesse hadn't shown up for work today."

Spring finished with a smug smile. "And one plus one makes two . . ."

So many emotions hit Clare so hard she had to bite her lip to clear some space in her head. She feigned indifference. "Maybe Jesse's sick."

"And Oksana's sick, too?" Amber smirked. "And instead of phoning her boss, she leaves her a note?"

The door opened. A gaggle of older women squeezed in, clustering around the counter to inspect the chocolates.

"Let's talk later, okay?" Clare said to the Barbies with fake sweetness. She smiled at her customers. "May I help you?"

315

* * *

The moment the Barbies left the store, Clare dialed Jesse's parents. They'd spent so many years protecting their son and listening to jilted women spewing their anger at them that they had developed thick skins. They gave away little, and never showed emotion.

But today, when Jesse's mother answered the phone, her voice was clotted, as if she'd been crying.

"Phyllis? It's Clare."

The older woman sniffed. Without preamble, she confessed in a rush, "Yes, Clare, yes, it's true, Jesse's gone, he's left, he's left the island forever, he's going to go live in *Russia*, of all the godforsaken places. Oh, Clare, we'll never see him again!"

Clare heard Jesse's father muttering something in the background.

"We never expected anything like this," Phyllis Gray sobbed. "We never thought he'd leave the island! All his friends! His family! And what if there are grandchildren? We'll never see our grandchildren!"

Well, Clare thought bitterly, you'll see one. But this was not her secret to tell. She wondered whether Jesse's parents even knew he'd been going out with Lexi. "I'm sorry, Phyllis."

As she hung up the phone, the Barbies returned, gleaming. "Moon Shell Beach is *closed!*" they announced gleefully.

"What?" Clare asked.

"Come outside, look for yourself! She's closed the store right in the middle of the day!"

Clare went outside and looked. The Barbies were right. "Well," she snapped at the Barbies, "probably she doesn't want anyone to come inside and gawk at her and *gloat*."

Insulted, Amber shot back, "Like *you* won't gloat, Clare?"

Clare rolled her eyes in reply and returned to her own shop.

Finally Amber and Spring left. Quickly she dialed Lexi's home number, but only got a recording.

"Lexi," she said. "It's Clare. I've heard about Jesse and Oksana. Give me a call. I'm . . . I'm so sorry. I want to help. Let me help."

All day long islanders collected at Sweet Hart's to exchange the news and check out in obvious or sly ways whether Clare knew more. At least they all bought chocolates, so her sales total that day was excellent.

But by the time she closed the shop, she was drained. Jesse was gone, really gone. At last Jesse was traveling. At last his wildest dreams were coming true.

And Lexi might be hurt, might feel embarrassed, but not, Clare thought, heartbroken. For while Lexi might not have Jesse, she would have Jesse's child. Jesse had given Lexi that much, and that was a prize beyond measure.

FORTY-TWO

She closed Moon Shell Beach early that day. She couldn't stay open until ten. She was too tired. She had to eat. She had to rest. She needed to be alone with her thoughts.

She locked the doors. The sudden stillness calmed her. For an hour or so, she moved around the store, smoothing the pashminas, rearranging the sarongs in order of size, adjusting the privacy curtains on the cubicles so they fell into harmonious lines. When her touch stirred the shimmering fabrics, they seemed to release an invisible mist of soft sounds into the silent air of the store. Jesse's laughter. Oksana's songs.

"Durak," Lexi said aloud. The Russian word for "stupid." "How could I have been so *durak?"* Jesse and Oksana must have fallen in love right in front of Lexi and she hadn't even noticed.

Out in the summer evening, people strolled along the cobblestones. Some tested her front door, then continued on. As dusk fell, Lexi noticed how the glow from Sweet Hart's patterned the lane with squares of brightness.

One practical consideration: she couldn't handle the store on her own. She would have to find a new salesclerk. She climbed the stairs to her second floor without turning on the lights. Enough late-evening sunshine shone through the windows to illuminate the long room, and she didn't want anyone outside to suspect that she was up here, sniveling into her solitude like a wounded bear into her cave. She was hungry but had no energy to cook, or even to call out for food. She meant to search for the local newspaper with its classified ads. It was buried somewhere on her desk. Instead, she collapsed on her bed, curling up into a fetal position.

On her bedside table, the message button on her answering machine flashed relentlessly. Her cell phone had rung so many times today, she had finally turned it off. She'd assured her mother she was fine, and Myrna had gone home, worry-free, which was exactly how Lexi wanted it. Myrna deserved to have her own life, unscathed by Lexi's continuing mistakes. Lexi hit Play. Myrna hadn't phoned, but Adam had, and Clare, and the Barbie Dolls, twice, and even Brittany Phelps, who had become a counselor/therapist, had invited Lexi, in her soft sweet voice, to come talk to her if she had any problems.

"Problems!" Lexi spoke into the empty air. "My problem is that I'm a big fat fool!"

She wanted to cry, but instead of the pressure of tears, she felt only hollowness. She buried her face in her pillow. *"Durak,"* she said aloud. "I'm so *durak.*"

A sudden violent pounding made her raise her

head from the pillow. "What now?" she demanded grumpily of the air. Someone was beating on her back door. It wouldn't be a customer, they only came to the front. Only her family used the back door. Her family, and Clare.

Grudgingly, she dragged herself down the stairs and opened the door.

Clare held up two bags emanating delicious scents. "Emergency rations. From Annye's Health Foods."

"How did you know I was here?"

"Oh, let's see, maybe because I've known you all my life?" Clare led the way up the stairs. "Good grief, your place looks worse than mine."

"You have a house to go home to," Lexi reminded her.

Clare set the food on top of a pile of catalogs on the coffee table. "Sit. I'll get utensils and drinks. What do you want?"

"Scotch," Lexi said, sinking into a chair. "Vodka. Gin. All of the above. Mixed together."

"Yes, well, pregnant mothers can't drink, so forget that." Clare bustled around in the kitchenette, finding a couple of glasses and a container of orange juice. She set them on the table, then went back for plates and paper napkins.

Lexi opened the bags. Delicious aromas wafted into the air. Her stomach growled. Fried rice with snow peas and spinach. Pasta with tuna and Parmesan. Grilled salmon with plum sauce. Caesar salad. Pasta ribbons with mushrooms and shallots.

"Thank you, Clare," Lexi said. "This is so nice of you."

Clare settled across from Lexi, filling her plate as she talked. "Glad to help. Adam's tried to call you, you know." She watched as Lexi ate ravenously. "I guess I can tell him your appetite is good."

"I know," Lexi mumbled around a mouthful of pasta. "Odd, isn't it?"

For a while they both ate in silence. Finally Lexi put down her plate. "Oh, man, I needed that." She looked at Clare. "I feel like the biggest fool on the planet."

"I know just how you feel," Clare said.

Lexi started to object, then reconsidered. She grinned. "I guess you do." She picked up a snow pea and munched it. "I don't know why I'm so surprised. It's not as if I was in love with Jesse, or he was in love with me. Right now, I can't even imagine why I slept with him."

Clare snorted. "Oh, please. Of course you know why you slept with him. Jesse is irresistible."

"Still. *I* should have resisted."

"Listen, Mother Teresa couldn't have resisted Jesse when he's full steam ahead."

"Do you think it was revenge sex, Clare? Because you dumped him? Or do you think he just wanted to finish off his list, and I was the last female in our high school class who hadn't slept with him?" Suddenly it all spilled out. "I never believed he was in love with me. He never said he loved me. I never said I loved him. I never thought I'd have a future with him. I never *wanted* a future with him. That wasn't even on the same planet when we were together. Then, when I knew I was pregnant, I guess I kind of began to imagine—but I hadn't spoken to him about it, so—Would he have married me if he knew I was pregnant? But even if he did, he'd still screw around, wouldn't he? I mean, maybe he's like an eternal optimist, the next one is always more desirable than the one he has . . ."

"Lexi, look—"

Lexi half-laughed, choking as tears began to well. "Maybe he's basically insecure, and needs to—"

Clare threw her hands up. "We are *not* going to psychoanalyze Jesse Gray! I've spent most of my adult years worrying away like a demented squirrel with a nut, trying to find ways to understand him, to explain his behavior. To *excuse* him. The fact is, he's just plain Jesse."

Humiliated by her own question, Lexi still had to ask, "Do you think he'll stay with Oksana?"

Clare snorted. "When he's got all of the European continent to conquer? Oh, I *doubt* it."

Lexi grinned. She blew her nose and wiped her face and caught her breath. She lifted her head and looked soberly at Clare. "Clare, I still want this baby."

"I know you do. And you can have this baby, Lexi."

"Geez, I'll be an unwed mother!" She laughed at the thought, and Clare laughed with her.

"No one cares about that stuff anymore."

"My parents might."

"Your parents will be thrilled to have a grandchild."

"You're right. They will." Lexi looked down at her flat belly. "I'm still not telling anyone else yet. I'll tell my parents when I'm in the twelfth week, but no one else until I start to show." She ran her hands through her hair. "I'm so tired all the time, Clare. I feel *drugged*."

"I've heard that's normal. Are you going to be able to keep the store open?"

"I'm going to have to. Oh"—she waved a hand—"I know my parents would always let me live at home and they'd take care of me, but they've worked hard all their lives and I don't want to be dependent on them. The store is doing really well, and I like it, well, most of the time at least." She leaned forward, thinking aloud. "This will be an April baby. That means I won't be really cumbersome until after the first of the year. So I'll be able to keep the shop open through the Christmas Stroll. By then I'm sure I'll have found some reliable help for the store, someone like your Marlene."

"You should advertise right away," Clare advised her. "You'll need help for the rest of the summer season. Besides, you'll need to take care of yourself and rest."

Tears welled in Lexi's eyes again. Reaching out, she took Clare's hand. "Oh, Clare, what a generous spirit you have! I'm so grateful."

Clare squeezed her hand. "It's easy to be nice when I'm so happy with Adam." A yawn suddenly overtook her. "Sorry about that. I'm just so tired."

"Are you and Adam getting serious?" Lexi asked.

"We're just taking it one day at a time, really. Which is what you should do. And right now it's time for you to rest." She rose and began gathering up the plastic food containers.

Together the two women washed the dishes and tidied the kitchen counter. Lexi walked Clare down to the back door. They hugged each other tight.

"How can I ever thank you?" Lexi asked.

"Oh, stop with the drama." Clare went out into the warm night. Looking back at Lexi, she said, "Take care. Take care of both of you."

For the next few days, Myrna came and helped Lexi with the store. She took money to the bank, brought in lunch, signed for UPS deliveries, and unpacked boxes with a practiced hand. Even so, Lexi was too tired to be open after six o'clock. She put an ad in the local papers and Myrna phoned everyone she knew, looking for anyone who could use a part-time job, but without success.

"Honey," Myrna said one morning, "are you okay? You look so tired, so pale."

Lexi had just come down from her bathroom where she'd quietly vomited away her breakfast. It was a struggle to hide her condition from her mother, but she kept her silence. She was too seasoned and too superstitious to admit how hopeful she was.

She tried to derail her mother's thoughts. "I'm fine. Just exhausted and running fast and falling behind." She looked out the back window. From here, she could see Jewel, sitting alone at the end of the pier. "You know, Mom, I've been thinking. I love this location. I like running a shop. But I'm not sure I'm comfortable with the kind of merchandise I'm selling. I want to sell clothing my friends can afford—Spring and Amber, for instance. I'm thinking teen clothing, too—Jewel's age. And maybe, oh, this is just an idea, teen jewelry, or maybe younger, jewelry you can make yourself . . ."

"I see where you're going," Myrna said. "It's not a bad idea. But you seem to be making a go of the store as it is."

"True. But in the winter, when there aren't as many summer people, it might be fun to have something else, something extra."

"Well, you'll have plenty of time to play around with new ideas when the summer's over," Myrna said. "You seem pretty content, being back on the island."

Lexi smiled. "I am, Mom. In spite of everything with Jesse, I'm really glad to be home."

FORTY-THREE

For a few days Sweet Hart's was flooded with customers, some wanting chocolates, others sniffing around for gossip. Clare was actually glad when a day arrived that was so intensely hot it kept everyone at the beach or in their pools or in their air-conditioned homes. She relaxed that evening by playing around with a new recipe for fish tacos, and was about to serve them to Adam and her father when Adam's beeper went off.

"Sorry about that." It was his night on call, and an islander's dog had been hit by a car. He had to leave for the animal hospital, so Clare served her father and sat with him and Ralphie while they ate.

It was two hours before Adam returned, and Clare could tell by the look on his face that he'd had to put the injured animal to sleep.

"Oh, honey. Sit down and have a beer. I've got your plate heating in the oven."

"Thanks, Clare." He collapsed into a chair at the kitchen table.

For a few minutes he just ate, staring into space, and Clare knew he was allowing the sadness of the past hour to evaporate.

She was dealing with her own emotions. She was still stunned by Jesse's absence—she thought of it as

Jesse's escape. She hoped he'd be happy, and yet the island didn't seem right, somehow, with Jesse gone.

And she was so secretly, fiercely, passionately jealous of Lexi and her baby. She loved Lexi, she wanted Lexi to be happy, and she didn't want to be filled with the poison that was envy; she knew how envy could eat away at one's heart.

When she looked at Adam, everything bad and sad and sorrowful vanished, replaced by a welling of tenderness and affection and hope. But it was too soon for them to discuss children. She was still on the birth control pill. Marriage, having a family . . . those were serious, important matters. So she kept her silence, feeling her heart swelling like the ocean during flood tide.

She forced herself to chat idly as Adam ate, about easy things—how Ralphie had fallen in love with one of her father's loafers, or perhaps she considered it a child, because she had taken to carrying it with her everywhere and sleeping with her head on it. That friends of hers had called to invite her and any guest she wanted to bring to a clambake Sunday evening.

"They're probably holding the clambake just to see who you'll bring," Adam said, and he grinned, and Clare was so glad to see him looking happy. "I wonder if they'll be surprised when you show up with me."

Adam had finished eating, and he sat in his chair,

large, masculine, relaxed, the sleeves of his blue button-down rolled up, exposing his muscular arms.

"Oh, and what makes you so sure I'll take you?" Clare teased. She moved around behind his chair and began to massage his shoulders, which were tight with exhaustion. "You aren't the only male in my life, after all." She could feel the tension leave as she rubbed his shoulders, and she bent down and teasingly drew her mouth across the back of his neck. He smelled so good, like soap and salt.

Adam groaned deeply and went lax in his chair, and all her thoughts vanished in the pleasure of touching this man.

Clare nibbled on his right ear, then slowly ran her hands up the side of his face and massaged his temples, nuzzling kisses into his hair, then kissing lightly across the top of his forehead. His head fell back, resting against her rib cage and the lower part of her breasts. She slid her hands down his face, down his neck, and continued kissing his neck while she unbuttoned his shirt and slid her hands inside. She brushed her fingertips across his nipples. She curled her fingers in his chest hair with one hand and slid the other down to his trousers. He was erect, straining his trousers.

Adam reached up and grabbed both her hands. "Clare. Your father."

"Is upstairs asleep with the bedroom door shut." She wriggled her hands free. She walked around and eased herself between Adam and the kitchen table. Without looking, she shoved his plate and glass away and lifting herself slightly, sat down on the tabletop. Adam sat in his chair and watched her as she did a slow striptease, pulling her tee over her head, unfastening her bra, lifting one hip and then the other to tug her shorts and silk thong away from her body. The kitchen light was bright, illuminating her every pore, the freckles above her bosom, the mole on her inner thigh, the moist, sweaty tangle of her pubic hair. She parted her legs.

Adam looked at her. His gaze was almost tangible. Her body trembled slightly under his intensity. He seemed to pull himself up from some profound place as he placed his hands on her thighs. He slid his hands up toward her pelvis, moving slowly. So slowly. She closed her eyes. His hands left her as he stripped off his trousers and boxers. She heard the rustle of fabric as they fell to the floor. She lay back on the table and he penetrated her, yanking her hips toward him to force himself deeper.

She raised her legs high, lifting her hips. Opening her eyes, she saw the dark thatch of his hair, and high above that, the kitchen ceiling, the ordinary ceiling. She wrapped her legs around his back. Her hairline grew damp with sweat; sweat broke out between her back and the table, allowing her to slip farther down the table, so that he was deep inside her. She clutched him against her as her body shuddered with sensation.

When he was through, he slowly lowered her hips

against the table. He was still inside her, growing limp, and she felt the sticky moisture like a glue between them. She lay against the table, catching her breath, feeling her blood thud in her chest and neck and groin. She stared at him as he leaned down over her.

He smoothed her damp hair away from her face. He put his mouth to her ear. He whispered, "Now which male do you think you'll take to the party?"

FORTY-FOUR

The hurricane started in Florida and screamed up the East Coast like a horde of hellions let loose from ancient myths. Through the night, it battered the coasts of the Carolinas. Toward dawn, it whirled toward Long Island and Connecticut. The waters around Nantucket grew choppy, the air howling as the gusts picked up speed.

When people woke on Nantucket that morning, they found gale-force winds assaulting the island. High seas surged up the beaches and crashed over the wharfs. Yachts, catboats, and Boston Whalers rolled and bobbed in the heaving water of the inner harbor, already congested with fishing trawlers looking for safe harbor. Rain slashed down over the streets, shops, houses, moors, and beaches. On TV, orange alert banners ran steadily, advising residents to remain in the safety of their houses. All ferries and planes were canceled for the day. Day camps, golf games, tennis matches, and picnics were canceled. The only shops doing any real business were the bookshops, where people flocked in, rain dripping off their slickers, to buy a good read for a stormy day. Heavy black clouds rolled overhead like tanks from an advancing army, and the birds, even the crazy gulls who liked to sail on high winds, had vanished from the sky.

The Weather Channel forecast was dire. Several merchants closed their shops and boarded up their plate-glass windows. Homeowners crisscrossed their windows with tape to keep the glass from blowing in if the hurricane hit hard.

Lexi spent a restless night, her own thoughts as turbulent as the wind that battered at her windows. When she woke at six, she was so nauseated her small apartment seemed to whirl around her. She staggered to the bathroom and vomited, then sipped warm 7-Up and chewed a saltine. The wind shrieked past her little island home like a freight train. Looking out, she saw the harbor waters tossing beneath a dark sky. She turned on the Weather Channel and watched the forecast. Should she try to open Moon Shell Beach today? Who would come out in this weather? Who would even want to walk out onto the wharfs in a storm like this?

She munched another cracker, drank more soda, and stood under a pounding hot shower. The tang of her jasmine-mint soap woke up her senses. She dried and dressed in a scarlet silk skirt and a turquoise cashmere sweater—the warmth felt good on this cold August day.

When she looked out the window again, she saw that lights had come on all over town. The beach around the town pier was empty, but the sea-green lights on the town wharf were still glowing in the gloom.

As Lexi watched, a small figure in a yellow rain slicker trudged determinedly down the beach.

"Jewel!" Lexi gasped. "You idiot!"

What was she doing? Why would the girl come out onto the pier in this storm? In a flash, Lexi knew what Jewel was hoping—so many boats had come in to shelter, perhaps a boat carrying her father would come in, too.

What the hell was Bonnie Frost thinking, letting the child out in this storm?

The wind was powerful, shoving at the girl so she had to push forward with each step to make her way down the pier. Lexi marveled at such sense of purpose, at how the power of Jewel's desires matched the towering storm.

But waves were leaping over the pier, breaking into foam, subsiding back into the water. Jewel grabbed a stanchion to steady herself against the drag.

Lexi couldn't allow the girl to stay out there. She'd bring her here; Jewel could sit here and watch from her window. Thrusting her feet into sandals, she clattered down her stairs and threw open the back door.

As she emerged from the shelter of the shop, the wind tore at her hair and clothing, whipping it in every direction.

"Jewel!" Lexi yelled, but her voice was lost in the wailing wind.

She forced herself forward, concentrating on putting one foot in front of the other as the relentless wind struck at her. Torrents of rain soaked her clothes, gluing them to her skin, while the wind yanked at her skirt like grasping hands. Her feet sank into the sodden sand as she raced over the beach.

Jewel was almost at the end of the pier now. The hood of her yellow slicker had been torn back by the wind and her red hair exploded up, flying around her head like flames.

Lexi reached the steps to the pier. She took them two at a time, and finally she was on the pier, advancing against the gale's resistance. She cupped her mouth with her hands, calling "Jewel!" The girl didn't hear.

Suddenly a monumental wall of water reared up. It crashed down on the pier with the elemental power of Niagara Falls, ruthlessly sweeping the girl off the pier and into the heaving waters.

"Jewel!" Lexi screamed, and ran.

FORTY-FIVE

Clare's dreams were turbulent. She woke early, exhausted, and agitated, to find the island under siege from gale-force winds.

Adam phoned to say he'd be at the MSPCA all day—the hospital was inland, and his calendar was full of appointments.

"Are you going to open your store today?" he asked.

"I am. Stormy days are often really profitable. Sometimes the crazy weather makes people crave chocolate."

"Well, be careful," Adam cautioned. "Keep your eye on the winds. This is going to be one hell of a storm."

Adam's concern warmed and calmed her. "I'll be careful," she promised.

She pulled on an ankle-skimming skirt patch-worked in lavenders and blues and a scoop-necked azure cotton sweater. She wrapped a striped red scarf around her hair to keep it away from her face as she went out into the wind, but the moment she set foot out the door, she knew today was not a day for her bike. She put the leash on Ralphie and took her into the yard for a quick toilet run, then let the dog back inside. Ralphie, freaked by the weather, raced back up the stairs and under her bed.

"Bye, Dad!" she yelled.

"Be careful!" he yelled back.

It was easy to find a parking space near Commercial Wharf. Anyone with half a brain would stay home, Clare thought wryly as she left her van and battled her way over the cobblestones to her shop. Lights were on all over town, but she could see *Closed* signs on some of the other shop doors.

She unlocked Sweet Hart's and nearly fell inside. It was a relief to get out of the tearing winds, but even inside the sound of the storm was overwhelming. Stripping off her raincoat, she hit the Play button on her answering machine.

"Clare," Marlene said. "You're not going to open today, are you? Let me know."

Clare phoned Marlene back. "I'm here, but you stay home. I thought I'd open, but it's pretty bad out here on the harbor, so I'll probably leave soon."

"You should," Marlene told her. "The Weather Channel's announcing a severe storm alert for the island."

"Well," Clare answered, "they don't always get it right. But I'll be careful."

She went around her shop, automatically making mental lists of all the tasks needing to be done—shelves dusted and restocked, the glass display case washed again, and if nothing else, she could spend some time in her office paying bills. She flipped her sign to *Open*, then headed back to her office.

She booted up her computer. While it geared up, she looked out the window at the harbor. Waves spewed upward like geysers, sending boats and small craft rolling and dropping. The town pier was reduced to a long ledge of gray, drenched with foaming surf—and a small figure in a yellow rain slicker was staggering toward the end.

"Jewel, what the hell are you doing?" Clare shouted. She had to call Bonnie Frost, tell her to come get her daughter. She grabbed her cell phone, then noticed a woman stumble up the steps and onto the wharf. The wind tore the woman's clothes into flags of red and blue. It was Lexi.

"Well, thank heavens for that," Clare said aloud, relieved. Lexi would bring Jewel back to safety.

A violent swell exploded over the pier and surged back, sucking everything in its path down into the harbor waters. Jewel was swept from the pier. Suddenly she was only a spot of yellow among small craft bouncing in the frenzied water. Then she disappeared.

Clare saw Lexi run.

Yanking open her back door, Clare raced outside, along the bulkhead and onto the beach. Her sandals slowed her down. She kicked them off. Her bare feet gripped the cold wet sand as she ran for the pier. She kept her eyes on Lexi and saw Lexi dive. Clare sprinted down the pier, her heart bursting with adrenaline and fear.

Rain stung her eyes as she searched the seething waters. She saw a smudge of yellow. Then she glimpsed Lexi, a blur of blues, lifted up on a wave and slammed into the side of a bobbing boat. Lexi sank into the perilous depths. Clare dove.

The water was alive, churning and bubbling, raging with power. But she spotted Jewel! The girl's limp body was being sucked downward by the relentless sea. Clare kicked her feet, struck out with her arms, and fought her way toward Jewel's shining yellow rain slicker. The sea tossed Clare upward, as if she weighed nothing, and she gasped, catching her breath, then dove again.

She saw Lexi flailing toward Jewel. Lexi's long blond hair floated out around her head in a halo, her clothes were pressed against her by the force of the current, her skirt streamed behind her like a tail. Lexi grabbed hold of Jewel's arm.

Clare clawed through the roiling waters, her lungs bursting, flailing, clutching, catching nothing. Desperately she reached out. She caught hold of Jewel's slippery raincoat. Her eyes met Lexi's. Immediately Clare and Lexi began kicking, making their ascent. Their hair streamed around them as they swam.

They burst upward, gasped for air, choked on water and together fought through the waves toward a wooden ladder nailed to the end of the pier. The wind made a sailboat veer hard at Clare, seeming to lunge right for her, but she jerked sideways out of its path.

Lexi grabbed the ladder with one hand. Clare grabbed it, too. Lexi yelled and pointed up. Clare nodded. While Clare kept a tight hold on Jewel, Lexi pulled herself up the three steps and onto the pier. She lay flat on her stomach. She reached down with both hands, grabbed Jewel's shoulders, and while Clare struggled to push, hauled the child up onto the wet boards.

Her sodden clothes were so heavy, Clare almost couldn't make her way up the ladder. She collapsed on the wood.

"Can't . . . stay . . . here!" Lexi panted. Blood streamed from her head and her arms.

Jewel was bleeding, too. Clare nodded and forced herself to her feet. Lexi took Jewel beneath her shoulders. Clare grabbed her feet. With the child swinging between them like a hammock, tripping on their soaked clothing, they staggered up the pier toward the shore. An onslaught of waves slammed against them, knocking them nearly to their knees, but they recovered and struggled on, dragging themselves and Jewel toward the solidity of land.

part five

FORTY-SIX

Suddenly, sirens screamed. Brakes shrieked. People shouted. The pier shuddered under the weight of men running toward them. Hands reached out for them. Waves spewed and slammed over them.

"We've got her!" a man yelled, but the howling wind deafened Lexi.

Someone tried to take Jewel, but Lexi's icy hands were clamped like vises around the girl's shoulders.

"It's okay!" The man put his arm around Lexi as another man caught Jewel's sagging body. "We're EMTs. We've got her now. We're getting her into an ambulance. You can let go now."

"Lexi!" Clare stumbled against her. "It's okay. They can take care of Jewel. You've got to let them take care of you."

As Lexi surrendered Jewel's weight, all strength went out of her and she fell to her knees.

A moment later, Lexi was lifted up into strong male arms. She was too exhausted even to reach around the man's neck, so she collapsed, head hanging down, heaving for breath, nearly fainting. He strode away from the frothing pier, toward the street, where police cars angled next to two ambulances, all lights flashing.

The man bent, laying Lexi on a stretcher.

"I don't need this!" Lexi tried to sit up. "I'm fine, I—"

Clare appeared, brown hair darkened and dripping from the water. "You're bleeding, Lexi. You've got to go to the hospital."

"No!" Lexi cried, struggling to get off the stretcher. "I'm fine!"

But she wasn't fine. As she crumpled back onto the stretcher, she knew.

Someone covered her with a blanket. She was elevated, riding through the air. She wanted to roll time back, she wanted the howling storm to retreat, she needed to be whole again. But she wasn't whole, she was injured, and gut-wrenching sobs shook her as the medics attended to her body, fastening an oxygen tube into her nose, strapping on a blood pressure cuff, slicing her sodden clothing to find her several injuries and staunch the flowing blood.

"I'm going with her." Clare, a blanket draped around her shoulders, pushed her way through the crowd into Lexi's field of vision.

"Sorry," the EMT said. "Rules—"

"Oh, shut up, Donnie!" Clare snapped. "I used to babysit you, for Heaven's sake. Think of the stuff I could tell your mother!" Clare scrambled up into the ambulance, managing to keep hold of Lexi's hand through all the commotion. "Jewel's going to be all right. I saw them put her in the other ambulance, they were doing CPR, she has a pulse, she's going to be okay."

"You're okay, too!" Donnie assured Lexi. "You've got some deep gashes along your left side and—" He glanced at the other EMT, an older woman, who was packing towels between Lexi's legs. "You're going to be okay!"

The ambulance swayed and screamed through the narrow streets to the small two-story cottage hospital. Lexi closed her eyes. She was aware of the movement of the vehicle and the chatter of the EMTs, of her wet hair dripping onto her face and shoulders, and of pain, and sadness, and how the violent thumping of her heart was slowing. She couldn't stop crying. Her chest heaved, her entire spirit raged like the storm tearing its way across the island. She was aware of Clare's hand tightly holding hers, security in the midst of pandemonium.

At the hospital, Lexi was carried into the emergency room. Immediately nurses and doctors were at her side. Clare was firmly detached and sent off to another room to be checked on. Lexi was undressed and redressed in a hospital gown. A nurse pierced her arm with a needle and threaded in an IV. A warmth spread through Lexi, calming her tears. Words floated above her like invisible birds: "local anesthesia," "stitches here," "swab, nurse."

"There's something going on down here," a doctor said, removing the packed towels from between Lexi's shaking legs.

"I'm having a miscarriage," she told him.

"Oh, hon," said the nurse, and Lexi was glad that it was summer, that the hospital was staffed with visiting medical personnel, that this nurse didn't know her, didn't know anything about Lexi at all.

The anesthesia took hold, and Lexi sank into sleep.

FORTY-SEVEN

She woke in a hospital room. She was warm, and woozy, and comfortable beneath the white blanket and sheet.

Clare was seated in a chair next to her, wearing sweatpants and a sweatshirt, her brown hair drying in a tangle of curls. "Hey, Hero," Clare said softly. "How you doin'?"

Lexi managed a smile. "How's Jewel?"

"She's fine. She's in the next room. She doesn't want to stay, but they're insisting on keeping her overnight for observation." Clare moved over to lean on the side of Lexi's bed. "Get this. Bonnie and Ken and the baby went off-island two days ago. They were supposed to come home last night but couldn't because of the weather. So Jewel was staying with Amber Young! Amber had no idea Jewel had sneaked out of the house. She feels terrible, I'm sure. But I should stop babbling, everyone's waiting outside to see you, I can't hog you like this, the nurse said only one person in here at a time and I forced them to let me be first."

"Wait, Clare." Lexi reached out to grasp Clare's hand. "I lost the baby, didn't I?"

Clare's face fell. She nodded. She put her other hand on top of Lexi's.

347

"Look," Lexi said urgently. "Don't tell anyone. I hadn't even told my mother I was pregnant. I hadn't even told Jesse. And I just couldn't stand it if Amber and Spring and everyone knew."

Clare smiled wickedly. "You'd probably get a lot of business."

Lexi snorted. "Great. Thanks a lot for that."

More somberly, Clare promised, "I won't tell anyone anything. Besides, this town's got quite enough to gossip about. Not that our little swim wasn't dramatic enough, but the storm destroyed the beachfront out at Sconset. Six houses went down. And—" she started laughing. "This is the best! Harsh Marsh was getting into her car when a tree branch blew down! She's fine, but she lay there on her front lawn, trapped beneath the branch, and getting completely soaked until a neighbor across the street saw her. She's in a room down the hall!"

"You girls!" The door flew open and Myrna came in, with Fred following right behind her. "I could hear you laughing!" She threw herself at Lexi, hugging her, kissing her face, smoothing back her hair. "You brave girl! We're so proud of you!"

Lexi's father stood shyly at the foot of the bed. He grabbed Lexi's toes through the blanket and squeezed them, as if he were shaking hands. "You did a magnificent thing, Lexi, saving that child's life."

Lexi's eyes met Clare's. "I didn't do it alone."

FORTY-EIGHT

Clare knew the day started early at hospitals, so she was up and dressed and striding into the doors of the Nantucket Cottage Hospital by eight.

She found Lexi sitting up in bed behind a hospital table, staring at a pile of undistinguished mush in a stainless-steel bowl.

"Morning, Lexi!" Clare greeted her brightly.

Lexi was crying, fat tears rolling down her cheeks. "Do they think I'm *toothless?*" She covered her face with her hands. "Oh, it's not the oatmeal, it tastes fine, I'm just . . . I'm just a total mess. Oh, Clare, I *hurt* so much. I don't mean the cuts in my thigh and side, that hurts, of course, but it's my . . ." She couldn't go on.

Clare moved close to the bed. "It's your womb. It's your womb, and your belly and your pelvic muscles and your heart and your soul."

Lexi nodded, stifling a cry.

Clare put a woven basket on the table. "What does the doctor say?"

Lexi lifted her head, sniffing back tears. "She said I can go home today, this morning. I have to have bed rest, I can't open the shop. Mom and Dad want me to go there for a few days. Mom says she's looking forward to babying me." The word *baby* caught in her throat.

"That's good. It will be nice for you to have someone taking care of you. Until then, I brought this." Clare lifted a plate from the basket. It was an antique china plate with a pattern of roses and blueberries rimmed with gold. "I baked these for you this morning." She unwrapped two blueberry muffins and a chunk of unsalted butter. She lifted out a small crystal glass and, opening a small thermos, she poured orange juice into it. "Fresh squeezed," she told Lexi. When she opened a larger thermos, the delicious aroma of coffee swirled into the air. She brought out a cup and saucer that matched the plate, and a set of flatware, and a cotton napkin printed with daisies and lilacs. She moved the hospital bowl of porridge to the top of the dresser across the room.

"Is this a bad moment?"

Bonnie Frost stood in the doorway. She didn't have her baby with her. Her hair fell glossily to her shoulders. She wore white trousers and a lacy sweater and her diamond ear studs glittered when she moved.

Clare looked at Lexi, who shrugged and nodded slightly.

"Sure," Lexi said. "Come in. If you don't mind my eating in front of you. Clare brought me breakfast and I can't wait to drink this coffee."

Bonnie sidled into the room, shutting the door behind her. "How are you, Lexi?"

"I'm fine. I'm leaving the hospital later today."

"They said you got pretty badly cut up."

Lexi took a sip of coffee and moaned in pleasure. "I'll be okay."

Bonnie moved cautiously closer to the bed. "I don't know how to thank you, Lexi, for saving Jewel. And you, too, Clare, I know you helped, I heard all about it. You were both so brave, and I'm so grateful." Tears filled her eyes.

Clare studied Bonnie quietly.

"I know," Bonnie went on, her words coming out in a rush, "I know you both think I'm a terrible mother, that I don't give enough attention to Jewel, that all I care about is Ken and the baby, but that's not true. You've got to understand, Jewel is such a *stubborn* child!" Angry tears welled in her eyes. "She's always been headstrong, independent, obstinate! Just ask any of her teachers! She's a very smart girl, she's precocious, but that doesn't mean she's easy to deal with! It makes it harder, in a way. Because she's so smart, she always thinks she's right, and she's *not,* she's just a child!"

"I'm not judging you, Bonnie," Lexi said quietly. "I wouldn't."

Bonnie tossed her pretty head. "Well, everyone else in this town does!" She glared at Clare and Lexi. "You both just wait, you just wait until you have your own child someday! You'll be surprised! They aren't little bits of clay you can mold, oh, no, they come out complete with their own personalities and *you're* the one who has to change!"

351

Lexi said quietly, "Jewel is a wonderful girl. You should be proud of her."

"Oh, yes, you see her out on the pier, the devoted daughter, with her books and her adult vocabulary, but I'm telling you, she's a child and she's a willful one. Do you think she'll help me with the baby? Oh, no. Do you think she'll give Ken a chance? Not on your life! The looks she gives him would cut glass! Sure, she's book smart, she's a clever little intellectual, but she's a child, and with all her smartness, she was stupid enough to go out on that pier during the storm yesterday, she was stupid enough to almost *die* looking for her precious father!"

Lexi said, "I'm sorry—"

Clare interrupted. "It's not Lexi's fault Jewel went out there yesterday."

"I'm not saying it's Lexi's fault!" Bonnie snapped. She reached in her shoulder bag, pulled out a tissue and blew her nose, scattering the floor with crumbs. "Frankie's crackers," she explained absentmindedly. She took a deep breath. "I didn't come here to criticize you, Lexi. I came here to thank you—and you, too, Clare. But I also came to ask you to help me. Jewel is *my* daughter. But for some reason, she adores you, Lexi, she hero-worships you. She thinks you hung the fucking moon, as a matter of fact, and it won't make any difference if I tell her I don't want her to hang around with you, she won't obey me."

Lexi gasped. "You don't want me to spend any more time with Jewel?"

"No, I'm not asking that. I'm not even asking you to tell Jewel to forget about her father. I'm saying, could you just not go out on that damned pier with her?"

Lexi looked relieved. "Of course." She leaned toward Bonnie. "Bonnie, I'm not trying to compete with you for Jewel's affection or anything like that. It's just that she's such a likable kid." She glanced at Clare. "She reminds me of myself and Clare when we were that age."

Bonnie snorted. "Yeah, I can see that."

"How's Jewel?" Clare asked.

Bonnie shrugged. "Do you think I'd be in here if she weren't okay? She doesn't have any injuries from yesterday—you got the worst of it, Lexi. She's full of energy. And she *still* keeps looking out the damned window, looking for her father's boat. I'm going to take her home and spoil her with ice cream and some new videos and books, although I don't want to be rewarding her for doing something stupid like she did yesterday."

"I'd like to see her," Lexi said.

Bonnie hesitated. "Well, all right. Sometime. But Lexi, come on, you've got to tell her you won't go out on the pier with her again. I mean, don't you feel *some* responsibility here?"

"I do," Lexi admitted. "And I agree. I'll tell Jewel I won't go out on the pier with her again.

I'll tell her she can come to my shop and hang out with me."

Clare suggested, "And maybe there's some little beach Lexi could take Jewel to, sometime. Lex knows a lot about shells, and marine life . . ."

Bonnie released a martyr's sigh. "I guess, Lexi, if you want to take Jewel to the beach now and then, that would be okay."

For the first time all morning, Lexi looked happy. She flashed a grateful glance at Clare, then said to Bonnie, "It's a deal."

FORTY-NINE

The day was dazzling with sunlight. The grasses and bushes made whispering noises as they wound their way toward Moon Shell Beach. Adam carried the wicker picnic basket and cooler while Clare brought the blanket and beach bag. They'd spent the morning entertaining Lexi, still convalescing at her parents' house. Then Adam told Clare he wanted to take her out to lunch. She thought a picnic for just the two of them on Moon Shell Beach might be nice, and now, here they were.

They stood on the small crescent of sand, just staring for a few moments at the sparkling water and all the colorful kayaks, sailboats, and power-boats crisscrossing the harbor.

"I can't believe you girls found this place when you were so young," Adam said. "And no one else I know has ever discovered it."

Clare flapped out the blanket, arranging it on the sand. "*I* can't believe I stopped coming here after Lexi left the island. Well, I was so busy with school and the shop, but still, I went to Surfside and Jetties and Dionis . . . I just never thought of it."

Adam set the basket on one corner of the blanket. As he pulled his tee off over his head, he asked, his words muffled, "You never brought Jesse here?"

Clare untied her sarong, letting the sun fall on her body in its little red bikini. "You know, I never did. Isn't that odd?"

"Works for me," Adam said with a grin. He wore ancient faded madras swim trunks.

"Madras is so yesterday," Clare mocked.

"Yeah, well, these are the most comfortable ones I own." He sat down next to Clare and rummaged in the picnic basket. He set out a plate of cheese and crackers, then, from the ice cooler, he lifted out a bottle of Dom Perignon.

"Champagne?" Clare was surprised. "On a Sunday afternoon?"

"You deserve it. You saved my sister's life."

"That's a gross exaggeration. I just helped her bring Jewel out of the water."

"In gale-force winds. While Lexi was hurt."

"Well," Clare said, "since you insist . . ."

Adam eased off the cork, working it upward with his thumbs. It flew out into the water, making a splash. He brought out two flutes and poured the bubbling liquid into them.

"Real glasses, not plastic? Wow. I'm impressed." Clare took her glass and for a moment just stared at the bubbles popping and floating upward toward the foamy top.

"Toast," she said to Adam.

"Toast," he agreed. "To life."

"To life!"

They sipped.

"Oh, man, this is so good!" Clare stretched out her arms expansively. "What could be better than this day and this champagne?"

"Also," Adam said quietly, "I have an ulterior motive."

"Oh, yeah?" Clare slid down, belly up, resting on her arms, letting her head fall back, exposing her neck to the sun. The warmth was so sweet. She glanced over at Adam, so large and male and real and solid. "You going to seduce me? I've never had sex on Moon Shell Beach."

"Seduction? Maybe later. Proposal first."

Clare blinked. She turned to sit, cross-legged, looking at Adam. "Huh?"

Adam wore an almost bashful expression. "Look, Clare. I've done a lot of thinking since you went into the harbor like that. I know you and I haven't been together very long, and I know I might be just the rebound guy after Jesse—"

"You aren't," she told him.

"I believe you. I believe that. And I know how I feel about you. I love you."

Clare's heart jumped. "Oh, Adam!" She threw her arms around him and hugged him. "Ooops. Sorry, I didn't mean to slosh champagne down your back."

"It'll wash off." He took her arms and pushed her back a bit, so he could look her steadily in the eye. "I want to marry you, Clare. I want to marry you and fill a house with children. I don't want to be sensible and wait a year until we're good and sure we want to be together—"

"But we *are* sure!" Clare laughed with delight. "I mean, *I'm* sure. And obviously you are, too, since you're proposing to me! Oh, Adam, I love you, I do! Oh, Adam, I want you to kiss me like crazy, but where can I put this champagne?"

He looked very sexy, with a big confident grin on his face as he took her glass and set both inside the cooler, anchoring them firmly in the ice. "So," he said, "are you saying yes?"

"Absolutely," Clare exclaimed. "Yes!"

"In that case . . ." He unbuttoned the small pocket on his swim trunks and brought out a diamond ring. He held it out to her.

"Oh, Adam." She gazed down at the diamond, which was a considerable rock.

"It's not a family heirloom. It's not my mother's. I don't want the kind of marriage they had. I want our own kind of marriage. And I want you to have a real sparkler."

"It certainly sparkles. Wow, Adam." She lifted her eyes to his. "Will you put it on my finger?"

She held out her left hand, and he slid the ring on.

She was astonished. "It fits perfectly!"

"I borrowed your jade ring to take to the jeweler to be sure I got the right size."

Clare tilted her hand left and right, watching the rainbows flying from the stone. "It's huge! Oh,

Adam, I'm going to cry!" She held out her hand in a stop signal and stared at the diamond. "Oh, *wait* till the Barbie Dolls get a load of this!" She clapped her hands over her mouth. "I can't believe I just said that! How petty of me! But Adam . . . I can't wait to show it to everyone! Oh, my gosh, we're going to have so much fun, telling everyone we're getting married! And we'll have a wedding, and wedding showers, and lots of parties!"

He settled back on the sand, arms around his knees, listening to her babble, amused by her excitement.

"And we'll live in a house together!" She felt her eyes go wide at the thought.

"That's usually what married people do."

"And we'll have children! Oh, Adam!" She launched herself at him so hard and fast she knocked him over backward, and she wrestled around on top of him, kissing his mouth, his face, his neck, his arms and chest and belly. "Oh, I love you! Oh, I'm so happy! I've never been so happy in my life!" Suddenly she rolled off him and sat up and held out her hand. "I don't know what I want to do more, kiss you or look at my ring!"

"Kiss me," Adam told her.

And she did.

FIFTY

Lexi lay in her old twin bed, the one she'd slept in as a teenager. She'd slept well, and the morning had passed quickly with Clare and Adam around. When they went off, she returned to her bedroom to rest. The doctors had insisted she rest. She wished she could fall back asleep. Her energy was returning, and her various aches and pains were subsiding, but her heart was heavy.

She heard her mother coming down the hall. She closed her eyes tight, playing possum as she had so many times as a child. She just didn't want to deal with her mother, or anyone right now. She didn't even want to deal with herself.

The bedroom door opened a crack. She heard her mother's breathing. The door closed. Lexi snuggled down into her pillow and tried to relax her body, to return to the comfort of sleep.

But no, it wasn't going to work. She couldn't will herself back to sleep. She couldn't even conjure up a fantasy to entertain her while she rested. For the first time, she wished she had a television in her bedroom. It would be a relief to let some show— *Seinfeld*, *Scrubs*, even *Lassie*—flicker before her, taking her from her own thoughts.

Beyond her door, her mother's dogs went into

barking fits. Voices broke the silence—laughter and shouts. Doors slammed. People clattered down the hall, and all at once her bedroom door opened again. Lexi opened her eyes.

"Wake up!" It was Clare, Clare smelling like sunshine in her red bikini and sarong and jeweled flip-flops and sunburned nose. She was glowing. "You have to wake up!"

Lexi shifted around in bed. "What's going on?"

Over Clare's shoulder, Adam appeared, and behind him their mother and father, and the Jack Russells Buddha and Pest yelping all around everyone.

"I'm engaged to your brother!" Clare bounced on the bed. "Sit up. Here, let me put another pillow behind you. Lean forward. Now look!"

Lexi looked. "Oh, *wow,* Clare!" She glanced at her brother. He was grinning as if he'd just invented laughing gas. "What a big fat diamond! Adam, you're the man!"

"Yup," Adam agreed.

"They're going to get married!" Myrna was practically levitating.

"That's usually what getting engaged means," Lexi said drily. She looked at Clare. "Congratulations. I'm so so glad for you. For both of you. For all of us."

"I'm going to be your sister!" Clare said. "*Finally,* we can make it official!"

Lexi laughed. "This is so fabulous."

"I'm thinking a church wedding," Myrna said. "Or maybe the beach. Or Brant Point, by the lighthouse? Of course it depends on what time of year—did you say when the wedding will be?"

"Mom"—Adam wrapped an arm around his mother—"we just this minute got engaged. We haven't set the date yet."

"But soon, right?" Myrna asked.

"Soon, right," Adam agreed.

"Penny can be my matron of honor, but *you* have to be my maid of honor," Clare told Lexi. Tilting her head, she said teasingly, "I'm thinking eggplant dresses with big puffy sleeves and a huge bow over the butt."

"Oh, Clare." Myrna looked horrified. "I'm not so sure . . ."

"It's okay, Mom," Lexi assured her mother. "Clare's just playing."

Adam said, "I brought a bottle of champagne."

"Oh, yummy!" Myrna clapped her hands. "I'll get the glasses."

"Do you feel like getting up?" Clare asked.

"Sure," Lexi told her. "I'm fine. Just give me a minute to pull on some clothes." On impulse, she reached out and hugged Clare hard. "I'm so glad for you. And I'm so glad for my brother."

"I'm going to call your father," Adam told Clare. "I want him to come over here and join us."

"Oh, good idea!" Clare said.

Myrna said, "Tell him to bring his dog."

Lexi pulled on loose cotton trousers and a big button-down shirt. She shuffled into the living room where Adam helped her settle on the sofa, her feet on an ottoman and a blanket tucked around her feet. She smiled fondly at everyone as the commotion continued. George Hart arrived with Ralph, and for a while the dogs stole the show as they got acquainted.

"I should go get Bella and Lucky," Adam said.

"Another time, maybe," Myrna told him. "There's enough chaos now."

George shook Adam's hand and congratulated the couple and sat down across from Lexi, looking slightly dazed. He'd shaved and dressed, although Lexi noticed he'd forgotten to put on socks. Lots of men wore loafers without socks, but few went sockless in wingtips.

Myrna brought out a platter of smoked bluefish pâté and crackers and one of smoked salmon and rye. The group gathered around the coffee table with their champagne.

The chatter died down as everyone munched, and into the silence, George Hart said, "I've been thinking."

Everyone looked surprised, not that George had been thinking, of course he was always doing that, but that he was speaking up.

"When Clare marries Adam, my house will be far too big for me alone. I've been wanting to spend more time in Boston—research for my book, you see. Clare, I think I might put the house on the market, and buy myself a smaller place here. I could give you and Adam a nice chunk of money for your wedding present, and still have some funds left over for something like a little flat in Boston for me."

Clare's jaw dropped. "Well, Dad!"

"I think that's a great idea, George," Adam said. "But look, don't you worry about Clare and me. I already own a house. It's small, and we might need to get a bigger one—"

Lexi shifted uncomfortably on the sofa, but kept a look of cheerful interest on her face. How lovely, she thought, even befuddled George Hart is getting his act together, and here Clare and Adam are already planning on getting a bigger house because obviously they want to have children soon, and lots of them. She saw the affectionate looks flying between her father and mother, and between Clare and Adam, and even George's dog Ralphie looked ecstatic as she trotted around, nosing Buddha's and Pest's butts.

I'll get well, she quietly assured herself. *I'll get over this. I'll get strong, and I'll have some tests run and see if any doctor thinks I'll ever be able to carry a baby to term, not that I'll ever be able to get pregnant again since I've so totally gone off men.* She would much rather be sitting here, with cuts on her legs and a cramping, empty belly, than back in New York with Ed Hardin, or anywhere in the world with Ed, for that matter. It was right for her to be here. She was sure of that. And someday she might meet a good man.

She wondered where Jesse was. Wouldn't he have needed some kind of visa to get into Russia? Did he even have a passport? She had really liked Oksana, and she found herself wishing hard, with complete sincerity, that Jesse would stay true to her. Labinsk, Russia, might just be exotic enough that life there would keep Jesse challenged and stimulated, and he would need Oksana to center him.

The dogs, all three of them, suddenly exploded into barking fits.

Myrna said, "Who can *that* be?"

The dogs paraded to the door in a little marching band of wagging tails. Myrna followed them into the hall, and returned. Behind her came Jewel and Bonnie, with baby Frankie on her back.

Jewel wore a blue-and-white-striped cotton sundress, the terribly simple Nantucket kind that probably cost the earth. Her hair was pulled back in a ponytail and tied with a sparkly flowered band. She looked shy, with her shoulders nearly squeezed up to her ears.

Bonnie announced proprietarily, "Jewel has a present for Lexi. And one for you, too, Clare. To thank you both for saving her life."

"Well, goodness, how nice!" Myrna went all hostessy. "Come in, come in, would you like some champagne? Jewel, how about a glass of apple juice? Or orange juice, but that's not very celebratory, or we have Coke, or diet ginger ale."

Adam lifted baby Frankie off Bonnie's back. "Hey, guy, are those teeth I'm seeing?"

Frankie chortled and squealed and drooled down his chin.

Myrna settled Bonnie in a chair with a glass of champagne, then went off to the kitchen for apple juice. Bashfully, Jewel handed Clare a small brightly colored paper bag, then sat down on the sofa next to Lexi and handed Lexi a bag, too.

"Oh!" Clare lifted out a beaded bracelet. A pink heart hung from it, etched with her name. "Jewel, did you make this?"

Jewel nodded proudly. "I have a kit. You make the shape and design, then bake it in a little oven. But be careful, the heart is fragile. It might break."

Clare looked over at Lexi and smiled.

"Look at yours!" Jewel told Lexi.

Lexi opened her little bag and reached into the nest of tissue paper. Her beaded bracelet was similar to Clare's. Dangling from it were three silver stars, a crescent moon, and a shining moon shell with "Lexi" written on it.

"It's perfect!" Lexi hugged the girl. "Thank you! Can you fasten it on me?"

Ralphie chose this moment to investigate Frankie's bare toes. She licked them, sending the baby into screams of delight.

"Oh, he's so cute, can I hold him?" Myrna asked.

"Are you okay?" Jewel asked Lexi shyly.

"I'm fine. Just a few cuts that need to heal. How about you? That's quite a bruise you have on your forehead."

Jewel touched it delicately. "It hurts a bit, but that's really my only injury. Did you know we're going to be in the newspaper next week? Maybe even pictures of us?" Her expression changed. Soberly, she added, "Not that I'm proud of what I did, I know it was stupid, and it endangered me and you and Clare as well and I'll never do anything like that again."

Bonnie nodded, satisfied by her daughter's speech.

"Would you like some more champagne?" Fred asked.

"Well . . ." Bonnie relaxed into the chair. "I don't know when I've had champagne in the middle of the day. But sure, I guess so. It's kind of cool to be with both my children—while someone else is holding that very heavy little boy!"

"I like holding him," Adam assured her.

FIFTY-ONE

Sunday afternoon, Clare and Adam lay in his bed, curled up with each other, lazy and sated after a long session of making love and a delicious nap.

"Hungry?" Adam asked.

"Mmmm," Clare responded, snuggling closer to him. "I'll be hungry in a minute."

Bella and Lucky, who had been ordered off the bed earlier, stood at attention, quivering with anticipation.

"I wasn't talking to you two fools," Adam told them. "I know *you're* always ready to eat."

They both jumped when the phone rang. Adam lifted himself up on one elbow to check out the Caller ID. It was his day off from the MSPCA. Miranda was taking the emergencies.

Adam frowned. "Logan Airport?"

Clare stretched and yawned. "Pick it up." She was so relaxed, she didn't know if she could summon the energy to shower. Perhaps if she made a new pot of coffee . . .

"Holy shit, man!" Adam exploded. "Clare—it's *Tris!*"

"Tris?" Clare sat up straight. "How can it be Tris? Tris is—"

Adam had thrown himself out of bed and was

pacing the floor, nodding his head as he listened. His energy was contagious—both dogs trailed him, watching him nervously. Clare found herself out of bed and pulling on clothes without realizing what she was doing, she was so focused on Adam's conversation.

"Thank God you're alive, Tris, thank God, thank God," Adam said fervently.

Where? Clare mouthed. *How? What happened?*

Adam waved at Clare, holding off her questions while he listened. "Yeah, I've heard about Sable Island, it's a notorious shipwreck site, man, what an ordeal, are you okay?" He listened for a while, then said in a quieter voice, "Yeah, well, I guess we kind of thought you'd gone under, Tris. It's been three months . . ."

"Jewel never thought he died," Clare reminded Adam. "Jewel's been waiting for him."

Adam nodded at Clare. "Jewel waited for you almost every day at the town pier, Tris. That's true, man, she really did. At the very end of the pier. She never gave up hope. I know, Tris, it's awesome." Adam's eyes filled with tears and his voice thickened. "I'm so glad you're alive, Tris. Man, I'm so glad." He strode into the bathroom, grabbed a handful of toilet paper and blew his nose. Returning to the bedroom, he said, "I don't know, I'll ask Clare."

Clare was nearly dancing with excitement. "Ask me what?"

"Hang on, Tris, let me tell Clare—" Clamping the phone to his chest, he said, "Tris is at the airport in Boston! The captain of the fishing vessel that found him loaned him money for airfare. His flight to Nantucket is about to be called. He'll be here in forty-five minutes! He's been trying to reach Bonnie and Jewel, but all he can get is their answering machine. Do you know where Jewel is?"

Clare shook her head. "I can call Lexi and find out whether she knows . . ."

"Look, man," Adam said into the phone. "We'll find Jewel. We'll meet you at the airport. Nantucket Airlines. Got it. Jesus Christ, Tris, this is a fucking miracle, you know? Yeah, Tris, I love you, too, buddy."

Adam tossed the phone on the bed, picked Clare up in his arms, and swung her around. "Tris is alive!"

The dogs caught the mood, dancing and barking and pawing at Adam and Clare, wanting to join the fun.

"You're making me dizzy," Clare told Adam. "Slow down. And put some clothes on before your animals scratch the family jewels."

"Right." Adam let go of Clare and stared around the room, dazed and ebullient. "Right."

"Your pants are on the chair," Clare informed him. "Now tell me, where has Tris *been?*"

"It's amazing, Clare." Adam pulled on his T-shirt and shorts as he talked. "His boat was wrecked near Sable Island, up in Nova Scotia. He ended up on a smaller island near Sable Island, completely uninhabited, but people have stayed there before, maybe to fish, because there were a couple of old shacks and some canned goods. He figures he spent the first month just mostly sleeping, he thinks he had a concussion. He was completely naked, he had no matches, no cell phone—he found some old jackets in the shacks—and then finally just early this morning some Newfoundland fishermen anchored near the island. He got their attention. The captain of the boat gave him some clothes, got him to Grand Manon Island, loaned him some money for airfare. He flew from there to Boston. He's been trying to reach Jewel, but Bonnie doesn't answer her phone." He looked wildly around the room. "Where are my car keys?"

"On the bedside table." Clare pointed to where the keys lay in clear sight. "Perhaps I should drive?"

"No, no, I'm fine." Adam grabbed up the keys. "Let's go." The dogs milled around his legs, whimpering, anxious now that he was leaving.

"Wait a minute," Clare told him. "Let's give the dogs their breakfast."

They emptied dry food into the bowls, then raced out of the house.

"Wait!" Clare stopped with her hand on the passenger door. "Let me get my cell phone. I'll try calling Bonnie and Jewel while we drive."

"Good idea."

When she returned, cell phone in hand, Adam had the engine running. Clare jumped in and they tore out of the driveway and down the street.

"Careful," she warned. "The last thing we want right now is to get stopped by a cop."

"Right. You're right." Adam eased up on the gas but his leg jiggled with excess adrenaline.

"Damn!" Clare stared at the cell phone. "I don't know Bonnie Frost's number, do you?"

"Phone Lexi."

Clare punched in Lexi's number and got her machine. She tried calling the boutique, but it was closed. She dialed Lexi's home number again and left a message: "Lexi! You won't believe it! Tris is alive! He's flying home now, Adam and I are on our way to pick him up at the airport. He's been trying to reach Jewel, but Bonnie's not home. Do you know where they are? Listen, phone me on Adam's cell." She recited the number, then clicked off.

Adam was focused now, steering through the narrow side lanes and one-way streets with caution as vacationing pedestrians and bike riders wandered dreamily into the traffic.

"Who else can we call?" Clare wondered.

Adam said, "Directory assistance."

But Clare was already punching in her father's number. "Dad? Listen, can you look up a phone number for me? Bonnie Frost, on Main Street." She shared the news with her father, got the number, and dialed. The machine answered. "Bonnie, it's Clare. Tris said he's been trying to reach you—I know he's left messages for you—isn't it miraculous? Listen, Adam and I are on the way to the airport to get Tris. Call us and tell us where you are—where Jewel is. He wants to see Jewel." She left Adam's cell number.

"Hey!" Adam slammed on the brakes and pulled to the side of Orange Street. "Maybe Jewel's out on the town pier."

Clare thought about this. "She promised to stop going . . ."

"But she's a kid. You know how kids bend rules. Maybe she's hanging out nearby . . ."

"It's worth checking."

"It won't take more than five minutes. We won't be late meeting Tris—"

"And it would be so great if we had Jewel with us when he gets off the plane!"

Adam steered the car to the nearest side street and then down to Dover and over to Francis and back toward town on Washington Street. There was just enough room for him to double park behind a truck in front of the Harbor Master's office. Adam and Clare both jumped out and ran around the small building and out onto the pier.

"Jewel!" they called. "Jewel!"

The day was sunny, the water throwing back spangles of light that half blinded them as they thumped down the wooden pier. Boston Whalers, sunfish, small motor yachts, and gray inflatable rafts bobbed gently at anchor, and at the end of the pier Bill Blount's fishing vessel *The Ruthie B.* rose, imposing and stately. A couple of kids chased each other over the boards and several people in shorts and scalloper's caps lugged coolers toward their boats, but there was no little girl sitting at the end of the pier. No Jewel. Clare approached a woman who was urging her yellow Lab into a boat. "Excuse me. Have you seen a little girl, about this tall, lots of red hair, hanging out down here this morning?"

"No. Sorry."

Adam took Clare's arm. "We don't have time. Let's just go. We'll find Jewel later."

They ran back down the pier, jumped into the Jeep, and with a scream of burning tires, Adam executed a three-point turn and headed back out of town.

"Who else can I call?" Clare muttered.

"Call my mom and dad. They might know where Lexi is, and Lexi might know where Jewel is."

"Great idea!" Clare dialed—and got a machine. "Damn. How can it be that with so much technology we still have trouble finding one another?"

"Never mind. We're almost there. Clare, I just can't believe this is happening, I can't believe I just spoke to Tris!"

"I wish I could be there when Jewel sees that her father's alive."

"Sorry, buddy, not today," Adam grumbled as he passed a truck waiting on a side street to get into the long line of Orange Street traffic. "I usually stop and let people in," he told Clare, "but right now I don't want to let anyone slow me down."

"Who else could I call?" Clare wondered.

"Never mind, we're almost there."

They turned onto the airport road. A few minutes later, Adam stopped the Jeep in the short-term parking lot. They jumped out and hurtled toward the arrivals gate, a long room with two wooden benches and a soft-drink machine. Windows opened onto the landing field where nine-seater planes sputtered to a stop or lumbered out for take-off. The lounge was filled with people waiting for friends and relatives, everyone in full summer dress. The men wore Nantucket red Bermuda shorts, polo shirts, and leather loafers without socks, or white flannels and striped button-down shirts. The women sported sleek floral Lilly Pulitzer sheaths or tennis whites and one chic brunette, Clare noticed, wore an indigo halter top with a Moon Shell Beach sarong.

"I think this is his plane." Adam took Clare's hand and squeezed it hard.

They watched as the small plane taxied into place. The attendant opened the door that folded down to become a ramp. The first person off was a woman with a baby. After that came a man with a dog. Then a woman with a straw hat tied with a navy blue ribbon.

And then came Tris.

"Good God," Adam whispered.

The Tris they had known had been slender but muscular. The man limping toward the terminal was gaunt. It wasn't just that his borrowed clothing—jeans and a baggy sweatshirt—were too big for him. His face was sunken and deeply lined. His red hair was streaked with white. He was thirty-three, but he looked fifty.

But when he caught sight of Adam, he smiled, and his eyes brightened, and he looked young again.

"Tris. Hot damn." Adam grabbed his friend up in a huge bear hug.

Clare moved back slightly, allowing the two men their privacy. She could see Adam's shoulders shake. Tris clutched Adam's arms, and she saw how his hands and arms were darkly tanned and scarred.

Other passengers looked curiously at the men as they passed, but quickly the room emptied out and for a moment there was no drone of airplane engine, no burst of chatter. In the silence, Clare heard Tris's muffled sobs.

"I thought I was going to die out there, Adam," he choked out. "I thought I was going to die."

Adam pounded his friend on the back hard, as if trying to drive out such an idea. "It's a miracle, man; it's a miracle." He held Tris away from him, studying him. "Tris, man, you look *rough*." Both men laughed, wiping the tears from their faces.

"Tris, I'm so glad to see you. I'm so glad you're alive." Clare reached out her arms and embraced him.

But Tris looked confused. "Um, Clare?" He looked from her to Adam questioningly.

"We're together," Adam told him. "We'll explain later. Let's take care of you first. Look, maybe you should go to the hospital."

Tris waved the suggestions away. "No, I'm fine. I need a bath and a good meal, but more than that, I need to see Jewel."

"We've been trying to find her for you," Clare said. "We can't seem to reach anyone on the phone. Not surprising, I guess, on such a perfect Sunday afternoon."

"Come to my house," Adam suggested. "You can take a bath and shave and we'll fix you a big meal, and by that time someone is sure to be home."

Tris grinned ruefully at his borrowed clothing. "I guess it wouldn't hurt to clean up a bit."

"You can borrow my clothes. Or we can go by your house and get some of your own."

"My house"—Tris shook his head in wonder— "I can't believe I'm here."

They were in the Jeep and buckling their seat belts when Clare's phone rang.

"Hi, Clare," Adam's mother said. "That was quite a message you left."

"Myrna! We've got Tris in the car with us! He just got off the plane. He was shipwrecked on an island up north of Maine. Listen," Clare rushed on, "do you know where Lexi is? We think she might know where Jewel is."

"Lexi has Jewel with her today. Bonnie and Ken are at some lawn party . . ."

"Jewel's with Lexi!" Clare told Tris and Adam. To Adam's mother, she said, "Do you know their plans?"

"I think Lexi was taking her to a special place . . . a beach—"

"Get out!" Clare shrieked. "Sorry, Myrna, didn't mean to break your eardrum. I know where they are, thanks, we'll phone you later." She leaned forward. "Adam, Lexi's taken Jewel to Moon Shell Beach."

Adam gunned the engine and did a U-turn back toward Polpis Road.

"I wonder if Jewel should see me looking like this," Tris said.

"She won't care how you look, man," Adam told him, punching his shoulder. "All she'll care about is *seeing you. Alive and kicking.*"

The mass of contractors' trucks and flashy convertibles and UPS vans and Marine Home Center flatbeds crept at a snail's pace.

"Tell me about Jewel," Tris said.

Clare was nearly bouncing in her seat. "Tris, she was amazing. She came every single day to wait for you on the town pier. She *knew* you would be coming home."

"And why is Jewel with your sister?" Tris asked Adam.

"Long story short," Adam said. "Lexi's back on the island. She's started her own boutique, a clothing store—"

"Right next door to me!" Clare interjected.

"And Lexi saw Jewel sitting out there every day and she started hanging out with Jewel and they became close."

Tris frowned. "Isn't Lexi married to that Hardin fellow?"

"She was. They're divorced. Lexi's back here for good." Clare met Adam's eyes in the rearview mirror. "Tris, we had a storm a few days ago. A bad one. Jewel went into the water, and Lexi ran out and saved her."

"Clare helped," Adam added.

"Is she okay?" Tris asked urgently.

"She's fine. The thing is, Bonnie has forbidden her from ever going out on the town pier again."

"I guess that's understandable," Tris said.

"So I think Lexi brought Jewel out to a little private beach where we played when we were girls. You can see the harbor from there. Jewel was obsessed with the idea that you'd be brought home by boat, she wanted you to see her waiting for you, she wanted you to know she never gave up hope."

Tris's shoulders heaved and he rubbed at his eyes.

"We're here," Adam said. He stopped the Jeep on

the side of the road and looked over at his friend. "You okay?"

"There's Lexi's Range Rover," Clare said, pointing. "They're out on Moon Shell Beach."

"Moon Shell Beach?" Tris asked.

Clare opened her door and jumped out. "Come on. I'll show you."

Her heart was leaping in her throat as she led the two men through the swampy marshland toward the secret path. The land squelched under her feet as she cut through the tangle of cattails, berry bushes, and beach grass. High overhead in the brilliant blue sky, a gull flew, shrieking. Clare parted the wall of grasses and stepped out onto the golden curve of sand.

Two figures were kneeling on the beach, making a sand castle. Jewel wore shorts and a yellow T-shirt and her hair was in braids tied with blue ribbons. Next to her, Lexi wore a white T-shirt and khaki shorts. Behind them, dozens of boats bobbed in the idle blue waters of the harbor. Tris came through the tall grasses, and Adam followed.

"Hi, guys," Clare said, and her voice came out high and squeaky, because her heart was pounding so hard.

Jewel turned and looked up. Her eyes went wide. She jumped up, screaming, "Daddy Daddy Daddy Daddy Daddy!" Sand flew up as she ran toward her father. Tris reached out and caught her in his arms and held her to him. "Daddy, *you're home!* I knew you'd come home! We've been waiting for you!"

Tris hugged his daughter, kissing the top of her head, smelling her, inhaling her, then looking at her face.

"Don't cry, Daddy," Jewel said softly.

"Happy tears, Jewel," Tris told her.

Adam came quietly to put an arm around Clare, who was smiling while tears ran down her face.

"Daddy, Daddy," Jewel squirmed, lifting an arm free so she could point to Lexi. "Daddy, you have to meet Lexi. She helped me hope for you."

Lexi had been standing by the water, watching. Now she came forward, her blond hair glowing in the sun.

"Hello, Lexi," Tris said, reaching out to shake her hand.

"Hi, Tris," Lexi said, and her smile welcomed him home.

Center Point Publishing
600 Brooks Road ● PO Box 1
Thorndike ME 04986-0001 USA

(207) 568-3717

US & Canada:
1 800 929-9108
www.centerpointlargeprint.com